SKAC

Mask of the Soul Eater

BOOK THREE
OF THE WULFHEDINN SERIES

Mask of the Soul Eater

CATHERINE SPADER

Littleton, CO

Mask of the Soul Eater – Book Three of the Wulfhedinn Series
Published by Quillstone Press
Littleton, CO

Spader, Catherine, Author
Mask of the Soul Eater – Book Three of the Wulfhedinn Series
Catherine Spader

ISBN: 978-0-9971535-6-9
Fantasy / Historical

Developmental Editor: J. Thorn
Copyeditors: Alexandra O'Connell and Thomas Locke
Cover designer: Nick Zelinger at NZ Graphics
Interior designer: Victoria Wolf

Littleton, CO

This story is a creative fusion of history, myth, folklore, and my imagination. It is inspired by travels with my husband, Craig, to far-off lands seeped in ethereal mysteries and buried truths. Thank you for your infinite support, patience, and faith in my storytelling.

For more information about the history and lore behind the story, see the afterword at the end of the book.

Europe 782 AD

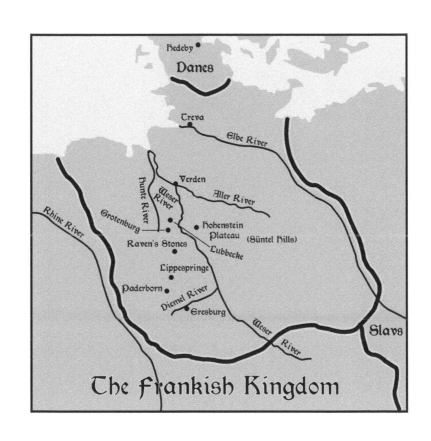

The Frankish Kingdom

Blood Moon

Saxony, 782 AD

The Monk

The Blood Moon glowed red with butchery. It ruled the season when autumn yielded to winter and animals were slaughtered for meat. But that night, the air reeked of human slaughter. I could not erase the stink from my nose, and I could not unhear what they had said—my friend Gerwulf was a dead man.

I stopped in my tracks and joined the group of five Frankish foot soldiers huddled around a smoky fire. They were warming their hands, stiff from the icy cold and the labor of beheading Saxon captives. The beer cask at their feet was evidence of their attempt to forget their grisly task as quickly as possible.

"What did you say?" I was tempted to warm my hands as well but kept them tucked away, hidden inside the sleeves of my monk's habit. I had failed to convince King Karl to show mercy to his Saxon prisoners, and the guilt of my shortcoming lingered on my dirty hands. I needed to wash soon.

"Have you not heard?" Clodio leaned forward and paused. The foot soldier was of low birth, and he beamed in the center of his comrades' attention. He stunk of beer, and his nearly toothless jaw clicked as he murmured, "King Karl's Royal Scout attacked the king himself—nearly killed him!"

"Who is spreading such ridiculous rumors?" I asked, hoping to discover Clodio's chatter about Gerwulf was a falsehood. His banal gossip usually was, but that night, I feared he had spoken the truth. Gerwulf had the temper of a rabid wolf, and if I were not there to moderate him, he might indeed attack the king.

I shifted from one foot to the other three times to calm my distress. My need to wash was soaring, making me jumpy, but I lingered at the fire to hear more.

"It is no rumor!" Clodio said. "My cousin, a royal guard, was there—witnessed the whole thing."

One of his companions, Asco, snorted, nearly gagging in the middle of a long swig of beer. "Your cousin is not a royal guard."

"He is, I say."

"Your cousin is a louse-ridden slogger who is freezing his balls off in this God-forsaken land, like the rest of us."

"Not *that* cousin, my second cousin. The royal guard is married to my second cousin. That makes him my cousin too."

"She is his whore, not his wife."

"I say she is his wife."

"I say you are a slogger."

Clodio reached for his seax, the weapon of the common foot soldier. The blade was longer than that of a dagger, but its quality could not compare to the swords of the nobility—nor could his skill. His blundering hand missed the hilt.

I stepped in and pushed the squabblers apart, revealing the filthy layer of guilt on my hands. "My sons! This is not the time for your petty dissensions, not while we are in the heathen lands where the Devil is about." I stuffed my hands back into my sleeves, hoping the drunkards had not noticed them. "Clodio, what else have you heard about the Royal Scout?"

"Well, my cousin told his brother, who is a captain of the Scola riders, who told his unit of horsemen, who told their squires, who told—"

"What, pray the Lord, happened?"

He leaned closer to me, and I drew away from the stink of his breath. If he had not vomited already, he would soon.

"The Royal Scout is a demon! One of those evil wolf warriors, he is!"

"A Wulfhedinn?" a soldier who looked old enough to be my father asked. "The thought of it quivers my bones." His thin body was as frail and brittle as a blade of dried grass. I doubted he would survive another of the king's campaigns. He pulled his woolen mantle closer around his narrow shoulders.

The biggest of Clodio's companions, a full head taller than the others, picked up the beer cask and shook the last drops into his mouth.

"For the love of God, Clodio! Mind what you say," I said. "King Karl holds the Holy Spear, the very blade that pierced the side of our Lord Jesus Christ as he hung on the cross. It is the most powerful relic in the kingdom and marks Karl as God's chosen king. He would never bring a Wulfhedinn into his court."

"But the Holy Spear's power is not enough for him, is it?" Clodio asked, raising a brow and grinning. "Nothing is enough for our good king. He made a deal with the Wulfhedinn, so he could wield its fiendish powers too."

"I still do not believe you," said Asco.

Clodio touched his eyelid. "My cousin saw it with his own eyes! He said the Royal Scout invoked the wolf spirit and grew fangs as long as your middle finger. His eyes erupted in flames, and he attacked the king with the strength of ten men. Then my cousin subdued the beast with his bare hands." He touched his fingertips together and shook his hands as though strangling someone.

"That is foolishness," I said, trying to curb the solders' rising panic and my escalating angst. "Why would a demon attack the king if the two were allies? Which, of course, they were not."

"Because the king betrayed the demon's people," Clodio said. "Karl deceived the heathen Saxons into surrendering under a white banner of truce. Then he condemned them to death and brought the rage of the wolf monster upon himself."

"The king did break his word to them," the old soldier said.

"The dirty heathens deserved what they got," Asco said.

The others murmured agreement.

"The betrayal was still a dishonor—in the eyes of God *and* the heathen spirits," Clodio said.

The soldiers at the fireside shuffled their feet, glancing around. For a moment, the only sound was the crackling of the fire. Asco licked and chewed on his lips.

"And *you* all carried out the king's sentence!" Clodio pointed at each of them. "The other wolf demons will take their vengeance on you for it, I tell you! They will stalk you in the darkness. Tear you apart. And you cannot defend yourself by spear or sword. Steel blades cannot pierce their hides. They will mangle your body and limbs, and the Eater of Souls will feast on your sinful blood before a priest can bury you. You will become one of the—"

I could hear no more of it. "For shame, Clodio! God-fearing Christians do not speak the name of ancient spirits, and the church forbids the spreading of superstitious babble."

"Why? I do not fear the Eater of Souls or the Devil's draugar."

Several of the soldiers' jaws dropped. Many years had passed since I had heard anyone speak of the roving soulless ones, gods be praised. Some things were better left forgotten.

"You beheaded as many of the Saxons as we did, Clodio," Asco said. "If—if what you say is true, the Eater of Souls will take you to Hell too. You will become one of them with the rest of us."

Clodio snickered, reaching under his mantle. "I have no worries. I am protected from her and all the evil spirits of Hell and the pagan forest." He pulled out a black feather hanging from a piece of leather. "By this."

The tall soldier tossed the empty keg. "What is that?"

"A raven's feather." It glistened with an oily green shimmer in the firelight. "I pulled it from the filthy scavenger while it was plucking the eyes out of a Saxon's head. Powerful magic it is—and rare to come by. It is not every day that one can kill a raven with a man's eye in its beak. But I do have a precious few of these charms to share with my loyal comrades, for a price."

I snapped the leather strap from his neck and threw the feather into the fire. It ignited quickly, smelling worse than searing flesh as it burned into ash. "My sons! Do not place your faith in pagan magic. Only God and prayer can save your soul from the Devil." I raised my cross to emphasize my words, but the symbol of God's power held no luster for them. Clodio's story had seized their minds, and they were too enthralled and terrified to listen to me.

5

Clodio grabbed me by the collar. "You destroyed my property! You will wish you had not done that, monk!"

I shoved him away, and he fell on his backside, his mouth hanging in surprise. The beer-soaked fool had not expected a monk to have any strength.

He stood cautiously, moving away from me. "Mark my words. The king has damned us all with the executions of the heathens," he said.

The fire crackled, popped, and collapsed. A burning branch rolled onto Asco's feet, and he kicked it back into the fire, sending a shower of sparks into the black sky. "Cursed to Hell or saved by God. Either way, I have had enough of King Karl and his war."

The others murmured in agreement. They wanted to be home, drinking by cozy fires burning behind barred doors, but the king still held them in service. Their yearly military obligation had long since passed, and the Blood Moon was upon us in a pagan land crawling with dark spirits. Worst of all, the king had ordered them to carry out a massacre of the people who worshipped those spirits. Desertion was on the minds of those simple soldiers, and I could hardly blame them.

"The Good Lord knows what you are considering, my sons," I said. "I urge you to be patient. You will be discharged and back home by Yule. I am sure of it."

"If I survive, I will return poorer than when I left," Asco said. "The booty ran out long ago in these lands."

"Nevertheless, you must fulfill your duty to the king and keep your mouths shut," I said. "You know the penalties for desertion and spreading lies about your sovereign king."

"But who can tell the lies from the truth?" Asco asked. "All I know for certain is that this place is filled with demon-worshipping Saxon savages."

Clodio rubbed his hands together over the fire. "Demon or not, the Royal Scout is surely a dead man. He was your friend, Brother Pyttel, was he not?"

His words struck me hard, stripping and exposing me, reminding me of my bare hands. "I am acquainted with everyone at court," I muttered, hiding them away again.

Clodio swiped the old soldier's beer cup from him, emptied the last sip, and sniggered. "The king will make it hard on your friend, monk."

Before I could reply, the tall soldier asked, "Can I see one of those feathers, Clodio?"

Clodio grinned and opened a drawstring bag tied to his belt. The others gathered around him. The old soldier had forgotten his stolen beer and asked about a price. Asco watched closely as Clodio pulled out several sleek black feathers. They could have been from any black bird. Clodio did not have the courage to approach a raven, but his companions were not thinking about that.

I slipped away, thinking what fools they were to believe a feather could protect them from the Eater of Souls. Hitching my habit, I ran to the king's pavilion. The tortured spirits of thousands of slaughtered Saxons wailed and shrieked behind me. The souls of the Frankish soldiers obligated to behead them would also haunt me someday. They all pleaded for my prayers, but I could not stop to help them now, even though it was the wise thing to do.

God had tasked me to save a thousand damned souls for every man I had killed, both on the battlefield and off. It was a massive penance, and rumors of the reappearance of Devil's draugar reminded me of how badly I was failing. My own soul needed saving.

I should not have been concerned with the fate of a heathen wolf warrior who had attacked my king. But I was. I should not have longed for the companionship of a Wulfhedinn. But I did. Under the Blood Moon, I could think of nothing else.

God's Price

The Monk

I crept through the shadows, climbing the hill toward the king's pavilion. Above me, ravens circled, black as the night sky. They hovered over King Karl's blood court, his field of victory over the Saxons—or the place of his greatest dishonor. The ravens' hoarse shrieking was deafening, but still it was not loud enough to overpower the sounds of steel hacking into flesh. The death blows had continued from that day into darkest night and would not stop until one of the Saxon prisoners betrayed their rebel leader, Widukind. Thousands had refused, and their heads were piled high around the field, yet I doubted anyone would cooperate. They would rather die as prisoners than betray Widukind.

The high point on the hill was the optimal site for King Karl's large pavilion. It gave him a fine view over the piles of heads on his killing field. A man who collected such trophies and would kill my friend could no longer be my king. Lamplight lit the pavilion, glowing like a huge emerald at the top of the hill. Karl's robust laughter wafted from inside, followed by the tittering of his entourage of courtiers and commanders. Twice the usual number of royal guards stood watch, and I feared Gerwulf was held inside, where I could do little for him. If I tried to plead his case, my own head might be on the block, rendering me useless to anyone.

No one would lift a finger to stop my execution. Many of the king's ass-sucking courtiers were suspicious of me or envied my position with him. They spoke to me with their shit-tainted tongues, as if I had committed more grievous sins than they had. Perhaps I had, but they did not scare me. I only feared one of them, King Karl's great friend and most powerful general, Theoderic. Everyone feared *the* General.

I slipped in a muddy spot and fell, scraping my elbows and uttering a brief curse. As I rose, a single torch across the hillside caught my eye. Beneath it, a soldier stood guard over a crumpled figure on the ground. Creeping through tall, dead grasses, I inched closer.

The prisoner lay naked, his limbs bound together behind him like a pig for slaughter. Bruises and dried blood covered his bare flesh. More blood matted his long hair and obscured his face, but his defined muscles and massive size marked him as clearly as a crown marked a king.

Gerwulf.

He lay still as death. The king's killing field was an unlikely place for hope, yet I had faith in the tenacious spirit of the Wulfhedinn. I held my breath until I saw his chest move. He was alive! As a monk and ordained priest, I should have gone to his side and offered him the opportunity to redeem his soul before execution. But as a veteran soldier, I was better at saving people than saving souls. Even a man possessed by a demon.

The guard was leaning heavily on his spear. His head bobbed as he nodded off. God was with me, and He whispered in my ear with the voice of all the gods.

Free him of this place.

I was quick to obey, and scoured the area for the best approach to ambush the guard. I had to act before a fresh, more alert guard replaced him. Before I could move, someone approached Gerwulf. I hesitated, noting his limping gait, the distinct hobble of General Theoderic. An old battle injury was likely festering again, causing his tottering stride. The wound would kill him someday, but not soon enough for Gerwulf and me.

The General wore full armor, his sword sheathed at his side. I was sure he was coming to execute my friend. He would enjoy the task. My fingers dropped to my seax hilt, itching to draw it and plunge it deeply into his innards, but I stayed my hand. I did not have the strength or skills—or the courage—to subdue both the guard and the General. Despite his injury and his age, Theoderic was formidable, and he would remain a great threat until properly rotting in the ground.

Gerwulf's fate lay in the hands of the gods. Nearly choking with fear, I admonished my cowardice.

Theoderic stopped within a couple paces of Gerwulf. In the flickering torchlight, Gerwulf stirred and rolled over, and they spoke together. My friend's voice was raspy, and I could not understand what either was saying. In my helplessness, I prayed and waited in agony for the General to draw his sword.

Father, Son, and Holy Ghost.

God must have seen purpose in my prayer, for he limped away, leaving Gerwulf alone with the guard. A small miracle—or perhaps the magic of the old gods. They often heard my pleas as well.

Free him of this place.

I rose, pulled my seax, and stole through the darkness behind the guard. As I crept up behind him, a raven screeched from somewhere overhead. The bird's shrill noise became the perfect cover. I leaped and plunged my blade into the guard's back. Mustering all the force I had, I cracked ribs and drove the seax deeply to the hilt. He fell to his knees, blood spurting. I jerked the blade out and shoved him to the ground. He would die quickly, but not soon enough, so I slit his throat, ensuring he remained silent in his last moments.

Crossing myself three times, I said a rushed prayer over the dying man. "Holy Father, forgive this sinner and welcome his soul into the glory of Heaven."

I cut Gerwulf's bonds and helped him to his feet.

"Brother, you risk too much," he said, wincing at his pain.

I wrapped the guard's torn and bloodied cloak closely around his battered body and handed him the spear. They were poor substitutes for his wolf skin and axe, but at least he was armed and clothed. "Do not concern yourself with me, my friend. I have done much worse. You must go now. Escape this forsaken place."

He grabbed me by the shoulders with more strength than a man so close to death should have had. But he was no ordinary man. Even stripped of his wolf skin and beaten like a dog, Gerwulf was Wulfhedinn.

"Did you see the Saxon woman they had taken prisoner?" he asked.

"Woman? No—what—?"

His tightened his grip on me, and he prattled on about some woman, his voice aching with panic and longing. Vala, he called her. He searched my face for an answer I did not have. I thought he might have been delusional from blood loss and the beating to his head until he said, "The woman! She flies through the sky as the Walkyrie and her Raven spirit."

He spoke of the Eater of Souls.

Gerwulf shook me, choking with panic—and passion. "What did they do to her? She carries my child."

So the fool had become her lover. I had always known, but my heart had blinded me, and I could deny it no longer. He was hers. No mortal woman or man, even a monk, could hope to steal him from the Walkyrie.

I tried to reassure him. "They could not possibly have captured the Eater of Souls—I mean, the Walkyrie."

His eyes flashed for a moment at the insult. The pagans had a different view of the Eater of Souls. They revered her as the Spirit of Three Faces: Vala the woman, Raven the spirit, and the Walkyrie. In her Walkyrie guise, she flew over battlefields in a Raven's cloak and brought the power of the wolf to the Wulfhednar. Then she selected the bravest fallen warriors for rebirth in the hall of Wodan, the war god. The powerful Walkyrie determined the fate of men.

"They took the mortal woman!" Gerwulf said. "They rounded her up with the rest. I saw her, battered and bleeding. They were dragging her by a noose around her neck. She…"

"I did not see any women among the beheaded," I said, feigning confidence. In truth, I could not swear her head was not one of the thousands on the killing field. "I heard a few of the prisoners might have escaped and fled into the forest. Maybe there was a woman with them, but…"

He burst into a smile, and his dark eyes lit up with a greenish hue I had not noticed before. He embraced me tightly, his savage scent filling my senses. I wanted to cling to him and lose myself in his warm touch, but I had to release him. The Wulfhedinn needed to vanish into the forest before someone came upon us.

I spoke quickly. "The king's executions of the Saxon captives continue, but so far, no one has betrayed Widukind. Not a single one of more than four thousand! The Walkyrie must be near, feasting on their honorable deaths. She will carry them to Wodan's Hall, but you must get far away from here. The safest place for you is at the Raven's Stones."

"You are right. She will come for me there," he said, clinching me again. "Thank you, my friend! I will never forget you."

"Nor I, you."

He ducked into the brush and escaped into the darkness, running back to his spirit lover.

I envied her and missed him already, but I did not regret what I had done. Someday, my soul would pay God's price for killing a man to save a demon, but the cost to my heart would have been immeasurable had I done nothing.

The Curse

The Monk

My bloodguilt had wedged itself under my fingernails and in the creases of my palms. The filth of it was a glaring reminder, a beacon of my sins. I had to purify myself before I was compelled to sin again. The camp's contaminated water supply would not cleanse me thoroughly, and even Holy water was no better. My latest offense demanded a sacrificial purging in a pagan spring—with blood.

Father, Son, and Holy Ghost.

I was unfamiliar with the thick forests around the king's killing field, so I waited until dawn to find a spring. To get through the long night, I had washed in a bucket over and over again. Still,

I longed for Gerwulf and would kill again for him—if I could get away with it. God said killing was my greatest sin, but Wodan and the pagan gods said it was cowardice. Both needed to be appeased.

At dawn, I snuck under the back wall of my tent. Hordes of ravens swarmed above, darkening the meager breaking light of winter. Many more winged black scavengers had perched in bare trees surrounding the army camp. They screeched with the ghastly cries of the thousands the king had murdered.

Unrighteous, no matter the god.

I wondered how close Gerwulf had gotten to the Raven's Stones. Maybe his wolf legs had taken him there already, far from this damned place. Throughout the night and into dawn, Karl's soldiers had stoked their campfires into raging bonfires to drive off the ravens. Like Clodio and Asco, they had gathered around the flames, trying to drown the ravens' song of death with beer. Every soldier had taken his turn as executioner and could not escape the minions of the Eater of Souls, the Walkyrie. I was not surprised rumors of the Devil's draugar had resurfaced in this cursed place.

I quickened my pace, hastening toward the forest edge, ducking behind a row of tents. Turning a corner, I ran into a soldier taking a piss. He belched, lost his balance, and splattered me.

"You swine!" I said, shaking drops of his filth from my habit. "This place is foul enough. Must you defile the pathway? Point your cock into the trees."

The soldier swayed and tucked himself back in his breeches. "A demon might bite it off!"

"What are you talking about?"

"There are wolf warriors, Wulfhednar, in the forest. They say one of them has even crept into the king's court."

Word about Gerwulf was spreading fast.

I shook a finger at him. "Our Lord God has cast out the demons, to Hell. No spirit will snack on your bits."

"But I hear they are rising again…Wulfhednar and the Devil's draugar…"

"Stop talking foolishness. Pray to God for his forgiveness of your superstitious idiocy and have more consideration for your comrades. Leave your filth in the shit pit."

He bowed his head. "Yes, brother."

I moved on, knowing he would continue to piss wherever he pleased, as all soldiers did. At the outskirts of camp, I slipped into the forest and quickly found a trail of crushed grass. It was littered with deer droppings, marking an animal track that would likely lead to water. The Weser and Aller Rivers flowed together just on the other side of Verden. The springs feeding them would be close, too.

I hurried, reminding myself of the king's council later that morning. If I did not appear, my guilt in the freeing of Gerwulf would be clear to everybody. General Theoderic would make certain of that. He was anxious to be rid of me, but all would be right once I purified myself. All would be right.

I had not gone far when I felt something in the shadows. I could still hear the sounds of the king's camp behind me, but dark spirits were near too—watching. Despite what I had told the soldiers, wolf warriors did exist in those woods. Gerwulf was proof of it, and he was one of many Wulfhednar, who would not favor me as he did. I drew my seax, knowing a mortal blade could not protect me from them. I might, however, have a chance against the bandits and army deserters who were fool enough to prowl the woods.

As the sun rose higher, fog rolled in, dispersing the light. The mist grew heavier until it swirled around me, obscuring the forest and the path. I lost sight of the deer trail. Somewhere, a raven screamed. When it stopped, the noises of the king's camp disappeared too. I was unsure what direction to take back.

By God's bones!

Cold sweat beaded on my forehead as I imagined what would happen if I missed the king's council. It scared me more than being lost in the pagan wood.

A black blur brushed past my face. I startled, and it disappeared into the mist before I could raise my seax. Then something grazed the back of my head. I turned and saw a raven landing on a branch. The only thing visible in the fog, it was the largest raven I had ever seen, and its flight had stirred a cold breeze that chilled my blood. Folding its wings, it opened its beak as though speaking.

Go to him.

It was her, the Raven, the black spirit of the Walkyrie, the Eater of Souls.

"Him?" I asked. "Who?"

She flew off, drawing me along with her whisper.

The wolf calls for you.

The wolf. My heart leapt. She wanted to take me to Gerwulf! He had not run back to his goddess lover and was waiting nearby for me! In my excitement, I forgot the council and followed her.

I trailed her through a maze of thickets and trees on the mist-shrouded hillside. After several hundred paces, the ground flattened and opened to a clearing. The fog shifted and partially cleared, revealing a horse on the far side of a small meadow. Wondering how Gerwulf had acquired a horse, I moved closer.

The Raven flew over the steed, and its legs swayed. They hung above the ground like phantom limbs, stepping across the air. Its body did not move, and its empty eye sockets stared downhill at the king's blood court.

It was a nithing horse, a pagan curse horse sacrificed to Wodan. Someone had staked the horse's remains above the killing field to scourge the Christian king and his army. The rebel leader Widukind had set nithing horses against the king in the past, and the dark magic had been effective. They had vexed the king with his massive defeat at Süntel.

I shivered and should have turned and run, but could not resist the urge to move closer. I crossed myself three times.

Father, Son, and Holy Ghost.

I should not have been in such a place, but Gerwulf would protect me if the other Wulfhednar were nearby and wanted to attack me. I was sure of it. I crouched low, keeping my blade at the ready. The sun burned through the mist, revealing the killing field and army camp below. A rotting stink was rising from the piles of bodies and heads.

Something moved from behind the nithing horse. Covered in fur, it had the head of a wolf and stood on two legs—a huge beast of a man or a man-shaped beast. Gerwulf! It must have been! I could spot his strong stance with one eye closed.

Relieved, I almost called out to him. Then he dropped his wolf hood, revealing blond hair. Gerwulf's was black. It was not him, yet he and this Wulfhedinn shared the same profile, heavy brow, and jaw. The manner and physical resemblance were so similar that they had to be kin.

Gerwulf's father. Widukind. The Saxon rebel and leader of the Wulfhednar.

I dove to the ground. This Wulfhedinn would show no mercy and tear me apart like the demon he was. And he would be righteous to do so. I was a Christian monk, despised by the Wulfhednar.

I held only one advantage over him; I was downwind. My fingers ached to cross myself for protection, but any extra movements might have attracted his attention. I inched back on my stomach, dragging my seax, terrified he would notice me, but he kept his eyes on the killing field as I crept backward. Just before I edged out of his line of sight, he pulled a dagger. I thought he might have seen me and would attack. Instead, he turned the blade toward his chest.

His eyes were soulful, his expression anguished as he gazed over the staked heads of eight of his wolf warriors and thousands of beheaded Saxons. He was a mortal man facing massive loss. Without a thought, I jumped up, sheathed my seax, and sprinted toward him.

"No! In the name of the gods! Stop!" I shouted.

I lifted the hem of my habit to avoid tripping. He froze, his jaw dropping at the sight of a monk running straight at him, baring his bouncing cullions.

"Stop! You cannot…"

I tackled him, and we tumbled to the ground. His initial shock passed quickly. Gripping his dagger, he leaped to his feet and pulled the wolf hood over his face. He slashed at my chest. I rolled away, but the tip of his blade sliced through my habit and tore off my cross. Blood seeped through the cloth. Clutching the wound, I scrambled to my feet and nearly stumbled.

"Father, Son, and Holy Ghost," I prayed in desperation.

Widukind pulled a sword, and armed with two blades, he raised them both to strike.

"Wolf, Raven, and Walkyrie!" I shouted, unsure how those words had come to me.

The Raven dove between us, tossing us apart with a wave of her black-fingered feathers. We landed hard on our backsides.

Widukind stood, watching the bird as it soared overhead. The wolf hood covered his face, but he looked like a man wearing a mask. The demon's fangs and claws had not emerged, and his eyes had not ignited into balls of fire like Gerwulf's had when the wolf possessed him. The fur cloak hung from his shoulders like a rotting, lifeless pelt.

"You must be a lunatic to attack a Wulfhedinn," he said without raising his weapons again.

"I am not mad. I am a mystic." I rose slowly, clutching my bleeding ribs. "And you are not a Wulfhedinn."

He did not deny it. "You have the strength of a warrior. And your face—"

"Crushed by a war club, years ago," I said.

"Who are you?"

"I am Brother Pyttel. I became a monk to atone for the murders I committed as a soldier."

He lowered his blade. "Killing in war is not murder."

I glanced over at the king's massacre in the valley below. "Sometimes it is."

He followed my gaze in silence.

"After I took my vows as a monk, my path led me to serve King Karl," I said. "I believed his mission to convert the pagans would save many souls, and my assistance with the task would redeem me for many sins. That was before the king betrayed and murdered so many in the name of God. I now believe he is the Devil himself."

The Raven dove and landed on my shoulder. She was heavy, and her claws pierced the threads of my habit. She ruffled her neck feathers, her breath heavy in my ear.

Tell him about Gerwulf.

"Yes, yes, Mistress Raven," I said, trying to shrug her off. "I am getting to him."

Widukind glanced from me to the Raven and back to me. "She comes and speaks to you?"

"She brought me here to tell you news of Gerwulf."

His expression hardened. "My son is dead to me. He chose a position in King Karl's court over his place in the Wulfhednar pack."

"He has left the king and returned to you."

He stared blankly at the field where the king had staked the masked heads of the Wulfhednar captives. "He made his choice. He cannot choose again."

"For the love of all the gods, he declared himself to be your son. Then he attacked and nearly killed the king!"

Widukind raised his deeply furrowed brow.

"Yes! It is true. Gerwulf took the Holy Spear from him. He held it to the king's throat and demanded he stop the executions." I paused to let him absorb my words. "But he was overpowered by the royal guards, beaten, and sentenced to die with the rest."

"Why should I believe you?"

"Because the Raven is sitting on my shoulder."

A smile passed his lips, half hidden by his untamed blond beard.

"I committed murder to help your son escape," I said.

"Why would a Christian monk do that?"

"Because I cannot let honorable men die of despair when there is hope."

He eyed me suspiciously. Then his gaze met mine and softened. The Raven took off, spiraling upward on a breeze rising from the valley. Her voice echoed across the killing field like a lonely, tolling bell. A massive flock of ravens rose from the mounds of corpses. They darkened the sky and screeched so loudly that I had to shout to be heard.

"Gerwulf has become my good friend, and King Karl has become a monster, a butcher," I said. "The butcher king."

He nodded. "Indeed."

"He offered to spare the life of any Saxon prisoner who would betray your whereabouts. Every one of them refused. They died with honor, as bravely as any who have fallen in battle."

"You are right," he said, his gaze following the hordes of ravens rising from the killing field. "The Walkyrie and her Raven spirit are carrying them to Wodan's Hall."

"If you reject your son and take your own life, there will be no one to lead the Saxons to avenge their sacrifice."

"It cannot be done." He hung his head. "We are defeated."

"You have the wolf."

"No longer. I have nothing but shame. I failed as leader of the Wulfhednar, and more than half of my wolf warriors surrendered to the king. My weakness and their dishonor broke the power of the pack. The Walkyrie has vanished and taken the wolf spirit away from us."

"But you have your son! He waits for you at the Raven's Stones, and the wolf might still be with him." I held my tongue. He did not need to know that Gerwulf had returned to the stones for his woman, not his father.

Widukind stiffened his spine. "Maybe he is there, and the wolf is still with him—maybe."

"The Walkyrie has not abandoned Gerwulf and will not abandon you," I said. "There is hope."

He thought for a moment and cocked his head. "You are not a good monk."

"I am a grave sinner, and the old gods often speak louder to me than the Christian one."

"So they do."

He sheathed his blades and trotted away, glancing once at me before disappearing into the trees. The Raven trailed behind him, heading south toward the Raven's Stones. She left me with one thought.

Killing in war is not murder.

Perhaps, but still, my hands were dripping with bloodguilt. I had betrayed my king and God, and worst of all, my efforts to convince the king to spare the Saxons had been futile. He had become the butcher king, murdering thousands of innocent souls because of me. All the gods were angry with me. I had to pacify them all, but I was out of time to find a spring. I would be late to council, and if I missed it altogether, my absence would draw more suspicion. I picked up my cross and dashed down the hill toward camp, grateful the fog had lifted and revealed a clear route back.

A chant rose from the trees as I ran, repeating itself with the beat of my heart and the pounding of my feet.

Bring us your flesh.
Bring us your flesh.
Bring us your flesh.

"Yes. Yes. I will appease you all!" I shouted, hastily tying the cross around my neck again.

I quickly outran their voices. They would catch up with me again someday, but I had helped my friend, which was more than a wicked monk and a mediocre mystic could have hoped for.

Judgment

Wulfhedinn

I was Gerwulf, a Wulfhedinn chosen by the Walkyrie, but my journey to the Raven's Stones from the king's blood court had not been easy. The wolf had not come to me, and I had been as weak and vulnerable as any wounded, hungry man. My spear would have been a pitiful defense if I had encountered the Wulfhednar pack. They were hungry for the blood of a traitor. But no matter. Losing Vala was my greatest fear, not wolf demons.

I was safe now, waiting for her in the stone chamber. The chamber had been carved into the top of Wodan's Tower, the tallest of the towering Raven's Stones. The Walkyrie had left my wolf skin for me on the altar under the little round window, and I was certain Vala the woman would appear soon. Wrapped in my fur, I stared out the window where her Raven spirit often perched. A single star twinkled outside.

I sniffed for Vala's scent of sweet musk and hawthorn. Her delicate white hawthorn blossom would not bloom for many months yet. Nonetheless, it accompanied the sweet muskiness of her body when she was near. So far, I had smelled nothing but decaying leaves and duff on the forest floor far beneath me.

The wolf skin fell open, baring my chest, and its magic escaped into the damp chill of early winter. My bruises ached, and my knees stiffened. I was young enough to tolerate such pains but felt them more deeply than in the past. Someday, the total of my injuries would cripple me. Even the wolf skin could not prevent it forever. Time was passing with every new pain—time I could never have back with Vala. She must have felt the same way. She would come for me soon.

A faint rhythmic sound rose from the bottom of the standing stones. I leaned out the chamber door, straining to hear more. Soft-soled boots padded lightly up the steps carved into the neighboring pillar. It was one of thirteen standing stones rising from the forest, like giants more than twenty times the height of a tall man. A damp draft whipped around the massive rocks, but I shivered with expectation, not the cold.

Vala was not sending her Raven spirit in her stead. She was not flying overhead as the Walkyrie on her black stallion in the feathered mask and winged cloak. She was coming to me as a mortal woman would, climbing one step at a time. She was coming as Vala.

My heart surged, and I sweated in the night chill as the footsteps came closer. For a moment, I thought of the monk. He would be happy to know she was there, that the risk he had taken to free me had paid off. I should have offered to bring him with me, away from the king and his war, but I had only thought of Vala at the time.

I clutched my spear and raised my hood to see better through the wolf eyes in the darkness. I would meet her as the Wulfhedinn, the warrior with the ferocity of the beast, the one she had chosen to father her child. I stared through the empty eye holes of the hood. The wolf was eluding me, so she would have to accept me as a man. I clung to the excitement of seeing her again. What would she say? Would she take me back?

She climbed steadily, disappearing around the far side of the pillar. She emerged again on the winding stairs. The figure was close enough now to see it was too large and robust to be a woman. Disappointed, I slumped against the threshold as the man rounded the stone a final time and emerged on its flat top across from me. A wolf hood concealed his face, but I recognized his scent. It was more familiar than I wanted to believe. He was Widukind, leader of the Wulfhednar and the Saxon rebellion. The man who had fathered me.

My idiocy struck me like a blow from a club. When I had escaped the king's killing field, I had not thought of anything but Vala. Her image had consumed me, pulling me back to the Raven's Stones, her stones. I had not considered that Widukind or anyone else might come in her place.

He stood at the edge of the sheer gorge between the stones that divided us. His chest rose and fell, his breath as rapid as mine. The chasm between us was as deep as the ravine between the standing stones, and I was glad the bridge was no longer there to join us together.

He lowered the hood. "I almost cut the throat of the lunatic monk who told me you had returned to the Raven's Stones," he said.

"Monk? What monk?"

"He had a smashed face and claimed to hear the voices of all the gods."

"Brother Pyttel?"

"That was the name."

How had Pyttel managed to find Widukind when the entire Frankish army had been unable to do so? And why had Widukind decided to spare his life? Pyttel was a favored court servant of Widukind's greatest enemies, King Karl and the Christian God.

Widukind's wolf hood hung lifelessly down his back, and he squinted like an aging man. Despite his years, his muscles were lean and strong, but he hardly seemed a wolf demon.

"Why did you come back?" he asked. "Maybe you thought to lead your Christian king and his army here."

"Karl is not my king."

He scoffed. "You deserted the Walkyrie and the Wulfhednar pack to return to him. Your actions reveal truth, not your words."

I could have begged him to trust me, to forgive me for deserting the pack. I could have pleaded for him to take me back. But I refused. He would not forgive me any sooner than I would him for abandoning my mother and me. The forsaken do not forget. Widukind and I were on even ground, and I would not bend to him.

Vala was coming for me, and I did not care about him and his pack of demons. The Raven had seen what I had done to defend the Saxon captives. I had risked everything, nearly dying for it and losing my chance to reunite with Vala. The Raven, the Walkyrie, and the woman knew everything, and that was all that mattered. I would rather have flung myself off the ledge than ask Widukind to bring something to bridge the gap between the stones and between us.

He glanced at the broken plank at the bottom of the rocks. "The Walkyrie has destroyed the bridge into the chamber. She has trapped you there to suffer her judgment," he said. "Your fate is in her hands, and she will free you if she has purpose for you."

I would not tell him how I had torn the plank bridge from between the stones and trapped myself in the chamber. I would not reveal the despair that had ripped through me when I had thought Vala was not coming. I had flung the plank to the ground, watching it splinter, imagining how my bones would have splintered had I flung myself after it. But before I could jump, the Raven spirit had appeared, and I knew the woman who carried my child would come too.

She had chosen me as the father by the Walkyrie, and I would be the father Widukind had never been. I owed him nothing.

As if sensing my thoughts, Widukind pulled the wolf skin around his shoulders and left. His footsteps faded quickly down the stairs. At the bottom of the pillar, he picked up a broken piece of the plank bridge. Tossing it aside like a gnawed bone, he vanished into the forest, leaving me alone with the twinkling star in the little window.

The Rope

Wulfhedinn

Neither Vala nor her Raven spirit came during the night. At dawn, I rose stiffly and went to the door, scanning the treetops and the sky, and found a rope. It was strung between the stone pillars, swinging in the breeze as though it had always been there. Someone—or something—must have come during the night to anchor it to the two rocks. No man could have competed that task. It required the power of flight, like that of the Walkyrie.

She had been there and given me a way to escape her chamber! I reached for the rope and ran my hand along the thin, brittle fibers. I hesitated. It would surely break under my weight. I knew then Vala would not appear until I had made the dangerous crossing to the other stone. It was a test of Vala's dark side, the Walkyrie, the Eater of Souls who wore the black feathered mask and flew on her great black stallion. I would have to suffer her judgment.

I spit.

Fuck her judgment.

I would use the bitch's own demon against her. Pulling the hood over my face, I listened for the wolf's howl. I expected the beast to come in my fury, as it usually did, but the forest remained quiet. My anger boiled with a force that felt like my rage would last forever. Still, the wolf did not come.

Fuck her judgment.

I hurled my spear across the chasm between the stones. It landed precisely on top of the neighboring pillar, waiting for me to make the dangerous crossing as a man.

I yanked hard and hung part of my weight on the rope. It stretched but held fast, so I reached across the gap and grabbed it. Swinging my legs off the ledge, I hooked them together in front of me. My wolf cloak hung limply from my back as I swung back and forth, the ground far below. The rope was holding, so I began to cross, sliding my hands and my feet, inching along it.

The rough fibers cut into my skin like razors. The farther I went, the more the rope stretched and sagged under my weight. Halfway across, a sudden gale gusted between the stones, rocking me like a blast of breath from Donar, the Thunder God. I clung on with every bit of strength I could muster, but my legs slide off the swinging rope. Dangling in the air, my gaze fell to the ground, so far below. My mind began to spin as my muscles writhed, stretched, and tore.

Vala, the woman, might have wanted me, but the Walkyrie had no intention of letting me survive. I had rejected her and the Wulfhedinn pack, and she was going to make me pay the price for it. Yet I still loved Vala. It was madness. I was one slip of the fingers away from death, and my heart still longed for the woman whose vengeful, Walkyrie face wanted my death. It was no wonder the Christians call her the Eater of Souls.

Fuck her judgment.

I put aside the pain and cramping muscles and locked my sights on the stone's ledge ahead. With a grunt, I flung my ankles back over the rope, hooking them together again. I continued scooting forward until my palms burned and the skin peeled. I was nearing the ledge when one strand of the rope snapped. The other fibers began to unravel. With every bit of resolve I had, I swung myself forward and reached for the pillar. The rope broke.

I slammed into the sheer wall of stone beneath the ledge. Loose rock shifted beneath me as I slid down the rock face, struggling to cling to a crevice. Clawing and scratching, I found a tiny handhold and jammed three fingers into the crack. My other hand and feet flailed in the air, unable to reach for another notch. My shoulder was tearing apart from the strain, and my grip on the handhold was weakening. Bits of gravel rolled past my face. For a moment, my fate was clear.

Fuck her judgment.

I rallied the last bit of my rage, hoping the wolf would come when I needed it the most, but the demon left me dangling off the great stone pillar by my human fingers. The Walkyrie was keeping the wolf from me, and I did not have the energy left to curse her. Images of Vala and the moments we had spent together raced through my mind.

Then one of my toes brushed across a small crack in the cliff-side. I crammed it into the crevice and lunged up, heaving my chest onto the pillar's ledge. The sharp rock edge cut into my gut, but I would not let myself fall now. With a thrust, I threw myself onto the top of the pillar.

Blood dripped from my mouth. I had bitten my tongue, but the blood tasted sweet. I had survived the crossing and was a few steps away from the staircase that would take me down to the ground.

Glancing back, I saw the rope was intact again, strung tautly between the stones.

Fuck her judgment.

Weave a Story

The Monk

My feet plodded toward King Karl's camp in rhythm with the Holy Trinity.

Father, Son, and Holy Ghost.
Father, Son, and Holy Ghost.
Father, Son, and Holy Ghost.

But God refused to hear my prayer and help me. I would be late for council. I needed to fly like a bird, so I beseeched the pagan trinity. It had interceded on my behalf once. Maybe it would again.

Wolf, Raven, and Walkyrie.

The spirits responded, and I soared down the hill, running faster and more surefooted than I had since childhood. Entering camp, I stayed off the main path through the tents to avoid encounters with soldiers. Inevitably, they would stop me and ask for penance and absolution. Their butchery filled the place with the smell of blood and the dark weight of regret on their souls. I could see across camp where the line of penitents outside my tent was growing impossibly long, so I detoured by way of another route to elude them. I had no time for their sins.

As I climbed the hill to the king's pavilion, I pinned together my mantle so it covered my torn and bloodstained habit. Looking up, I saw something else was wrong. Large swaths of the pavilion's linen walls were shredded and blowing loosely in the breeze. It looked like the king's campaign residence had been sacked by marauders. The royal guards were not at their posts, and I found them huddled together halfway down the hill, talking in low voices. They quieted as I passed and failed to question me about my business with the king. Something was truly amiss.

I entered the pavilion cautiously, and a steel dagger sailed past my face. I ducked in time, avoiding grievous injury, but it had come so close the blade's metal had chilled my cheek. Karl's hand was still raised from his throw.

Father, Son, and Holy Ghost. He is going to kill me.

He was still dressed in his sleeping shirt. Eyes bulging, he clutched the Holy Spear in the other hand. Tangled clumps of hair framed his ruddy, blustering face. Quills and sheets of vellum maps and scrolls lay scattered across the floor, and ink splattered the tattered walls he must have torn with the spear. Standing in the middle of it all, he looked like a madman—even more than I did.

His mother, Bertrada, stood behind him, holding his tunic and mantle. "Where have you been, monk?"

"I came as soon as—"

She was never interested in hearing my excuses. "Council has been postponed until this evening. The king needs you now."

"Did you see it?" Karl demanded.

I touched my cheek. "Your dagger? Yes—just before it nearly stabbed me in the face."

"No! No! How could you not see the *demon*? It just flew over your shoulder!"

I looked behind me and shook my head. The king pointed at his crown lying on the table.

"That thing had perched on *my* crown," he said.

I examined it. The gold had been splattered with white filth. "Bird shit."

"Not any bird, a raven—*the Raven*! The minion of the Eater of Souls."

Bertrada and I exchanged glances. The appearance of the Raven spirit was a grave omen for a Christian ruler who had just executed thousands of pagans.

"You simply had a bad dream." Bertrada offered him his clothes. "Now get dressed."

"Shut up, woman. Do not talk to me like I am an infant."

"You are acting like a babe pulled from the breast of his nurse."

"I am *king*!"

"Not the king your father was."

I cringed. Karl turned his spear tip toward his mother, and I almost wished he would launch it. The woman riled him at the worst times.

"Do not cross me, or I will send you back to the Thionville palace with the other women of the court. Queen Hildegard is with child again, and she needs her mother-in-law."

Bertrada did not flinch from him. "I am no midwife, and you need me here to manage the situation."

"I will manage it."

"Can you? You broke a trust with the heathens, just when we had the upper hand with them. Both Brother Pyttel and I warned you against executing them all, but you refused to listen. I have worked too long and hard and sacrificed too much to allow you to destroy the kingdom I have built for you."

"This is *my* kingdom, old woman! I fought and spilled my own blood to hold and expand it."

"It is time you learn to rule with your head, not your pride and your temper. Too much bloodlust does not suit a Christian king."

Karl sneered. "Or a queen mother. *You* ensured I would rule alone—without my brother."

Bertrada dropped his clothing, strode past his spear tip, and slapped him across the face. "Your brother died of a nosebleed. The royal physicians declared his death to be the will of God."

No one could prove it, but some courtiers believed Carloman's death had not been so natural. They whispered about it when they were out of earshot of the queen mother, but I had overheard them often enough. I had not been part of the Frankish court at the time of Carloman's death and remained happily ignorant of the truth.

Seething, his cheek inflamed, Karl turned his rage on me. "This was your idea, monk! You brought the Wulfhedinn to me. You and Mother told me I could control him and use his powers against the Saxon rebels."

My mouth dried, and I could not speak. I was picturing my head staked on a pole or thrown into a pile with all the others.

Undeterred, Bertrada put her hands on her hips. "The Wulfhedinn *was* under our complete control until you broke the terms of the savages' surrender. Your actions stirred the half-blood's defiant, heathen side."

"The half-breed wolf bastard tried to kill me!"

"None of that would have happened if you had listened to me," she said. "Now regrets are haunting your dreams."

"This was no dream! The Raven has foretold my death. She will take me to Hell to become one of them, the draugar…"

The queen mother shot me another troubled glance. "Nonsense. You are God's chosen king, my son," she said in a hollow tone. "You hold the most powerful relic in history. When your time comes, the largest army in Christendom will protect your body from ravens and other demons."

I had not heard Karl or his mother refer to the Devil's draugar before. Hearing talk of the roving soulless ones twice in one day troubled me. Karl's disregard of his mother's advice was another bad sign. Bertrada wielded a shadowy command over everyone in court—especially her son. We were all a bit afraid of her, but her counsel was often practical and wise. Karl's refusal to listen to her was ominous. Worst of all, his hysteria might panic his entire army, intensifying fear and hatred of the Saxons. More innocents would suffer.

I laid a hand on Karl's arm, keeping most of my fingers covered with my sleeve. "Listen to the queen mother, my son. She knows the difference between a dream and a vision."

"Are you an idiot? This is no dream!" With a massive effort, he overturned his great wooden bed, cracking one of the finely carved posts. "The Raven will come for you too, Mother!"

"She already has," Bertrada muttered through gritted teeth.

Before I could ponder the encounter she might have had with the spirit, the king picked up the table and threw it. I startled and ducked, but Karl had not aimed it at me. It crashed, and the crown fell to the ground and rolled away.

Bertrada came to my side and whispered, "This is a catastrophe. The nobles who are against us will use this situation to their advantage. They are already calling Karl a tyrant, and nobles must believe they have some measure of control in court if we are to keep their support."

"Yes, yes. Something must be done," I said.

He continued to rage. "The Raven is here again! Do you not see her? Are you both blind?" He thrust the Holy Spear at the invisible spirit, tearing more holes in the pavilion walls. Then he threw a bench. He had to tire soon. He was running out of furniture.

"This must be dealt with quickly," she said to me. "The whole army will soon know their king retained a wolf warrior in his service—the son of the rebel leader, no less—and made him his Royal Scout. You must weave a story about it in our favor before it is too late."

Weave a story. It was a task I performed regularly for them, but it would not be so easy this time. The situation with Gerwulf would be as devastating to the king's reputation as his massacre of the Saxon captives. I had already prepared and rehearsed something, but I could not focus on it while he ranted. My priority was to protect myself from the tip of the Holy Spear until Karl's tirade ran its course.

He slashed through the wall a few more times, and his temper finally began to cool. Panting and seething, he clutched the Holy Spear as though his life depended on it. Then I saw it, a small miracle. A water basin sat undisturbed on a stool in the corner, the only object left intact in the tent. With great relief, I dunked my hands in the water and rubbed them together three times. I paused and repeated the process twice more, squirming to keep my mantle from falling open and revealing my bloodied habit.

The flush in Karl's neck and face was fading, and his eyes cleared. My handwashing ritual soothed him as much as it did me. I shook water from my fingers, and the brief sense of peace evaporated as my hands dried. I wet my lips and washed my hands again, giving myself time to think.

Father, Son, and Holy Ghost.

I pulled my mantle close, and Karl shivered, his breath hanging in the damp air. Dipping his fingers in the water, he crossed himself.

"I feel as if the Eater of Souls has flown over my corpse," he said. "What has God told you? Will He deliver me from her?"

Weave a story.

"He will," I promised.

He did not question me, so I continued. "You have a special calling from God. It is a heavy burden to carry, and God understands it may cause you to stumble." I paused, pacing my words carefully. "The Devil sent the Wulfhedinn to tempt you with his power, and you were led astray for a time. But you saw through the demon's deception before it was too late. With the power of the Holy Spear, you cast him down and punished thousands of his evil followers, to the glory of God."

"Yes. Yes, that is true," Bertrada said.

Karl stared at his distorted reflection in the wash basin. "I was deceived, but I defeated evil in the end."

I raised my cross. "Kneel now and accept the Sacrament of Penance. Free your soul from the demons, and move forward in God's work. Repentance will also ease the consciences of all the men who have followed your orders. It is needed to keep order in the ranks."

He knelt on his bare knees. "Then let it be done."

He will pay a high price.

The voice cut through my veins like ice. I clutched the cross, trying to squeeze some warmth from it, but my whole body was frigid. God was telling me He was displeased with the executions and was not accepting the king's token gesture of repentance. The Lord's voice grew louder, becoming a clamor, booming through my head like the deafening tones of a bronze church bell.

The butcher king will pay a high price.

I covered my ears but could not unhear the judgment of all the gods, ancient and new. It struck me so hard, I fell to the ground.

In the distance, I heard Karl ask, "Monk, is it God? Does He speak of me?"

—a high price.

The king and his shredded, waving pavilion walls whirled around me. My tongue swelled, filling my mouth and throat. I choked, the struggle to breath consuming me. The Holy Spear glowed with a blinding light, obscuring everything else with the fires of Hell. A scream arose from deep within the flames, dousing the fire with an icy cry, the voice of death. I drifted into a vast cold darkness stretching endlessly in every direction. The scream called again. Something brushed across my face, soft as feathers.

A huge black bird soared past me, the radiant Holy Spear in its talons. Then she disappeared with it.

"Is God speaking to you? What does he say?" Karl asked.

His emerald pavilion emerged from the darkness like a sunrise after a bitter cold night. Breathing became easier, but I was still shaken by the Raven and the voice of God. I could not rise. He yanked me up by the collar. "What did He say?"

I could not tell him the truth. He had to believe he had triumphed over the Eater of Souls so he would withdraw his army and leave Saxony in peace.

"Yes, my king. The Lord spoke to me." My raspy throat struggled to say more. "God…the Lord…absolved you…no penance."

He crossed himself, grinning like a child who had gotten away with stealing a tart. His eyes dropped to my chest. The mantle had fallen open, revealing my bloodied habit.

"What has happened to you?" he asked.

My heart pounded, and in my panic, a prayer came quickly to mind.

Wolf, Raven, and Walkyrie.

And the lies poured from my lips like a fine Frankish wine. "God's word is manifest, my king! He decrees Verden as your final victory against the Saxons and commands you to cease further attacks on them." With every falsehood, I was digging a deeper hole to Hell for myself, but it had to be done—for peace, for Gerwulf, for the innocents. "You have crushed the Saxons and destroyed more than half of the Wulfhedinn pack. The resistance is broken. They will not rise against you again. God calls you to attend to greater matters now."

I stood and tossed his breeches to him. He caught them but hesitated to dress, frowning in thought.

"If God has deemed I have won, so be it," he said without conviction.

King Karl never gave up so easily. I knew he would not relinquish the hunt for Gerwulf and his father, Widukind, the Wulfhednar leader. He might, however, withdraw most of his army from Saxony for the winter. That would buy Gerwulf and the Wulfhednar more time.

I helped him wrap his legs with strips of fur. Then I combed the knots from his hair, taking great care to be gentle until his golden mane was tamed and shone brightly. Finally, he buckled his sword belt, and I placed his ermine fur-lined sapphire mantle on his shoulders, patting him like a mother hen. He grasped the Holy Spear, his back straight and his gaze as sharp as an eagle's.

"Shall I summon the tentmaker to make repairs on the pavilion?" I asked.

"Burn it. I will lodge in General Theoderic's tent."

I found the crown among the broken pieces of his bed. "May I take my leave to purify and bless your crown? You will need it for the council this afternoon."

"Go, but return quickly. God is close when you are near."

"Indeed."

I crossed myself three times, and Bertrada threw me a faint smile. Then her dark brows furrowed as she thought of things I did not want to know. Before she could speak to me again, I headed for the door.

Sacrifice

The Monk

The forest beckoned me like a whore from a dark alley, but I had to bide my time and ensure no one was following me. The camp was erupting with activity and noise as officers shouted at soldiers to return to their normal duties, but that morning was far from normal or routine.

I detoured around the most heavily trafficked areas, ducked into the woods, and found the deer path again. It led me quickly to a freshet feeding the Weser River. I followed the little stream to its source, where a spring flowed into a small pool. I set down the king's crown, stripped my monk's robes, and waded into the water with a dagger. Only my own blood would suffice for sacrifice, and it would have to flow from a new cut. The scratch Widukind had given me had stopped bleeding and would not impress the gods. I had to draw the blood myself.

The pool was deep enough to cover my legs. My teeth chattered as I waded in and lifted the dagger. The first slash was painful, making me hesitate before making the second cut, but the third was easier.

"I tried to do what was righteous," I said, watching the blood drip. "But thousands have died because I have failed. I offer my body as a living sacrifice to you and remain dedicated to your service and to pleasing you."

The Shepherd materialized in the blood-streaked water. His long beard waved in the ripples. He held a long white staff, and a hood covered his face. A white dove was perched on his shoulder, cooing softly, and a halo encircled his head, sparkling like gold. In the glow of the Holy Ghost, I had a moment's hope the Shepherd, the embodiment of God and our Lord Jesus Christ, had come to relieve me of my burden of sin.

Then the Shepherd's hood fell back, and his halo faded into a crown of thorns. The thorns grew longer, penetrating his scalp. Blood flowed, streaking down his face. Christ had paid dearly for our sins. So would I.

"Your blood will not atone for the blood that has been spilled," the Shepherd said.

With a flap of its white wings, the dove transformed into a black bird, the Raven. The Shepherd's staff became a spear, and the ripple in the pool mutilated his face. One of his eyes disappeared, leaving a hollow cavern in its place. Wodan, the Traveler. The Saxon god of wisdom, war, and fury had gouged out his own eye in exchange for greater vision. I feared he would require the same sacrifice from me.

"What do you demand?" I asked.

46

"No amount of flesh will amend what has been wronged," he said. "Keep your body strong so you can achieve what must be done."

"What must I do?"

The blood from my cuts was washing downstream toward the Weser River. It created long scarlet fingers pointing at the king's camp. As the bleeding eased, the water cleared. The Traveler disappeared, and the Shepherd did not return. Above me, the Raven hovered, floating on the breeze. As the spirit of the Walkyrie, she was also the eyes and ears of Wodan—and his messenger. She shrieked, her shrill voice etching his decree into my mind.

You must kill him.

"Who?" I feared the answer.

She dove and alighted on the crown. She cackled at me as if I were an idiot, but I knew what she meant.

The butcher king.

"I cannot murder the king! I am a monk now. My killing days are over."

She preened the feathers of one wing and flew off, leaving the golden crown streaked with more shit. Circling above, she cackled at me.

You have killed many before. A murder just last night.

"Do you not see my cross?" I shouted, holding it aloft. "I am a peacemaker who walks in the footsteps of Our Lord Jesus Christ.

I will temper the king and try to make peace between him and the Saxons, but my killing days are over, I tell you."

She made jeering, *cr-r-rucking* sounds, tumbling through the air as if rolling with laughter.

The butcher monk.

I threw a rock at her and missed. "Stupid bird!"

My cheeks burned with the shame of hypocrisy and guilt. The Raven saw it, and every day I lived with the fear that others would see it too. I had only killed to defend my life or when justice had demanded it—and the risk of being caught in the act was low. Even so, I struggled to keep my hands clean of the bloodguilt that proclaimed my sins to the world. I could kill Karl, but I would never get away with the murder of God's chosen king. That was the sacrifice the gods demanded of me.

Coward.

The Raven flew away, but her cackling persisted, lodging itself in my mind like the ceaseless squeaking of a wheel.

Justice demands it.

She was right. My killing days were not over yet, and I was running out of time to make amends for them.

Treulogo

Wulfhedinn

J bolted down the stone steps, gloating in my victory over the Walkyrie. I had passed her test and was expecting Vala to show herself soon.

A few dead leaves blew up from the ground below. They scraped lightly across a step in front of me and sailed off the edge. At the bottom of the staircase, I waited, but she did not come. The morning passed. At midday, more dead leaves blew across my feet, followed by a delicious scent rising softly from the forest floor.

Sweet musk and hawthorn.

Vala's ethereal scent. It carried the memory of her warmth and her body pressing against my flesh. At the same time, I felt the jolt of her sword striking against mine. I lingered in the competing sensations, enjoying both at the same time. Then the feelings faded like a retreating mist, revealing a female form standing on the shore of a small lake. We had swum naked together there last Midsummer Day, and the echo of that moment brought tears to my eyes.

"Vala!" I cried, my pulse racing.

She dissipated into the sparkling lake's ripples, and the water flattened. It lay smooth as glass, reflecting a perfect image of the Raven's Stones rising into the sky. Vala's world. She had brought me to this place, and I yearned to share it with her again.

Falling to my knees, I threw water into my face and bathed my blistered hands in its coolness. My splashing broke the stillness of the water, and I saw something bobbing on the waves I had created. A small cluster of white flowers floated in the middle of the lake. It was a circlet of hawthorn like the one Vala had worn in her hair on Midsummer Day. Its scent drifted to me with a deep, moist richness.

Sweet musk and hawthorn.

I had to possess her flowers, sure they would bring her touch back to me. I dropped my wolf skin and dove into the icy water. Exhilarated by my excitement and the shocking cold, I retrieved the circlet, swam back to shore, and buried my nose in its sweet, musky scent. The petals were impossibly alive for winter, and I imagined they had been enchanted by crowning Vala's long, black hair. Droplets fell from my beard onto the petals glistening with moisture. She had to be nearby.

I sensed someone outside the clearing. A figure emerged from the shadows, but it was not Vala. It was a fur-covered beast. A Wulfhedinn. Then a pair of eyes gleamed to my right and faded back into the forest. Another emerged to my left and vanished. A beast's husky breath came so close behind me, I felt its heat on my bare back. I turned, and it was gone. Another dark shape leaped from behind a tree and dissipated into the thickets. The smell of old fur hides grew stronger as Vala's flower petals withered into dust, leaving thorns that pierced my hands. A crown of thorns. I had been stalked and baited by the pack, the Wulfhednar.

Aware of my nakedness, I threw on my wolf cloak and grabbed my spear. Four Wulfhednar emerged from the shadows. They aimed spears at me and carried sheathed swords, axes and seaxes in their belts. I had no chance of surviving their attack, but I crouched low, ready to defend myself as best I could.

They moved closer, and I could see human jaws under their furry muzzles. They were bare-chested under their wolf skins, and each bore the mark of the Raven. Their scars matched the cut the Walkyrie had given me on my chest when they had brought me into the pack. Despite that, they were not possessed by the wolf. They were men wearing wolf cloaks, not demons with eyes of fire.

I spun around, trying to face them all. They kept their weapons low, more cautious than aggressive, but I was not fooled. Even as men, they were fearsome warriors. I gripped my spear, poised to fight. One by one, they lowered their hoods, and I recognized Widukind among them.

"You have survived—again," he said.

I turned steadily, measuring the threat each one posed. One Wulfhedinn was completely bald, but he was not old. He had a hungry look in his eyes, and his body was lean, muscular, and covered with scars. The tallest Wulfhedinn dwarfed the rest of us like a massive, ancient oak. A thick mass of fire-red hair topped his unnaturally large head, and his enormous hands could probably choke a horse. Most striking was the size of his wolf mask.

Such giants existed in the mists of time long past—but also in the figure of this man.

The fourth Wulfhedinn was smaller than the others. His white hair was braided to his waist and shimmered like silver in the sun. Blindness clouded one eye, but his expression was cunning. He focused intensely on me with his ghost eye. The old warrior might see better half-blinded than the rest of them put together.

"You have much to prove to the Walkyrie," Widukind said.

"Where is she?" I demanded. "Where is Vala?"

He was in no hurry to answer.

We were standing in a tense silence when a plump youth ran out from the forest. His embroidered mantle was pinned with a silver brooch that looked too large for him. He held a sword like a child at play and screamed, "Treulogo! Treulogo!" He shouted with so much spite that his voice cracked. "Truth liar, oath breaker! He is not one of us." He stopped next to Widukind, clearly afraid to get any closer to me.

Widukind put a hand on the boy's shoulder and moved him backward. "Neither are you—yet."

The color rose in his smooth cheeks, highlighting his little upturned nose, pouty lips, and unblemished face.

The bald warrior studied me, tapping his second finger on his spear shaft. "The boy is right. You rejected the wolf skin and returned to our enemy, the butcher king."

"The butcher…?"

"King Karl, *your* king, the one you swore an oath to. But you betrayed him as well. You are without loyalty, a treulogo." His wolf skin smelled of killing, of languishing in blood. He rubbed his mouth and licked his lips, hungry for my flesh. "I would happily slay you now, treulogo."

He wanted to tear out my throat, yet he had not come closer

than ten paces, the length in which he could safely defend himself from my spear. None of them had come nearer.

"Where is the Walkyrie?" I demanded.

They remained silent, as though guarding a secret. I wondered where the rest of the pack was. Lurking just beyond the clearing?

"Where are the other Wulfhednar?" I asked.

"Why did you come here?" the older one with the dead eye asked.

If he was waiting for me to swear loyalty to them, he would be disappointed.

Lowering his spear, he approached me cautiously, without menace. "I am Erhard," he said, "and you are a riddle, treulogo."

"My name is Gerwulf."

"So you acknowledge your real name." His good eye twinkled, taking me off my guard. "Tell us why you risked your life to forsake a rich and powerful king who gave you an honored place in his court."

"That is obvious," the bald one said, grabbing his crotch. "He wants the Walkyrie."

"We all want the Walkyrie," the giant said.

They laughed, but not at the joke. They were amused by me.

"You cannot possess the Walkyrie," Erhard said. "You *belong* to her, like the rest of us."

The bald one spat. "He still licks the balls of the Christian god. I can smell it on him."

"I think his taste has changed," Erhard said. "The Walkyrie chose him as one of us. He bears the Raven's mark we all share." His gnarled finger traced the scar on my chest. "She and the Walkyrie may still be with him."

"Is this true?" Widukind asked me. "Has she brought you the wolf spirit?"

I did not want to answer him.

"We cannot trust him, no matter what he says," the bald one said.

"He has survived the Walkyrie's trial in the tower," Erhard said. "It is a sign we cannot ignore."

"Erhard is right," Widukind said. "We will accept you, but I will watch you closely, treulogo."

"So will I." The giant one stepped between Widukind and me, ensuring I took in the full measure of him. "I am Abbo, Widukind's guard."

His warning was clear; I could not threaten Widukind without killing him first.

The bald warrior loomed so close to me, I could feel his heavy breath. "Remember my face, treulogo. It will be the last thing you see if I smell the faintest stink of betrayal on your dirty Christian flesh. The last thing you will hear is my name, Rotgrim."

I held his gaze. I could have declared I was no longer a Christian. I could have defended myself by telling them many things—how I had tried to stop the executions of their Saxon kinsmen at Verden. How I had attacked the butcher king and had nearly died for it. But I refused. Fuck him.

Widukind pulled the pretty young boy forward. "This is my son, Wichbert."

Son? I should have expected it. The rebel leader probably had many more. Not that I cared. The boy scowled and curled his upper lip, like an overindulged nursling who thought himself more important than he was. I was not this brat's brother in any way, and I could not think of his father as mine.

"This talk is done," said Widukind. "We must move on. We will see how you choose to walk your wolf path with us, Gerwulf."

Without a glance at me, Widukind stole away into the forest.

Wichbert tried to follow, but Abbo's giant hand stopped him, allowing the senior warrior Erhard to go next. Then Abbo shadowed Erhard and Widukind. Rotgrim popped Wichbert in the gut with the butt of his spear and trotted after the others. The boy fell hard on his soft backside, and I thought he might cry.

"No one wants you here, treulogo," he said, struggling to hold back the tears. He rose slowly and scrambled after the others.

I could hardly believe the same man had bred both of us. He and his Wulfhednar would fight again—soon and often—and my half-brother would not survive long. That was certain. Maybe that is what Widukind intended.

I wanted to return to the familiarity of the chamber in Wodan's Tower, where I had spent so much time with Vala. I ached to lie with her in the place where she had cared for me, healed my wounds, and loved me. I was sure it was where she would come for me. And the rope bridge was still in place.

I climbed the stairs back to the chamber and was halfway there when the Raven appeared. She hovered on the updraft between the stones briefly and dove to the rope, grasping it in her talons. It unraveled and dissipated in the breeze. Flying after the Wulfhednar, she carried away any hope of returning to the chamber. Her message was clear.

Go with the pack.

The Farm

Wulfhedinn

J caught up quickly with the Wulfhednar. They had taken a well-worn path leading west from the Raven's Stones. No one seemed to notice I had lagged behind. Wichbert was right; they hated me. The sting of their scorn was not a new feeling. I had run away and hidden from worse contempt many times. Neither pagan nor Christian welcomed a bastard half-breed like me—especially one they believed to be a traitor. I could run away and hide from them too, but I knew Vala would never come to me if I did. The Raven had made that clear.

Erhard dropped back from the others and whispered in my ear, "Well, well. I had my doubts about you. I still do, but here you are. This is a good day for you. You are ready to begin."

"Begin what?"

"Earning your place." His clouded eye burned through me as though it saw all my secrets. "I know what you really want," he said.

"You think so?"

"You will not see the woman or the child she carries until you satisfy the Walkyrie. If you fail, your own dark spirit will destroy you, and the Walkyrie will not save you from it a second time."

"I do not need her to save me. I win my own battles and have done so my whole life."

He shook his head. "You have much to learn about yourself and the Goddess of Three Faces. And you have a long journey to become the kind of man and the kind of Wulfhedinn your father is."

"I am my own man."

"Indeed."

Erhard hastened his step to join the others. I fell behind, embracing the extra space between me and them. They were full-blooded Saxons, pure Wulfhednar who belonged to their pack. They did not understand the pain and darkness I had endured as a half-blood, a lone man possessed by a wolf demon.

Rotgrim stopped to wait for me, leering. "Thinking about her?" His upper lip curled and twisted. "Missing the feeling of sinking your cock into her warm cunny?" He leered. "We *all* do."

Smashing my bare knuckles against his face was the only thing that would set things right. My punch landed square, and his nose cracked under my fist and bled. The fury and strength had come from me—the man with the sore fist—not the wolf. I liked the pain the punch gave me, glad to settle the matter man-to-man. I expected Rotgrim might call upon the wolf to get even, which would tell me what kind of man *he* was. Dropping my wolf skin and spear, I took a wide stance and waved on his retaliation.

"Call the wolf if you must," I said.

The others had stopped to watch.

Rotgrim brushed the blood from his face and rose slowly. "Good punch."

"Sorry to mar your pretty face."

The Wulfhednar chuckled. Rotgrim already had a crooked nose, a brawler's nose, and when the bleeding stopped and the swelling faded, it would not look much different than it had.

He dropped his wolf skin and weapons, balled his fists, and scanned me, searching for my weaknesses. He glanced at my belly scar, an old wound that should have been fatal. It had healed through the love of Vala's care and the power she wielded wearing the Walkyrie's Raven mask. Now that scar was tougher than armor.

Rotgrim swung hard, and my gut took the jolt. It hit me like a boulder launched from a catapult. I doubled over. God's bones, the man was strong. The strength he would possess when he invoked the wolf would be staggering. I had no desire to hit him again. We had traded blows, and the matter was finished in my mind.

As we moved on, I wondered if he had truly wanted to fight man-to-man. Maybe he could not call the wolf and *had* to fight as a man. I had not seen the wolf come to any of them yet.

I quickly forgot the incident as the scent of smoking salt pork filled the air. Rotgrim's nose was still dripping, but he seemed not to care as he licked his chops. The smell of meat grew stronger as we came to the edge of the forest. A large farmstead spread out below us, nestled in an open glen. Plowed fields thick with stubble surrounded a handful of sturdy buildings. The black soil smelled rich and fertile. An orchard of hazelnut and apple trees covered the southern part of the glen. Naked berry bushes grew thickly on the fringes of the forest, having been carefully harvested by the farmer, no doubt.

Several dozen cattle and horses grazed in the field stubble and drank from a stream flowing through the farm. Milk cows and goats with heavy teats chewed their cuds near a manger stuffed with hay. More hay was stacked high for the winter, protected under a roof structure. Fat sows snorted and wallowed in their pens. Chickens clucked softly, pecking at surplus grain scattered around a bursting granary.

The entire glen was ringed by a wattle fence. In the center of it stood a sturdy wattle-and-daub hall, roofed with thick thatch. Smoke seeped from under the eaves, heavy with the aromas of roasted barley, beer mash, and curing pork. A small cottage stood alone on the other side of the farm. Despite the sunny day, the door was closed, and the shutter pulled shut across its single window. The life of the farm was centered around the hall across the glen where a woman sat in the sun outside the open door, nursing an infant. She was surrounded by other children and baskets overflowing with vegetables, herbs, and eggs.

A man, three older boys, and two dogs emerged from the forest, driving several fat pigs toward the hall. The younger children ran and greeted them, nine in all. The man kissed the woman and stroked the infant's cheek.

Everything about the farmstead heralded abundance and fertility, including the rich, black soil in the fallow fields of early winter. The family and its farm bore no scars of famine, strife, or war. There were no burned-out buildings, no skeletal, sickly children. The Christian priests said such a place only existed in the Garden of Eden. Even King Karl's rich estates paled in comparison to it. My mouth watered for it all. I wanted to share such a place with Vala and the baby.

Abbo sighed, almost like a woman. "I do not want this to change."

It was a strange sentiment from such a giant of a man whose last words were grim threats to me.

"We cannot alter our fate, but we can meet it with honor," Widukind said.

He trotted down the glen. Abbo, Wichbert, and Rotgrim followed, leaving Erhard and me at the top of the rise.

I wondered what Widukind had meant. "What is this place?" I asked Erhard.

"Our home."

It had not occurred to me the Wulfhedinn pack had a home, a real home. I had assumed they lived in a dark hole in the ground like I had. No wonder they looked down at me with scorn, but I had experienced rich dwellings too, places they could hardly imagine. When I was King Karl's Royal Scout, I had lived in a stone palace. Despite feather beds, many people, and more food than I could eat, I found life there as lonely and impoverished as a wolf's hole, but in a different way. Neither my dark hole nor the king's palace was anything like the farm.

"Is it real?" I asked.

Erhard grinned. "Of course."

"And these people are your servants?"

"Never!" His eyes flashed for a moment, as though I had insulted them. "They are sacred farmers and the guardians of the Raven's Stones, a position more honored than the highest nobility. Odilia, Kuno, and their children dedicate their lives to the Wulfhednar. They grow crops and raise livestock to feed us and provide respite for us." The wizened lines on his face deepened, and his eyelids drooped with years of fatigue. "They *were* protected by the Walkyrie, but...anyway, we will rest, eat, and gather our strength here. This may be the last time it is so."

"The Walkyrie and the wolf spirit are not with you and the pack, are they?"

He shook his head. "You have a quick and clever mind. Good. We need all the wit and muscle we can muster."

"What happened?"

"I am not sure I should tell you yet, but you have already figured out the worst of it. Might as well know everything now, but you must be sworn to secrecy."

"Who would I tell? I can never go back to the king. Anyway, I do not really care if you tell me anymore or not."

"But you just asked." He considered me for a moment, his ghost eye probing deeply into mine. "You are right. Karl will skin you alive the moment he sees you, so I will tell you everything and consider your secrecy your first trial." He paused, examining my face. "More than half of the Wulfhednar deserted the pack and surrendered to the butcher king at Verden."

That surprised me. "You had won a great victory against Karl. Why would they surrender?"

"The victory at Süntel was *too* great. They were afraid."

I snorted. "I thought the Wulfhednar were fearless."

"The Wulfhednar are, but the men under the masks are not. Many Saxons were frightened after the battle because so many of the king's commanders—his friends and kin—had been killed. They feared the vengeance Karl would take on them with his massive army and the power of his Holy Spear. Even the Wulfhednar were losing faith in the pack and the Walkyrie. We began to fight among ourselves, and some gave up their wolf skins and surrendered."

"So?"

"A pack divided destroys the Walkyrie's magic. Because of our dissension and dishonor, we lost her and the wolf with her."

"I ran from the pack, back to your enemy. My dishonor did not seem to break her magic."

He put a hand on my shoulder. "The other Wulfhednar abandoned the pack. You simply were not ready to stay."

"And still, you call me treulogo."

"As men, we do not trust you, but if you bring the Walkyrie back to us, we will all become one wolf pack again."

"I do not control the Walkyrie or the wolf and…" I stopped myself from saying more. I did not want to admit the Walkyrie and wolf spirit had not come to me either since Verden. Let them think I still had her favor.

"No one rules the Walkyrie," he said. "You belong to her, like the rest of us."

I pulled away from him. "You already told me that. I do not belong to anyone."

He tittered. "I have hope for you and the rest of the pack. The Raven spirit still flies with us, and that is a good omen." He rubbed his hip. "But for now, I am hungry, and my bones ache for the comfort of beer and a warm fire. Stay here by yourself, if you please, but the company is far better in the farm hall than in the forest."

He ambled down the glen with a slight limp, still rubbing his hip. In front of the hall, Odilia was hugging the Wulfhednar as if each one were her own son returning from war. She gave Erhard the longest hug of all. Kuno greeted them all warmly, and the children petted their wolf skins, their faces glowing. They clearly worshiped the Wulfhednar and were too young to smell the stink of desperation on their pelts. The pack was made up of defeated men forced to accept a treulogo and a spoiled, useless brat tagging along to a hopeless war.

They went inside, and no one seemed to have noticed me at the top of the glen. Even the dogs and livestock had not raised their heads in my direction. But something was watching me from the woodland shadows. Raising my spear, I spun around. Three sets of eyes confronted me, reflecting the fading light of dusk in a way no human eyes could.

"Who is there?"

The eyes vanished, but I still felt their presence. My heart pounded. Spirits or demons? Was it Vala?

"What do you want?" I asked.

You, Gerwulf.

I had heard the voice many times before. It had haunted me in the Walkyrie's shriek across a thundering sky, in the call of the Raven, and in the wolf spirit's howling. She was there, and so was her scent.

Sweet musk and hawthorn.

I was sure I smelled it, hawthorn, the witch's bloom. I had been six moons since the budding of the thorny hawthorn thickets, but her magical flower always blossomed in my mind.

Sweet musk and hawthorn.

I followed her heady fragrance into the woods. The forest sank into complete darkness and silence, and the scent vanished. I turned several times, trying to pick it up again.

A rumbling of distant thunder echoed through the bare trees. Complete silence. The sound came again and again, growing louder, coming closer. The fur stood up on the back of my pelt. Lightning flashed, striking nearby and nearly knocking me to the ground. An ear-slitting boom shook the ground, and the Walkyrie burst from the sky. She straddled her huge black stallion, wearing a black feathered cloak. The Raven's mask covered most of her face, but it did not hide her sky-blue eyes—Vala's eyes.

She spurred her mount and charged me, spear poised. I rolled out of the way and jumped to my feet.

"Vala!" I reached for the horse's reins. It reared, hooves kicking, sharp as knives. One of them sliced my arm and knocked me down and kicked grit in my face. Before I could get up again, the Walkyrie flapped her great winged cloak and rose into the sky.

"There is no Vala and Gerwulf." She spoke with a crack of thunder that shook my bones. "We are wolf, Raven, and Walkyrie."

"Vala!" I screamed, scrambling to my feet. "Come back!"

She left me holding my bleeding arm. My flesh burned with the Walkyrie's sting, but my heart could not forget the eyes of the woman. I swallowed deeply, fighting the disappointment Vala had not come. I told myself the appearance of the Walkyrie had to be a good sign. She had come to me—and to no one else in the pack. Underneath the Walkyrie's mask and feathered cloak, Vala must have still loved me, and I needed to stay where she could find me.

I walked to the farm, the heathen Garden of Eden, holding my bleeding arm. As I joined the others in the hall, the Raven flew in after me.

Ƅonor is Victory

Wulfheðinn

The Raven perched on one of the hall's rafters, and several children jumped from the table and ran to my side. Erhard and the others had made themselves comfortable at a long table. They joked together and gulped beer, ignoring me, but the children clustered around me, stroking my wolf skin.

A boy of about five clung to my leg. "I want to be a Wulfhedinn too."

A young girl asked if she could hold my spear, and a boy of about ten asked, "Are you going to be the pack leader someday?"

Odilia herded them away. "Let Gerwulf be," she said, carrying an infant on her hip as easily as a warrior carried a blade in its sheath. She knew my name, so they must have discussed me. She smiled, her cheeks like ripe apples, round as her full bosom and bottom. Then she frowned and took my arm to examine it. "You are hurt."

"It is a scratch," I said.

"Nonetheless, I will clean and bandage it, but you must eat first—before the rest of those wolves devour everything. You look like you have not eaten in days." She ran her fingers across my face. "My, my, you have endured a terrible beating, but you can rest and heal now. You are safe here." Her voice was as comforting as melting butter on fresh bread.

Her husband stood, a drinking horn in hand. "Welcome, Gerwulf. I am Kuno, and you are welcome at the table we provide for the Wulfhednar."

Wichbert scooted down the bench, leaving no room to sit between him and Widukind, but Kuno made space for me next to him. Wichbert scowled as Kuno formally introduced Odilia and his nine children.

Odilia and the older girls brought us platters of salted pork, vegetables, and cheese. I grabbed a haunch of salted pork and tore it apart. After devouring much of it, I gulped half a horn of beer before I realized no one was eating. They were all staring at me. Had I done something wrong?

Odilia and the girls were still serving food, and when they finally sat down, the meal began. The wolf warriors gorged themselves while the younger children bickered and stole food from one another's plates. The older boys discussed hunting rabbits. Food fell from their mouths as they argued about who was the best with a sling. The girls stared at me, whispered, and giggled.

The food was so rich and the beer so strong that I thought I had fallen into a dream. But if it were, Vala would have been there. The only hint of her was her Raven spirit, perched above, preening its glossy feathers.

When the eating slowed, Odilia sent the children outside to bring in the pigs and chickens for the night. A couple of dogs trotted after them. She brought out a linen cloth and water to tend my wound. I was too full and contented to argue. Then she brought out more beer, and when she served her husband, he grinned and pinched her behind.

With a giggle, she smacked him lightly. "I have work to do," she said.

Kuno sighed and turned to Widukind. "There is always work to do, but our labors have been blessed. The barley harvest was good, plenty to brew beer and bake bread. The pigs are fat, and the cows and goats are bursting with milk. The cellar is full of cheese. There is plenty to keep the Wulfhednar strong through the winter."

"And enough for your young ones?" asked Widukind.

Kuno glanced at several dozen hams hanging in the smoky rafters. "More than enough for my ravenous brood, gods be praised. They eat like they have holes in their guts, especially the boys."

"Good. Now you must gather the livestock and as much of the food stores as you can carry. You must move your family north and seek the protection of the Danes."

"What?" asked Odilia. "Why?"

In this isolated haven in the Teutoburg Forest, they had not heard about the massacre yet.

Widukind wiped beer from his mouth. "There has been a massive Saxon surrender to the Franks at Verden."

"You have just won a huge victory over him at the Süntel Hills. You destroyed him, killed twenty of his best commanders. Why would anyone submit to the Frankish king now?"

I knew the answer, but it was not my place to tell them.

"The slain commanders included many of Karl's close kin and friends," Erhard said. "Many Saxons feared his retaliation—and the revenge of his god."

"The Christian god is weak," Odilia said. "Everyone knows this."

"But his king is a snake without honor," Widukind said. "Despite his promise of clemency, Karl ordered his army to surround and capture those who had surrendered and kill them all."

Odilia's rosy cheeks lost their color, and Kuno's jaw dropped in disbelief.

"How many?" he asked.

"Four thousand or more. Perhaps another six or seven hundred. All beheaded."

"And the rest of the pack?" Odilia asked. "I was afraid to ask. Where are they? Did they...?"

Widukind dropped his gaze.

"Seven Wulfhednar submitted, and another was captured," Erhard said.

"Then the pack is broken," Kuno said.

Odilia leaned against her husband, and he put his arm around her. Widukind rose and went to the window. Silence fell on the hall as everyone waited for him to speak. He stared outside for a moment. Then he closed and barred the window as if knowing he would not see the Walkyrie that night. I did not want to tell him how near she had been.

"The Walkyrie and the wolf have not come to us since the surrender at Verden," he said.

Odilia glanced up at the Raven. "But the Raven is with you. And Gerwulf has returned. These are good omens."

Widukind turned and looked at me. "Maybe we can win the favor of the Walkyrie and the gods again. Maybe—but right now we are without the wolf. We are like other mortal men, and the Teutoburg Forest, the Raven's Stones, and the farm have lost the Walkyrie's protection. You are as vulnerable to the Frankish butcher king as any other Saxon farmers."

"We have never been like other farmers," Odilia said. "We are the caretakers of the Wulfhednar and Raven's Stones and will not flee. The gods have seen this coming and blessed us with a rich harvest and thick layers of meat on the animals. We have bounty enough to nourish you well through this fight. The Walkyrie and the wolf *will* return to you before the butcher and his army can get to us."

Kuno agreed. "It is our sacred duty to stay here," he said. "If we abandon you, everyone will know you have lost the Walkyrie, and they will believe the gods have abandoned us all."

Widukind thought for a moment and said, "You are right. No one else can know the pack has lost the wolf."

Odilia planted her fists on her round hips. "We will not run away, and neither will anyone else when they hear of the massacre."

Even Widukind dared not argue with her. "Then I will make careful plans," he said. "We will work together to bring the Walkyrie back to the pack and build a rebellion. Gerwulf will be crucial to this."

He stood and took the axe from his belt and presented it to me. "Vengeance is honor, and honor is victory," he said.

Vengeance? Crucial to his rebellion? Everyone was staring me, waiting for my reaction. The smoke in the hall grew thick and hot. I felt smothered and could not breathe. Sweat ran down my face and chest, and the thick daub walls swayed like they would collapse on top of me. I had to get free of them and their desperate war. I shoved the table, upsetting the cups of beer. Snatching the axe from Widukind, I went for the door.

As I left the hall, Wichbert asked, "Where is he going?"

"Not far," Erhard said.

Mark of the Beast

The Monk

I dipped my quill into the inkpot and blotted it three times. The tip scratched across the parchment, making the lone sound in the king's council. I was glad my hands could stay busy writing an introduction to the meeting while King Karl's commanders languished in tense silence, waiting for him to speak.

The king sat at the head of the table, General Theoderic on his right and Bertrada and his oldest son, Prince Pepin, on his left. Karl grasped the Holy Spear as if he were God Himself, and his crown shone in splendor on his royal head. He displayed no sign of the unhinged madness of earlier that day, but I feared his rational, calculating mind all the more.

I squirmed under the gaze of the high-born nobles. Would anyone suspect the crown had been sullied by the Eater of Souls and purified in a pagan spring? I was still hiding my blood stained habit under my cloak, but would any of them see the blood beneath the ink stains on my hands?

"Brother Pyttel, what is the final tally?" Karl asked.

I startled and shuffled through various documents, glancing at the numbers. "My king, the executions have barely been completed. I need to check each entry for names and ranks to determine how many Saxon nobles have been eliminated. And then I must compile those names on a separate register and..."

"The number. Just give me the total number."

My hand tingled from the tight grip I had on the quill. A drop of ink fell onto one of the parchments, spreading like a churning thunderhead.

"I have collected the counts from each of the scribes, compiled the overall numbers," I said. "Let me recheck my figures." I added the numbers again, hoping for a different result. Damn it all—4,666—those last three numbers were the mark of the beast. The butcher king.

"Well?" asked Karl.

"The final number is...well...4,667."

One beheaded Saxon, give or take, made no difference. The commanders would not know any better, but they would not overlook a number that contained the mark of the beast.

Karl stood, clutching the Holy Spear. His nostrils flared, and the flushing in his neck rose to his face. "More than *four thousand* savages watched as their comrades were beheaded, and *not a single one* was willing to save his own neck by offering some small piece of information? Is that what you are telling me?"

General Theoderic shifted in his seat. His old leg injury was paining him, no doubt. The pus-filled swelling was likely growing again. Despite that, he wore the same stone-cold expression he always did, concealing his pain and his thoughts.

"My officers all concur," he said. "The prisoners in their charge all refused to talk."

"What about the rest of you?" Karl pointed the spear at each of them.

Fulco, commander of an elite company of Scola horsemen, spat. "None of the soulless barbarians would talk, no matter what I did to them before taking their heads."

The other commanders were sons of the generals slain by Saxons at the Süntel Hills ambush. They were all hastily appointed as commanders and had enthusiastically supervised the executions to prove themselves worthy of their new titles. They felt justified in avenging the killing of their fathers. They would never admit their fathers had disobeyed the king's orders and foolishly walked into the disastrous ambush. Despite their fathers' impulsiveness, Karl would take vengeance for their deaths, and their sons were glad to be a part of it.

"None of the prisoners in my charge talked," said Engel, son of Chamberlain Adalgis. He had the same pointy nose as his father. He would embrace his role as chamberlain so he could stick his long nose into the king's treasury, just as his father had.

"None of the captives in my charge did either," said Guillaume, son of Gallo the Horsemaster, leader of the light calvary. He was also like his father, born to the saddle, riding before he could walk.

"I was happy to execute every last ruff-sniffing heathen," said Gasto, son of Count Worad, who had died of his wounds after the ambush. "We have won a huge victory, eliminating thousands of their warriors, including eight Wulfhednar. They are finished."

Karl's jaw tightened, and he spoke through gritted teeth. "The leader and strongest of them all, Widukind, still lives. Enough of his wolf warriors and other rebels are still alive to attack settlements and churches in the borderlands and threaten trade on the Rhine River." He slammed his fist on the table. "I have not won until the rebel leader and his bastard son are taken and we destroy the Walkyrie witch and the Raven's Stones."

No one dared accuse the king of what we all knew—that he had consorted with a demon himself. Their indictments were clear on their faces, but even the brash young commanders held their tongues.

Bertrada smoothed the front of her tunic casually, breaking the tension. "I know we have all heard the rumors about Tracker, the one called Gerwulf," she said. "He came to court disguised as a loyal soldier of God and deceived us all, even Brother Pyttel."

I stopped writing and bowed my head. "Yes, my lady, to my great shame and disgrace."

"The clever demon masqueraded as a loyal servant," she said. "When the Holy Spear was stolen, he tracked down the thieves and returned it. For months, he faithfully reported the movements and tactics of the Saxon rebels. He did not show his true nature until last night when he attacked the king and dared hold the Holy Spear to his throat."

The three young commanders leaned toward Bertrada with wide eyes, eager to believe her version of the story. She made a practiced smile that showed all her teeth. "Despite what you have heard about the Saxon wolf warriors, they are not the monsters you imagine. They are simply men who dress in wolf skins. Savage barbarians. Able warriors, yes, but not devils, hellions, or evil spirits. When we executed eight of them, their heads dropped and rolled on the ground like any mortal's. Their gods were powerless to help them."

"But their gods did help Gerwulf to escape," Prince Pepin said.

His grandmother gave him a sneer of disdain that could have silenced a mad boar. She despised him for his physical weaknesses. His hunchbacked deformity shamed her and the entire family dynasty, but she underestimated his strengths. He had a sharper mind and more determination than his father.

General Theoderic cleared his throat abruptly. "We have to consider the possibility Gerwulf escaped to join the Wulfhednar, which might inspire the barbarians into another rebellion."

The king pounded the Holy Spear on the ground. "Of course he returned to them! And we cannot let him and his father rally another fighting force."

Engel lifted his pointy nose, his face glowing with keenness. "My king, I pledge to continue God's battle to destroy the heathens and their Wulfhednar demons!"

The other young commanders would not be outdone.

"My calvary will run them into the dirt," Guillaume pledged.

Gasto stood and jammed his knife into the table. "My soldiers will burn every inch of their land and choke them out of their holes."

The General shifted again. "Sit, you foolish boy. We cannot win this war on your naive enthusiasm. Winter is upon us, and the army has already been detained in the field beyond the required service." He pointed a gnarled finger at the young generals. "I know there are deserters from each of your contingents, and there will be more if we press the men too long."

Gasto sat, face flushing. I knew he and the others were itching to refute the shameful accusation. Only weak commanders lost men to desertion, but they knew better than to argue with the General.

"The lesser nobles and infantry want to return to their warm halls for winter," Theoderic said. "After they plant the spring crop, it will be time for war again. That is how it has always been done."

Engel scratched his pointy nose and spoke up. "Perhaps the General is right. My father said there is no booty left in this God-forsaken pagan land. We need silver to inspire soldiers to fight into winter, and..."

Theoderic cut him off. "Most importantly, fighting men need food. There is not enough fodder left in Saxony to support any army through winter—ours or theirs. Widukind has lost too many skilled warriors. He has little left but hungry peasants without arms or armor. Let him and his few wolf dogs shiver through the winter in their hole."

"He will not overwinter like a rodent," Karl said. "He will prey on easy targets through the dark months and may seek refuge and support again from his brother-in-law, King Sigfred of the Danes."

The General grunted, always cunning enough to consider a reasonable argument. "That is possible. Brother Pyttel, you know these barbarians better than anyone. What do you say?"

The General never consulted with me, and I doubted he actually wanted me to side with him. I could never tell what game the old goat was playing, but he had given me an opportunity to sway the king toward peace, and I would not pass it up.

"Half of the wolf warriors and thousands of the Saxons' best fighters have been executed," I said carefully. "There simply are not enough pagans left to mount a serious threat. They are soundly defeated and will be willing to submit to God's will."

Commander Fulco pulled a louse from his hair. "I would not take military counsel from a monk," he said, crushing the parasite between his fingers.

"I was fighting battles before you were born!" I immediately wished I had kept quiet.

Fulco glared at me. "So you think you know something about war, old man? I think you know more about heathen magic than anything else."

I dropped my quill and hid my hands inside my sleeves. Had he seen me at a sacred spring?

"Commander Fulco!" Karl snapped. "I will not allow you to

levy false accusation against my loyal scribe, a man of God, and my trusted confessor."

Fulco sat back and shrugged his shoulders. "Forgive me, my king, but we cannot underestimate the evils of the savages' dark magic—especially that conjured by their women. I am hearing reports that the Eater of Souls will bear a child this spring. They say a mortal woman, a witch, carries it in her womb and will bear it for the pagan spirit. The savages believe the child is a descendant of Wodan, a redeemer who will bring the wrath of the old gods down upon all Christians."

Theoderic waved his hand. "We have all heard this superstitious gibberish. We cannot push the army to continue on campaign through the winter based on archaic fears. There is more to be lost than gained, including the loss of more men to desertion."

"Many of the soldiers do not feel right about the executions," Prince Pepin interjected.

Bertrada gave him a scathing look. "Perhaps it is Prince Pepin who does not have the stomach to carry out God's war," she said.

Pepin scratched the back of his head and fell silent.

Karl shot him a scowl. "My son knows as well as any of you the executions were a just act in the sight of God. The heathen barbarians broke their oaths to me and murdered my best commanders at Süntel, and they continue to flaunt God's laws and worship the old gods."

In truth, many of the Saxons had never taken an oath of loyalty to Karl, but no one mentioned it. They dared not suggest that what happened at the Süntel Hills was a fully engaged battle between two armies, not murder.

"This is true, of course" the General said, "but it does not change the realities of staging a continuous campaign in a barren land. Men need time to rest and attend their farms, and we cannot run hastily into the pagan wilds in winter without supplies."

Before they could debate the issue any longer, one of the royal guards broke into the meeting. "My king, urgent news—the bodies of three foot soldiers reported as deserters were found outside camp." He paused and swallowed. "They have been torn apart by wolves…and …and a heathen curse horse has been found staked on a hill above the camp."

No one moved or spoke.

Theoderic laid his hands on the table decisively. "The sooner we conclude the campaign for winter, the better," he said. "This incident will spread panic throughout the ranks, especially among the peasant infantry. We must pull back to Paderborn and send the bulk of the army and the conscripts home for the winter. We will leave an occupying detachment to hold our forts in Saxony through the winter."

Karl tapped his fingers on the shaft of the Holy Spear, thinking. "Agreed. We will dismiss most of the army, but during the withdrawal, all commanders must keep their units under a tight rein. They must pack up and march with discipline and order, like a victorious army. We cannot flee like retreating cowards. General Theoderic will send a few men to destroy the curse horse, and you will reassure your men the deserters were attacked by wolves, not demons. My holy counsel and God deem this to be so. Is this not correct, Brother Pyttel?"

"Of course, my king," I replied hastily. "It is always righteous to glorify God and reject pagan superstitions. God will be with us as we retire for the winter and travel back to our homes to celebrate Yule."

"Yes, yes. Tell them that too." Karl waved his hand, dismissing me. "But the hunt will continue for the rebel and his Wulfhednar through the winter. Commander Fulco, you will assemble a squad of your most elite riders to track them down. You will find the witch who carries the offspring of the Eater of Souls. I give you a free hand. Do what you must to get the locals to talk. Someone must know where Widukind is and how to break through the Teutoburg Forest to get to the Raven's Stones."

Fulco grinned and bowed. "With pleasure."

"I will also send a diplomatic envoy to King Sigfred of the Danes," Karl said. "General Theoderic, you will lead the envoy. Find out if Widukind has fled there, and if he has, negotiate with Sigfred to turn him over to us. Brother Pyttel, you will go with him."

The thought of accompanying Theoderic all the way to King Sigfred's court was more than I could bear. The General would rather throw me into the marsh to drown in mud than tolerate my presence.

"But my king…" I said.

"As a missionary, you understand these heathen Danes," Karl said. "You will make them understand they have more to gain by bowing to me than by standing against me and sheltering a renegade."

The General tilted his head, his hardened eyes latched onto me. He was always looking to find guilt with me. I had little choice but to act compliant.

"A righteous idea, my king," I said. "It will be a wonderful opportunity to convert more pagan souls to God."

"Good. They will all soon see how embracing me and the One True God is their only path to salvation."

The commanders murmured in agreement and voted unanimously to accept the plan. Council adjourned, and I busied myself by rearranging the meeting documents, avoiding further conversation with anyone. I was the last to leave, relieved to be alone, but Prince Pepin was waiting outside for me.

"You say the final count of the executed is 4,667?" he asked, staring up at me due to his crooked back and bent posture.

"Yes."

"Are you sure?"

"Yes, yes. Now I must go and ..."

"That is only one number removed from 4,666."

"One removed, as you say."

"You are lying, like the rest of my father's lackeys," he said. "That number marks my father as the beast, and we both know it."

The butcher king.

"The number is 4,667," I repeated, keeping the rest of my thoughts to myself. I had held my tongue about much that day, including a critical piece of information that would have revolutionized Karl's campaign against the Saxons. Only I knew the magic of the Wulfhednar and Teutoburg Forest was broken.

One Thing

Wulfhedinn

Outside the farm hall, the sun was setting. The bleak light of winter was waning, and my mind cleared in the rapidly chilling air. I hid behind the granary, watching the children chase one another with sticks as though they were swords. They were lost in their game, without a thought of the chores their mother had given them. Their swordplay was clumsier than the moves of noble boys who were trained to fight. They were farmers' children who could scare nothing but their own chickens. Their fat hens and rosters had gathered near the door, clucking softly, waiting to go to their safe roost inside. Tonight, the family's biggest fear was a fox in the woods. That would change quickly if the Walkyrie did not return to the pack soon.

Kuno and Odilia were fools to believe a few men in wolf skins would shield them from the strongest army in the world. This family and every remaining Saxon farm and family would soon face a fate far worse than hungry foxes. The old gods and the new were at war, and they did not care about the mortals who would be crushed beneath them. I wanted no place in it on either side. Neither did the Walkyrie, for she had abandoned them and come to me. She and Vala belonged to me.

I bolted toward the woods, upsetting the chickens. They squawked and flapped their wings, and the children called and chased me, surely alerting everyone inside. I dashed into the trees, losing them quickly, and ran in the direction the Walkyrie had flown earlier. I would find her. I knew she could have been anywhere, but I could track anything, even a spirit. Within one hundred paces, I located the scent I knew so well.

Sweet musk and hawthorn.

I heard small claws and wings flitting through damp leaves—a bird, the size of a raven. The fluttering grew louder and heavier until it sounded like human footsteps. I turned and glimpsed the dark form of a cloaked woman through the branches but quickly lost sight of her. She took shape farther away through the tangle of branches. Instead of calling out, I followed, trying to get close enough to grab her. Every time I neared, she disappeared behind a tree or darted away. She turned once toward me, and I saw a quick shimmer of her blue eyes through a thicket's thorny bare branches.

Sweet musk and hawthorn.

Intoxicated by the smell, I tripped and scraped my knee on a sharp rock. Cursing, I jumped and rushed after her. Soon, I was almost within arm's reach. Leaping, I grabbed her mantle and pulled her close. I held her loosely, not wanting to hurt the baby she carried. She slipped out of my embrace, as if a ghost, and was gone.

"Vala!"

Silence. I strained my ears, listening for any sound she might have made. The forest remained unearthly quiet, but the pounding of my heart seemed deafening.

"I should not be here," she said from the darkness.

Her voice was as I remembered, as soothing as the tiny swallows of warm broth she had spooned into my dry mouth. It was as comforting as the potion she had fed me to relieve my pain while my belly wound healed.

"Show yourself. I want to see you," I said. "I need to know you and the baby are well."

"We are fine. The baby grows every day and kicks like a Wulfhedinn warrior."

I spun around. "Where are you? I cannot see you. Come closer."

"I must go before…"

"Before what? Why have you not come to me sooner?"

"I could not, and this is not the right time yet, but…"

"Why not? I am here now. I want to talk to you. When I saw you at Verden, rounded up with the others who were to be executed, I thought…I could not stand it. I…"

She emerged from the shadows. "You saw what you needed to see."

Her words made no sense until I saw the black-feathered mask lying at my feet in a stream of moonlight. The mask of the Eater of Souls, the Walkyrie. The Walkyrie was using her again to entrap me—or perhaps Vala was a willing participant. I did not want to believe it, but standing face-to-face with her and the mask between us, I could not tell for sure.

With all the strength I had, I swung my axe and cut the mask in half. "Why did you bring this thing here? I want to see only you—not her. You, she, or both of you are using dark magic to confuse me and draw me into war. I thought you, Vala, wanted me, but perhaps you are deceiving me again!"

"*I, me, the woman*, have never deceived you," she cried, clutching her chest. "But the Walkyrie does what she must to reveal truth when you refuse to see it."

"Stop it!" I swung again and again at the feathered mask, hacking it into pieces. "I am freeing you from her."

She waited until I had decimated the mask into a pile of feathers and did not try to stop me.

"I am her, and at the same time, not her," she said, "but you are still too much of a Christian to understand." Her voice was cool, almost icy.

I panted, nearly choking with outrage. "Too Christian? Are you mad? I have been damned by the Christian god, not once, but twice for what I have done to come back to you. You know that. Your Raven spirit and you were there."

"I was not there. Not *me*."

"I cannot believe I let you fool me again. I now see that you are the Walkyrie's master, not her prisoner. *I* was her prisoner— and you are trying to make me her captive again."

"You were never her captive. Once you had healed in Wodan's Tower, no one was holding you there," she said. "You were free to go, and you chose to leave the pack—and me. You returned to the court of King Karl, and he gave you everything a Christian man could want. Why would you come back here?"

"I thought you had been captured and were to be executed with the rest of them. I risked my life to stop it! And when I heard there was a chance you might have escaped, I came to find you. I…I thought I lov…" I locked my jaw to stop myself from saying more.

"You did it all for yourself."

"Do not talk to me like I am one of those filthy, carnal wolves in your pack. I am nothing like them."

I had no more words for her. How could I love such a creature? The Spirit of Three Faces, they called her, and I was hopelessly enchanted with only one of them. Was she even real? My pulse pounded in my head, and I needed to lash out at something. So I swung my axe at the nearest tree several times, taking out large chunks of bark and wood. When my outburst did not soothe me, I stormed off, unsure which direction I was going.

"You had all you needed here with me and the pack," she called after me. "You ran away like a coward, and now you are going to leave me again. I…"

She choked, unable to finish; she was crying. I should have kept going but could not help myself. I turned around, and she appeared behind me, tears gleaming on her mortal cheeks.

"Please, stay," she whispered. "I need you, as any woman of flesh and blood needs a man. I am not supposed to want you in that way, but I do."

Her charms were as strong now as they had ever been. I knew it, yet I could not take another step away from her.

She wrapped her arms around herself and clutched tightly. "I was pledged to the Walkyrie as a young girl. She took my body and gave me her mask. It is the same with you and the wolf. We belong to them. We cannot be what we want, but we can be what we are together."

My rage melted away, and I had the sudden longing to take her in my arms, protect her, soothe her. But I did not move, still distrusting her tears and the feelings they roused in me.

"Go away with me," I said. "We will leave the Walkyrie and the pack."

A breeze stirred, lifting the butchered raven feathers in the air. They whirled around one another, spinning more and more rapidly until they bonded together to restore the Walkyrie's mask. It settled gently on the ground, and Vala picked it up.

"You cannot destroy her so easily," she said. "There is only one thing you can do to free us."

"What?"

The Raven called from above, bellowing like a moose calling for its mate.

"She needs blood....I cannot...I must go. Before she..."

"Whose blood? What...?"

I could not tear myself away from those eyes, the color of the Midsummer Day sky. I knew they would disappear in a flash, so I asked the question I most wanted answered. "Is the child mine?"

She gazed up to where the Raven beckoned her. "Yes," she said.

Then the mask was upon her, and she vanished. Her scent faded. A stiff breeze blew through the trees and shook a few shriveled leaves clinging to the hawthorn thickets.

Her absence was a vice crushing my heart, but she had told me what I most longed to hear. She had chosen me above all the others. The woman was mine. I yearned to smell her skin and hair, to touch her, and I no longer cared if she was bewitching me.

I screamed into the emptiness, "What do you want of me?"

I tried to make sense of what she had said and longed to take back my angry words. One thing she had said was clear though; the child was mine. I clung to the thought, and as much as I wanted to run away, I could not leave her. Not yet.

Strike a Blow

Wulfhedinn

Odilia was shooing the children up the ladder to their pallets when I closed the hall door behind me. Kuno and the Wulfhednar were talking, and the conversation did not stop as I heaved the heavy timber bar in place.

Erhard slid down the bench, gesturing for me to sit between him and Rotgrim. "Have a good piss?" he asked.

"Delightful," I said.

"Enjoy it while you can." He shook his head. "It grows more difficult with age."

Rotgrim sneered. "I hope to never live so long."

The children roughhoused in the loft above our heads. They screamed and giggled until something or someone hit the floor, hard. No one cried, but dust filtered through the floorboard cracks, upsetting the roosting chickens at the far end of the hall. The cows and goats bleated in their stalls. Lost in thought, I hardly noticed the ruckus. I was thinking of Vala, still trying to understand what she had meant about freeing us from the Walkyrie.

"Go to sleep, or the Wulfhednar will put you to sleep!" Kuno shouted.

The noise stopped abruptly. Odilia smiled and filled our drinking horns. "You must come more often."

I refused more beer. She and the rest of them were trying to force me into their war. Every proud and desperate one of them, from the smallest toddler in this family, to the honorable leader of the Wulfhednar, to the one I could not refuse, Vala.

Rotgrim elbowed me in the side, jolting me into the middle of a heated discussion. Abbo was bickering with Widukind and Kuno.

"Treulogo, what do *you* think of the cowards who surrendered to your king?" Rotgrim asked with a mouth stuffed full of meat. His nose had swollen, and bruises were forming under his eyes, but the injury had not slowed his eating.

I glared at him. "I saw frightened men and boys who were too young to know any better. They submitted to Karl to protect their families and themselves."

Rotgrim slammed his fist on the table. "They were cowards!"

Widukind pulled his heavy brows together. "Wulfhednar, nobles, warriors, or peasants—they may have surrendered with dishonor, but they refused to betray us. We owe them blood vengeance."

"But the wolf warriors who submitted to Karl broke the pack!" Rotgrim said. "We have lost everything because of them! We will have to run and hide like mice if the butcher king mounts a full-scale campaign against us."

"He already thinks he has defeated us," Erhard said. "I think he will withdraw his army from Saxony for the winter."

Rotgrim sneered. "Perhaps he will spend the dark months warming his sagging royal balls in one of his palaces. It is what he always does. The treulogo should know. As the Royal Scout, he as close to the King's balls as his whores' lips."

The others laughed, but I jumped up, axe in hand. Rotgrim pulled a short seax and stood. He raised a heavy brow, daring me to make the first move. I thought we had settled our differences, but Rotgrim was like a surly bear whose jaws had locked onto prey it wanted to maul thoroughly before eating.

"Calm yourselves, you blaggards," Erhard said. "The Walkyrie will never return with the wolf if we keep fighting one another. We must forget the past and join together as a pack again. That requires thinking with our heads, not our cullions."

Wichbert drew his sword and waved it in the air. "I can fight with the pack!"

Rotgrim shoved him off the bench, and he fell on his ass. "You can stay here and squeeze goat teats and make cheese."

"We must strike hard, hit the king boldly," said Widukind. "We will attack his church at Paderborn."

Abbo shifted on the bench and it swayed under his great weight. "The palace church? With just five of us? Their god will strike us down before we even break down the door."

"The Christian god has never stopped us from attacking churches," Widukind said.

Abbo fidgeted with his sword. "Small churches, shitholes. Easy pickings. How can we fight the sorcery of Christian priests in the palace church without the wolf?" The giant seemed more fearful of Christians than anyone else.

Erhard clapped Abbo's huge shoulder. "You have seen enough

dying priests to know their blood is real, and their Christian prayers are powerless."

"And they are unarmed and untrained," Widukind said.

"Priests." Rotgrim licked the edge of his dagger. "I *do* like the taste of their blood. The five of us could take a hundred of those mud suckers, with or without the wolf. The palace church is just another Christian shithole, and I am not afraid of getting a little shit on me."

Abbo and Erhard laughed in agreement. I remained quiet, delaying the inevitable, knowing how much they needed me.

"We will create a diversion at the Lippespringe garrison," Widukind said. "That will draw the Paderborn guards away from the city walls and leave fewer protecting the church."

Erhard was looking at me with the cunning of one who had lived longer and knew more than most. "As Royal Scout and Huntsman, Gerwulf is familiar with the garrison. He must know its weaknesses—and his way around Paderborn." He tilted his head, waiting for my answer.

Widukind locked eyes with me, expecting a response. He too had thought of this.

"This is a fool's errand," I said. "Even if we get inside the walls and burn the church and the whole stinking royal city, you have no chance of defeating the most organized and powerful army north of the Alps."

"True," Widukind said, "but we will not be fighting his whole army. The king may not have returned from Verden to Paderborn and Lippespringe yet. The city and garrison might be nearly empty, lightly defended. We must take the chance and act now or not at all."

"The treulogo could help us, if he wanted," Rotgrim said, "but I do not trust him and will not follow him right into our enemy's garrison."

"Nor will I," Widukind said. "Gerwulf, you will scout the garrison first—alone. Then we will decide if we should trust your word. If we do, then we will determine how to attack."

I did not care about proving myself to them, and I resented Widukind for acting like my commander. The Walkyrie had come to me alone. She and the child were mine, not his, and I had far more knowledge about the Franks than any of them. I, not Widukind, should have been giving the orders to the pack.

"I am not your underling," I said.

Erhard was studying me with his ghost eye. "The Walkyrie brought you back to us for this purpose."

The Raven squawked in the rafters, ruffling the feathers on her head, appearing to grow horns. Her beak hung open.

Strike a blow to the king's god.
I thirst for their blood.

The Raven had made it clear. Vala and I would not be free until I had given the Walkyrie the blood vengeance she craved. The vengeance the Saxons all craved. How I hated that bird.

"I know a way to get inside the garrison," I said.

"How?" Widukind asked.

"There is a place in the palisade wall where a timber can be shifted enough to let a man squeeze through. I have done it before."

Rotgrim scoffed. "It sounds too easy."

"I will get inside the wall and see how many soldiers have been left to hold the garrison. Likely not many. We might be able to take them if we surprise them at night from inside their own walls."

Widukind searched my face for signs of deception. He took his time and did not rush to a decision. Finally, he said, "We will do as Gerwulf says."

Abbo had been busy stuffing food into his huge mouth. He washed it all down with several gulps of beer and slammed his cup. "If Widukind says we do this, we do this."

Rotgrim muttered an agreement—not because he suddenly trusted me, but because I would be carrying all the risk on my shoulders. Surely, he wanted to see me fail.

"First, we will sacrifice at the Raven's Stones," Widukind said.

"The king could return with his army at any time, if he is not back already," I said. "How long will a sacrifice take?"

Erhard patted me on the back. "As long as it needs to."

"Then let us not waste time," I said. "We should take the farm horses. They look like good mounts."

"Wulfhednar do not ride," Widukind said. "We use the wolf legs."

"We do not have wolf legs."

"And no one can know that."

"But no one would see us riding in these woods in the dark."

"The Raven will."

I glared up at the black bird, wishing it would fall into the fire, but I was not going to win the argument, so I gave it up.

The children were peeking over the loft's edge, spying on us, thinking we did not notice them. Odilia offered us packs of salted meat for the trip and a goat for the sacrifice. We bade the farm family goodbye and stepped outside in the crisp, moonlit air. It was a good night for a raid, and despite the need to hurry, I paused to admire the farm one more time.

"Thinking about becoming a farmer?" Erhard sniggered. "Well, forget it. A wolf is born to hunt and fight, and the Raven feasts on the blood we spill. That's our destiny. You are us, and we are you."

"You are nothing to me."

His face lit up as if I had made a joke. "Why, we are all you have." He followed the others up the glen, snickering. "He thinks himself a farmer."

The old man is wrong, I thought, taking a final look at the farm, tucked into the glen like a sleeping infant bundled in its mother's arms. I had twice damned myself to the Christian Hell, but that night, I had beheld a heaven where I might dwell with Vala and our baby in this lifetime.

Signs in Entrails

Wulfhedinn

*T*he sacrificial goat dug its hooves into the dirt and refused to budge any farther. It bleated and pulled at its lead, wanting to return to the security of the hall. I did not want to leave the hall either, but fate was taking me and the goat to dark, unforeseen places, and we could not change it.

"We would save time by slitting its throat and saying a quick prayer here, now," I said.

"We do not fight until we have made proper sacrifice," Erhard said.

"But the Raven's Stones are a mile out of our way, and the army could return to the garrison at any time."

He shrugged. Fools, I thought, scooping the stubborn goat into my arms and setting a quick pace to the Raven's Stones. The sooner we got there, the sooner we could move forward with the plan. The rest of the pack followed. Despite the wolf's absence, they were strong runners, conditioned to navigating through the thick woods. Wichbert lagged behind, but I did not slow my pace for him and neither did the others. With luck, we would lose him altogether.

The stones towered above us, and Widukind led us past Wodan's Tower to a square-shaped pillar with a flat top. Wichbert had managed to keep up with us and wanted to join us in the sacrifice, but Widukind told him it was only for Wulfhednar. The boy pouted and stayed at the bottom of the pillar while Widukind led the rest of us up the stairway. We climbed quickly to a large platform open to the sky. The pillar was not as high as Wodan's Tower but tall enough to fall to one's death with a misstep over the edge.

I set the bleating goat next to a stone slab that served as an altar, and the others gathered around. They began pounding their spears on the rock and chanting gabled words that sounded more like animal grunts than human speech. The noise grew into a pulsating drumbeat echoing across all the standing stones. I waited at the top of the stairway, ready to go the moment they were done, but their chanting and pounding droned on and on. I was about to ask how much longer it would take when Erhard called for me.

"Hold the goat," he said.

"Anything to quicken this process," I mumbled.

I lifted the squirming animal onto the altar and held it tight while Widukind grabbed the nose and jaw and pulled back its head.

"Mighty Walkyrie, Raven Spirit, Chooser of the Living and the Slain," Widukind said. "Bless us with the courage and ferocity of the wolf so we may fight and die with honor among our brothers. May we prove ourselves worthy of Wodan's Great Hall if we fall in our quest against the butcher king."

He ran his seax across the goat's throat. Blood spurted like a pulsating spring, splattering us and flowing over the altar.

He continued the prayer. "Great Wodan, Ancient One, Father of All, God of Victory, and Ruler of the Slain, accept our offering and bless us in seeking vengeance for the slaughter of your people."

I held the animal until it stopped kicking and its life had drained. Soaked in the blood, I was oddly comforted by its warmth. When it cooled, I was chanting with the others, repeating the strange words as though I had known them my whole life. Their meaning was clear to me yet unexplainable in any human language.

Erhard smeared blood on face and chest and then on Widukind, Abbo, Rotgrim, and me. He told me to turn the goat over, and he made a long, deep cut into its gut. The slimy entrails spilled out onto the stone. Narrowing his ghost eye, he examined the steaming guts. He frowned, scratched his beard, and walked around them, cocking his head to see the innards from different angles.

"The signs are unclear," he said.

I knew the wolf was not going to come to them. I was about to demand they stop wasting time when I saw her.

The Walkyrie.

Her great wings carried her black stallion across the moon. The others followed my gaze to the sky, but no one reacted. They had not seen her. Good. I kept her to myself, watching her dark beauty until it vanished.

When I looked down, Erhard was staring at me.

I shivered and pulled my wolf skin tighter around me. "Stop gawking at me with that dead eye, old man."

He winked with it, as though we shared a secret. "Did you see something in the sky?"

"No."

"Then what do you see in the entrails?"

"I have no knowledge of reading the slimy guts of goats—nor do I want any."

The wizened warrior recognized a lie when he heard it. He had not survived so long by trusting the word of dubious men like me.

I knew victory would be mine. The Walkyrie's appearance—not the entrails—proved it. Victory could imply many things, including winning the woman I wanted. The Christian god had never given me such an omen, despite my many prayers to him.

"Perhaps you saw something else?" Erhard asked.

"I see a bunch of warriors who will never defeat their enemy by waiting all night for magic," I said.

"Agreed," Widukind said. "It is time."

He led us down the stairs. Wichbert was dozing on the bottom step, and Rotgrim kicked him.

The boy whined and asked, "Did the Walkyrie bring the wolf?"

His father answered him with a dark glower.

"No?" Wichbert pouted and pointed at me. "She is not coming because of him. Treulogo! His dishonor is keeping her away."

"You are keeping her away," Rotgrim said. "She does not like simpering brats."

Erhard stepped between them. "You are both wrong. The Walkyrie will return with the wolf when we lay the flesh of our enemies at her feet—no sooner."

Wichbert stood and stomped his foot. "I am my father's legitimate son and cannot become a Wulfhedinn until she returns to send me on my journey to the wolf. And this bastard half-breed is stopping her."

"Enough!" Widukind snapped. "You will take your journey when the time is right—if it is ever right."

No Use to Anyone

The Monk

Father, Son, and Holy Ghost.

I had been riding with General Theoderic for less than a day, and already his temper was ready to erupt. He shifted uncomfortably in his saddle, and I nearly retched from the stink of the old goat's rotting leg. When would it finally kill him?

"Where are the Saxon villages?" Theoderic snapped at our Saxon guide.

A crude, freshly carved wooden cross hung around the guide's neck. It was strung on a worn leather thong that had likely borne a pagan amulet recently. I had not noticed the cross until after the General offered to pay him for services.

"I told you to take us on a route through as many villages and farmsteads as possible," Theoderic said. "Our mission is to find Widukind. If we can do that by questioning Saxons along the route, we will not need to go all the way to King Sigfred's court in Daneland."

I knew he wanted to do more than question local Saxon peasants. He had chosen twelve of the roughest Scola soldiers for our escort. Like their captain, Lothar, they were the kind of men who would rather wield weapons through the winter than return to their wives and children for Yule. They were itching for an excuse for violence and pillaging.

"There will be plenty who are willing to talk in Treva," said the guide. "It's a trading town, and Saxon traders are as greedy as any. They want to stay in the graces of King Karl so that they can keep doing business with the Franks. They will talk."

"We should not have to go that far," Theoderic said. "The rebels staked a curse horse at our camp in Verden. Widukind is likely nearby, hiding in a midden pile in one of the local peasant villages."

The General's leg wound had not dulled his instincts for sniffing out a renegade, but he was wrong that day. I knew Gerwulf and his father were far from us at the Raven's Stones. I was doomed to go all the way to the Danish court with the General and his vicious riders. The journey did, however, take him farther from Gerwulf, so I was willing to make the trip.

I reined my mount closer to him. "The coward rebel likely fled to King Sigfred. They are kin by marriage, and Sigfred has offered him refuge in the past."

He sneered. "Is that what God told you?"

"Why...yes...but it is commonly known."

He leaned close, and the stench of his leg wound nearly

overwhelmed me. "I never believe what is commonly known—or a word you say. I know what you are, you demented monk."

Father, Son, and Holy Ghost.

"My lord! I am a mystic…"

"Shut your blathering mouth, and stay out of my way."

He spurred his horse toward our guide. "Take us to the nearest village. Now!"

"Yes, my lord." The guide bowed his head. "But there is not much there."

"Take us!"

The guide led us farther east. Within moments, the smell of thick smoke filled the air. We soon came to a clearing and found a handful of hovels and several smoldering, earth-covered charcoal piles. The place appeared empty of people despite the well-tended piles.

"Filthy charcoal burners," the General said. "Find them, Lothar."

The captain grinned, and he and his squad spurred their horses through the squalid hamlet. They shouted for the residents to show themselves. When no one came forth, Lothar ordered his thugs to burn their homes.

"But, General…" I pleaded.

He silenced me with an impatient scowl, and I sat quietly in the saddle as his men tore open one of the charcoal piles, grabbed several smoldering timbers, and set the thatched roofs ablaze. I prayed silently for the poor souls inside. The flames took hold quickly, and the roofs collapsed, but no one screamed or ran out. The place was abandoned.

"Someone warned them we were coming," the General said,

"which means either Widukind or other rebel sympathizers were here."

As we pulled away from the burning compound, I prayed all the villages and farmsteads along our route were empty. One of the gods must have heard my prayers because the next village was abandoned, as was the next and the next. The Scola riders tore apart every hovel and hut in each place and found no people, livestock, or anything of value to pillage. They cursed the lack of booty as they fired each village. Theoderic's mood darkened, but I was smiling inwardly.

"We must be right on Widukind's heels," the General said, shifting awkwardly in his saddle. He had always had an iron ass in the saddle, but his leg was paining him more as the day wore on. His breeches were wet from the pus, and sweat beaded on his forehead.

We continued on the north road, and soon our horses were stepping in fresh goat shit. Within moments, we overtook a group of twenty women, children, and old men. Some of them pushed handcarts loaded with a few possessions. Three skinny chickens battered their flapping wings against their small coops as the carts bumped over the rough road. One woman struggled to push a cart carrying an elderly man. Others hauled loads on their backs, and three children were scrambling to herd several goats.

Two gaunt dogs trotted alongside the procession. They turned and growled at us, hackles rising. Lothar launched his spear and hit one of them in the back. The poor creature squealed, fell, dragging itself by its two front legs. Then Lothar's men threw their spears and hit the other dogs and one of the goats. The group panicked, and several women dropped their loads and picked up small children. They all scattered into the forest.

"Round them up. See what they can tell us," Theoderic ordered.

The riders dug their heels into their horses' flanks and herded the villagers back to the road.

"We are the soldiers of God's chosen king, Karl of the Franks, to whom you owe your allegiance," Theoderic said in a rough, common Germanic tongue. "We are seeking the outlaw rebel Widukind, his wolf warriors, and a pregnant woman who travels with them. Who will tell us where they can be found?"

The women held their infants close, and the toddlers clung to their mother's tunics. Some were crying. One woman handed her infant to another and came forward. She wore wool dyed with bright woad, and she had an amber and gold hammer of Donar hung around her neck.

"We know nothing about Widukind," she said.

"Why are you fleeing your village in winter?" Captain Lothar asked.

"We heard about what the butcher king did in Verden. We are not safe in Saxony any longer."

"Who are you?" the General asked.

"I am Adelais, wife of the elder of the clans who live in these forests," she said. "My husband and sons were murdered at Verden, and I am in charge of these people now. Are you going to kill us all too?" She asked as if it were a practical matter.

"You will help us locate Widukind and his Wulfhednar, by order of your king," Theoderic said.

"We have no king."

"The Saxon tribes are sworn to King Karl."

"We made no such pledge."

"Many Saxon noblemen pledged their fealty, and you are bound by their oath. Reveal the whereabouts of the outlaw Widukind, and we will spare your lives."

She sniggered. "Why should we believe you? Our men

trusted in your king's word and he murdered them for it."

Lothar signaled his soldiers, and they began to kick and poke the villagers with spears, prodding them into a tighter group.

The old man in the cart moved his toothless mouth, trying to make a sound.

Lothar reined his mount next to him. "Do you know where the rebel is?"

He coughed, wheezed, and choked out a few words. "You will…dance with the draugar."

The color drained from Lothar's and his men's faces. The horses whinnied and fought the reins, and it took several moments to get control of them again. Lothar flipped the cart, and it landed on top of the old man, crushing him. His legs moved feebly a few times and lay still.

"General! Stop this," I said, spurring next to him. I lay a trembling hand on his arm, trying to bring Jesus Christ's spirit of tolerance into his cold heart. He pulled away from me so abruptly that my hand popped back against my face.

"These heathens are aligned with the Wulfhednar demons, like their husbands and brothers," he said.

Several women screamed.

"Leave us alone!" one of them cried, clutching her infant tighter. "Widukind cannot be found by anyone, Saxon or Frank, unless the Walkyrie allows it. If so, she sends the Raven spirit to lead the way. Widukind has not been here. That is all we know." Her baby wailed, and she bounced it frantically, trying to hush it.

"You are lying." Lothar kicked the woman in the face. Her head snapped back, and she fell with the infant on top of her.

"My lord General, these peasants are ignorant and harmless," I pleaded. "They are not rebel warriors."

"They were smart enough to run from us," he said. "And the old man spoke of the draugar. He tried to curse us."

"He was just a senile old man—a dead man. You and your soldiers cannot possibly fear him. Let me approach the others. I can convince someone to talk."

Theoderic's gaze was icy, but he gestured for his men to stand down. They withdrew a few paces but kept their weapons poised.

"You have one chance, monk," he said. Tapping his heel, he rode to one of the women and yanked a small boy from her arms, setting him on his lap. The woman collapsed, trembling with tearful pleading while her boy laughed and played with a loose ring on the General's mail.

"I will count to fifty," he said, stroking the boy's head.

I slid off my horse so rapidly that I lost my balance and almost fell. Running to them, I held my shaky cross aloft. "Peace be with you! May God give his blessing on you."

Adelais set her jaw and furrowed her brow with scorn.

"Quickly now," I said. "You must renounce the old gods and ask for God's forgiveness for your pagan ways. Show yourself to be good Christians, and they may spare you."

"Fifteen, sixteen, seventeen…"

"Now! I beg you. Plead for mercy. Pray to the Christian God. Swear to relinquish the old gods!" I lowered my voice and spoke through my teeth. "Even if you do not mean it."

The woman who had lost her son to the General prostrated herself and pleaded, "Forgive my pagan ways, holy Christian man! Bless me with the word of God!"

All the others, except Adelais, followed along, repenting in a confusion of words that sounded more desperate than sincere.

"Twenty-six, twenty-seven…"

I almost fell to my knees myself to beseech the chieftain's

wife. "You are the leader. You must kneel too to save the others. If you are all killed, who will be left to take up the sword for the old gods and fight with the Wulfhednar?"

Adelais narrowed her eyes. "You know much about us, Christian," she said.

"I know Widukind, and I have seen him within a fortnight," I whispered. "His eldest son has joined the Wulfhednar, and they will need every able-bodied man and woman to help them fight. Please, my lady. I speak the truth."

"Thirty-five, thirty-six, thirty-seven…"

She relented, going slowly to her knees, spite and anger in her deliberate movements. I blessed them all loudly, forgiving their pagan transgressions, but the chieftain's wife did not bow her head like the others. Her cutting glare was locked on Theoderic.

"Forty-seven, forty-eight…"

"Now, live as good Christians in fear of the Lord God," I said quickly, hoping their hasty repentance had satisfied Theoderic and his men.

The General clapped slowly four times. "A fine Christian display," he said. Then he wrenched the boy off his lap by the leg and dangled him upside down. "Now who will tell me where the rebel is hiding?"

The boy twisted and writhed, screaming.

I ran toward him. "My lord, they have asked the Lord God for forgiveness for their transgressions!" I protested. "They are good Christians! One of them will talk. I just need more time with them."

The boy's mother wailed. "Where do you *think* Widukind has gone?" she said between sobs. "Where he always goes to flee from you. To the Danes, King Sigfred's court."

"She lies," he said.

He was going to drop the child, and I had but a moment to catch him, but I stopped in my tracks. Nothing I could do would save him. The peasants had pushed the General's patience, and his brutes were impatient for the slaughter. They would gladly kill me too. I was of no use to anyone as a dead monk, so I stood and watched it happen. My stomach turned as Theoderic released the boy on his head and trampled him under his horse's hooves.

"Kill them, and take the livestock."

His men needed no second order. The General watched without blinking as they speared, slashed, and trampled them all. They ransacked the carts for booty and fought one another for the amber amulet that had fallen from Adelais's mangled body. It was the only object of value they had found, and Lothar claimed it for himself as their captain. Then they slit the throats of the goats and chickens for fresh meat and tied the carcasses across the back of their saddles.

Unrighteous by any god!

I had failed again. I needed desperately to cleanse myself.

Father, Son, and Holy Ghost.
Wolf, Raven, and Walkyrie.

As we rode on, I could barely contain the sickness in my soul, but Lothar and his men were in high spirits. Their blood was surging with energy from their slaughter, and they made crude jokes about the old man. They turned my stomach, but I was helpless to do anything about it.

I needed to wash as soon as possible. Fortunately, their blood lust had roused their appetites, so we stopped early to make camp and cook the meat. I excused myself to pray and found a quiet place where a tiny spring trickled between stones into a stream. I rubbed my hands raw, but my bloodguilt was not eased.

When I returned, the soldiers were tearing pieces of roasted meat from the carcasses. I interrupted them to say a blessing—a good long one. In my heart, I prayed Theoderic's leg would kill him before I did, and I prayed the hardest to see Gerwulf before they did.

The hot goat meat smelled heavenly, and I forgot my queasy stomach. I was ashamed of my earthly longing for the taste of flesh, but I ate my fill. As I chewed, I could not stop thinking about the old man and his draugar curse. I prayed someday it would come true, and Captain Lothar and his Scola riders would dance with the roving soulless ones.

An Opportunity

Wulfhedinn

J ran with the Wulfhedinn pack southwest toward the Lippespringe garrison. Widukind was leading us on well-defined paths, ignoring my advice to cut through the forest. He did not explain himself, but he likely thought the danger of twisting an ankle or knee on mole holes, tree roots, or fallen branches was greater than the risk of arriving too late. The eyes of mortal men were weak in the dark, and with only five warriors, we had no one to spare to injury.

Wichbert managed to keep pace with the pack, if only to prove I could not best him. He struggled and fell a few times, but he got to his feet and kept going. The boy's fear of being left behind in the Teutoburg Forest must have been as powerful as his need to prove himself. The boy was learning how fast and lithe he could be when he had to be.

We were tired by the time we neared the garrison. Wichbert was panting and ready to collapse. Our journey would have been faster had we not wasted time with the sacrifice, but luck was with us, and the garrison was quiet. The army had not returned yet, and perhaps my victory omen in the goat's guts would prove right.

The Raven had disappeared. She and the Walkyrie would not come until we had blood and souls to feed them, which did not bother me. The others scanned the sky often, hoping to see her, but I knew Karl's army and his garrison well and had more faith in myself than in omens and spirits.

Nearing the garrison walls, we passed the place where Brother Pyttel and I had first met. He had been on his way back from the nearby spring where he had secretly performed his rituals. The Eye of Wodan dwelled there in the glowing blue waters. It was a sacred place for the Saxons—a place Karl had desecrated, allowing his most favored commanders to soak off their filth in it. But he had not defeated the old gods yet, and the Eye of Wodan still lived there, as it did in other sacred springs. It still appeared to some people in the soft, blue glow it cast through the rippling water. The last time I had been there, it materialized, seeing everything I could not face. I still feared it.

I alone knew about the sacrilegious rituals Pyttel performed at that spring. He said he was trying to placate Wodan and the old gods with his sacrifices, and I held no judgment of him for it. He had befriended me and had risked his life to free me before my execution. He was unlike any holy man I had known. Returning to that place, I missed him and his crooked face and unkempt tonsure.

Leaving the memory of him there, I led the pack to a place overlooking the Lippespringe palisade. I climbed a tree to get a better view of the walls.

"What do you see?" asked Widukind.

"Four guards." I jumped down from the tree. "Must be raw recruits or men with little care for their duties. They are clustered together in one place the far side of the garrison, and they let several of the torches burn out. We can approach the loose timber in the wall in darkness."

Rotgrim climbed the tree to see for himself. "They are throwing dice! A child could get into the garrison under their watch."

"Perhaps the Walkyrie is beginning to favor us," said Erhard.

"Perhaps," Widukind said.

"I want to go with Gerwulf," said Wichbert.

"No, you little piece of maggot shit," Rotgrim said, shoving him. "You will get in the way."

Rotgrim had said what we all were thinking, and Widukind did not reproach him for it.

I left them and headed to the back of the garrison, feeling confident until I neared the palisade. It had changed since I had been there. The clump of brush that had concealed me in the past had been cut down. Some officer had finally gotten wise and ordered it to be cleared away. I feared the loose timber might have been discovered and shored up as well.

I listened, sniffed the breeze, and sensed no one nearby. The guards were likely still engrossed in their dice game. I took the chance and dashed through the dark from the forest's edge to the wall. Wedging my hand into a crack between the timbers, I found the same one was still loose. Shifting it just enough to peek inside, I saw the pile of firewood that concealed the secret opening. I push harder on the timber, opening the gap, and squeezed through. Several large splinters lodged themselves in my shoulders and arms before I was inside.

Hidden by the woodpile and the walkway overhead, I stole a glance at the garrison. Empty except for a large tent pitched near the gate across the empty field. The tent glowed faintly from a couple oil lamps or candles inside. Next to the tent, a campfire burned low, producing more smoke than light. Two palisade torches cast little more brightness, leaving most of the empty field in deep shadow.

Darkness was my cover on the open expanse of dead, flattened grass and mud where the army had been camped. Crouching low, I moved toward the tent, avoiding the shit trenches. They still reeked, although the army had been gone for weeks. Clearly, the contingent of soldiers left to hold the garrison had slacked in their duties.

I dropped to my belly and crawled. About a dozen loud, drunken men were laughing and talking inside the tent. Outside, a boy had curled up with several dogs next to the smoldering fire. Karl was so cocky that he had left fewer than twenty men to guard his garrison—and a sloppy unit they were. That was all I needed to know.

I scooted back toward my escape hole when one of the dogs lifted its head, perked its ears, and stared in my direction. I froze, sure it would bark and expose my presence. Before it could open its mouth, a soldier came outside from the tent and kicked the boy. The dogs jumped and scrambled out of his way.

"You worthless turd-eating blaggard of a squire," he said. "Get more fucking wood and keep the fire going, or I will kick your carcass back into your mother's cunt."

The boy stumbled to his feet, dodging the soldier's fist, and ran into the tent. He returned quickly with an oil lamp, placed it in a nearby handcart, and pushed it across the garrison toward the woodpile.

"Bring back my lamp, or I will…" the soldier said.

"Yes, my lord. I promise."

The captain returned inside, grumbling about lousy squires and bad beer. The squire pushed his cart between me and my escape route. I would have to wait for him to finish his task before I could get back to the loose timber. I followed him at a distance as he dragged his feet, taking his time. When he finally arrived at the woodpile, he sat on the cart and pulled a small dagger from his belt. He toyed with it, balancing the blade by the tip on his finger. He was surprisingly good at the trick and must have spent a lot of time there, playing with his dagger. He was in no hurry to leave that night either.

The captain shouted for him from across the field. He dropped the dagger and threw logs haphazardly into the cart. Then we both heard it, the raw, creaking sound of wood rubbing against wood. The squire stopped and listened. More creaking. Someone was pushing through the secret entrance, whining as he scraped past the rough timbers.

Wichbert.

The squire grabbed his dagger with one hand and a large piece of wood with the other. Wichbert came around the woodpile, and the boys saw each other at the same time. They froze. The squire raised his wooden club, but Wichbert had not pulled his sword yet. They were about the same age and size, but the squire was smarter than I had thought, and Wichbert more senseless.

I could not predict what the young urchins might do next. Would the squire scream for help, run back to the tent, or attack? Would Wichbert try to fight or run away? I laid low in the shadows, ready to retreat farther back if the guards and soldiers were alerted and came running with torches and weapons drawn. I would leave Wichbert on his own. He would become a convenient diversion when they jumped on him and hauled his simpering ass away. Then I could slip back out the hole unnoticed.

The squire rushed Wichbert with more aggression than I had expected. Wichbert ducked behind the woodpile and fell back against the palisade, clawing for the loose timber. The squire wacked his shoulder with the club. He swung again and clipped him on the opposite side of his head. Wichbert crumbled, knocked speechless. In a blink, the squire would scream and alert everyone. I could let it play out as expected, but Wichbert's dazed expression was pathetic, and he was frozen with shock and fear. My little brother. How I hated him.

I stole behind the squire and hit him on the back of head with the handle of my axe. He fell, stunned. Pushing the timber aside, I shoved Wichbert through the hole, his face scraping the wood. Then I squeezed through and threw him over my shoulder. I would have to carry him across the clearing into the forest, but voices were approaching on the palisade walkway. Four guards had turned the corner and were walking toward us. They carried two torches that lit the wall's perimeter as they approached. I could not run across the clear-cut area without being seen. My chances of staying undetected were better inside the wall, hidden under the walkway.

"If you make the slightest whimper, I will slice your throat," I whispered to Wichbert.

Before he could respond, I shoved him back though the hole and followed, hoping the squire remained unconscious. But he was stirring. He moved and moaned softly as the guards passed over us on the walkway. Their steps stopped above our heads, but the squire had quieted again, and they moved on. Their voices faded as they walked, arguing about their dice game and grumbling about how bad the beer had been since the king had left.

I was ready to shove Wichbert back out the hole when the squire vomited, making the loudest ear-piercing retching noise

I had ever heard. The guards came running back, the wooden walkway creaking under their pounding feet. They would be down the steps and see us within moments.

I should have killed the squire when I'd had the chance. I should have left Wichbert to his own devices. I should have done a lot of things, and now my options were few, and none of them were good. If we tried to run for the forest, the soldiers would see us and launch their spears into our backs before we were out of range. My best choice was to take on the guards myself, and my best offense was my wolf hood, even if the wolf did not come.

"Who is there?" one of the soldiers asked.

He was answered by more of the squire's retching noises. I gripped my axe. A wolf howled in the distance and the fur on the back of my wolf skin rose. It was coming. It would take me, and I embraced it.

Fire surged through my veins, and the tips of my fangs brushed my tongue. I saw through the darkness, lit by the fire in my eyes, and leaped at the soldiers as they came down the stairs. With one swipe of the axe, I cut across two of them, flaying their chests. Thrown off their feet, they crumpled in a shower of blood. The third soldier gasped, frozen in shock. The fourth one turned and ran to the walkway screaming, "Wolf demons! We are under attack!"

I bounded up the stairs after him, but it was too late. His cries had carried across the field, alerting the dogs. They barked wildly and would soon bring the rest of the soldiers. I sunk my claws into the guard's flesh and threw him over the wall. His body landed on the ground below with a thud. I bounded back to the remaining guard, who still had not moved, and slashed his throat. The dice he was clutching dropped as he fell. He had rolled snake eyes.

Wichbert was trembling and smelled like he had pissed on himself. For a moment, I wished he had been captured, but I grabbed him by the scruff and shoved him back through the timbers.

I crouched behind the woodpile, peeking around it as the seven soldiers and the dogs approached. The captain and the largest man wielded swords. The others carried spears and daggers or small seaxes. The dogs, mad with excitement, sniffed the bodies of the guards. For a moment, I thought they would tear into them. The dogs had a ravished look, and their ribs were visible in the semidarkness, but they tucked tail and backed away. The soldiers stopped short of the sight.

"Holy Mother of God," one of them said, crossing himself.

"Who could have done this?" another asked.

The squire was trying to get up, but his eyes rolled back, and he fell. "Demons," he muttered. "Demons ..."

The captain dragged him to his feet and shook him. "What happened, boy? Who? Where did they go?"

The stunned boy's head wobbled limply. The captain shook him, and when that did not reveal any more information, he dropped him. "Break into two groups, and search the garrison. There is little place for them to hide here."

"Are you mad?" another soldier asked. "This was not done by mortal men."

A soldier wearing a ragged mantle and threadbare breeches agreed. "Wulfhednar! I have seen their victims in the woods around here."

Another soldier backed away with short, jerky steps, terror in his eyes. "They have gotten inside the walls and will kill us all. The dogs know it and have run away. We have to get out of here!"

One of the men, the largest of them, spoke calmly, "Rebels. We should ride to Paderborn and raise the alarm."

"No," the captain said. "This is the work of bandits or vagabonds who have found a way inside the wall."

The first soldier covered his throat with his hands. "Bandits and vagabonds do not tear open flesh like this."

"You drunken louts! Search the field," the captain ordered.

Several of them tried to protest. The captain threatened to take away their beer if they did not obey, so they broke into two contingents to search the field.

Once divided, I could have easily trounced them one-by-one, but only one more needed to die that night—the captain. I stalked him and his group until they had separated far enough from the others. Then I tossed a small stone at his shoulder. It tapped him like a finger. He stopped, turned, and raised his torch. Squinting into the darkness, he strained to see beyond the limits of the meager light.

"Do you see something?" the soldier with the sword asked.

"I…"

My wolf legs coiled and sprang, launching me across the air at his throat. In a mad fury of snarling, I tore through flesh and crushed his windpipe. Then I dragged him into the darkness, knowing the others would not follow. They dropped their torches and rushed back to the tent. Their screams alerted the other group of soldiers as the captain gurgled his last bloody breath.

I grabbed two of their torches, ran back to the woodpile, and lit it on fire. The seasoned wood ignited quickly, spreading flame up the walkway and the wall. The squire was still stunned and had not moved. He whimpered and inched away from me, and I grabbed his collar, dragged him to the gap in the wall, and heaved him through it. Then I carried him a safe distance from the burning garrison and left him there.

Wichbert was gone. He must have run back to his father like

a pup to its mother's tits. I lowered my wolf hood and returned to the pack. As I had expected, Wichbert was there, his scratched and scuffed jaw trembling. He gasped and bit his lip when he saw me. I did not know if he was more afraid of me or the wolf spirit that had erupted from within me. Good. He needed to be afraid and uncertain. Let him wonder if I would tell his father what he had done, or if my demon would tear him apart while he slept.

I glowered at him with a silent warning to keep his mouth shut about how he had seen the wolf demon. If he did, I would not tell Widukind and the pack of his fool's adventure. He was an idiot, but even he must have understood the silent bargain.

The pack glanced from me to the growing fire of the garrison walls.

"What happened?" Widukind asked.

"I had an opportunity, and I took it," I said.

Widukind raised an eyebrow, and Rotgrim snickered, shaking his head.

"What kind of opportunity?" Widukind asked.

"One I made for myself."

"How many did you kill?"

"Five are dead, including their captain. There were fewer than twenty of them total, mostly boys, old men, and second-rate soldiers. The survivors do not have the mettle to stay. Watch the gate, and soon you will see them flee to Paderborn to raise the alarm."

My words had barely left my tongue when the gate opened, and the remaining soldiers tore out of the fortress, whipping their horses. The riders on better mounts left the others behind, but soon they were all gone. In their panic, they lost any military discipline they might have had.

"Fate is working in our favor," Erhard said.

"So it seems," Rotgrim said.

Widukind grinned and clapped me hard on the back. "Perhaps the wolf is near."

Wulfhedinn Devil

~~~

Wulfhedinn

We ran to Paderborn with renewed energy as the Lippespringe garrison burned behind us. We took the king's road, the Hellweg, but veered off it as we neared the Lippe River. We could not risk being seen on the bridge where soldiers were posted, so I led them to a remote ford where the water ran wide and shallow. Stripping our breeches, we piled them and our wolf skins on our heads and began to cross. The frigid water rose slowly until it reached my thighs. As the water climbed to my groin, something caught my attention. It floated in a quiet pool behind a fallen log. A familiar shape wavered in the little ripples shimmering in the moonlight. It drew me closer, and I stopped to gaze at it while the others continued the crossing.

Rotgrim splashed past me. "Better move your ass before your little prick disappears altogether. The women will be disappointed in me if I stay in this river much longer."

His eyes flashed with an impish spark, and I realized he was jesting with me. He waded on, oblivious to the face I saw in the water. I had expected to see my own image, but instead, a distorted face ringed by an unkempt tonsure looked back at me. Brother Pyttel.

The pack was climbing onto the opposite bank of the river, but I lingered by the monk's image. He was so unlike the monks I had known as a child, the ones who had tried to beat the wolf spirit out of me. Pyttel had tried to use it to help his Christian king and redeem our damned souls. Both ideas had failed, but I had grown fond of him, nonetheless. I missed his company but still despised other holy men. They wanted to damn me forever. Despite their vows to save souls, they did not want to save a wolf demon. No one did, except Brother Pyttel. He was my friend, my only friend.

I tried to block the memory of the dark times before I had met Pyttel, but it was too late. I was back there again—an eight-year-old boy dragged by the ear by one of those blessed holy men. Brother Gotthard was reciting the Lord's Prayer as he pulled me through the icy creek flowing past the monastery.

"Our Father, which art in Heaven, hallowed be thy..." he stammered and grunted.

The monk had never moved so quickly. He usually relished sloth, but he had found me outside the monastery walls in the forest again. His terror of the evil spirits drove his lumbering steps, and he would repeat the prayer many times until we were back safely inside.

"Thy kingdom come; thy will be done..."

His grip was fierce, and I struggled to keep up in the water without stumbling and losing my ear. I was still dizzy from the first blow to my head when he punched me a second time.

"I told you to repeat the Lord's Prayer with me, you evil, worthless half-blood," he said. "It is the only hope you have. Your demon cannot protect your mortal flesh from the retribution of the all-powerful God. This time I will not be so lenient. Your flesh will suffer the worst of God's judgment."

I swung recklessly at him and fell in the stream, splashing and soaking him. He released my ear and grabbed my arm in a piercing grip, twisting it behind me. Then he kicked me in the stomach, grunting with the effort, and he shoved my head under the water.

Water flooded into my nose and mouth. I choked. He was right. The wolf would not protect me. It always bounded away when Brother Gotthard found me in the forest. No matter how hard I tried to call upon the wolf spirit, it never saved me from the monk when he stripped me and forced me into the dark, secret place. Neither the wolf nor the Christian god ever went there.

I had to fight the monk myself, scrawny boy that I was. My head and lungs were bursting with the desire to breathe, but I managed to grab his ankle and trip him. With a great splash, he released me. Choking and pulling myself onto the stream bank, I heard the distant howl of the wolf. It had never left me, but it had not rescued me, either.

I had grown up thinking all holy men were like Brother Gotthard until meeting Brother Pyttel. I would take my vengeance soon on the rest of them. Brother Pyttel grinned at me from the water, as if he were giving me his blessing. He had no great love for many of his monk brothers and priests.

Bidding the monk farewell, I finished crossing the river, threw on my breeches, and caught up to the pack. We were all shivering.

Erhard pulled his wolf cloak tighter around his shoulders. Then he took me aside and spoke in a low tone. "You are always tarrying, separating yourself from us, but yet, you have not run away. Did you see the spirit Walkyrie in the river?"

"I told you. I do not command her."

"No, of course not, but I know she and the wolf have come to you. You cannot hide it from the others much longer."

"I hide nothing."

"Bring her to us when you are ready, but do not wait too long, or she will disappear forever."

He did not wait for my reply. I knew he was tired of hearing my lies. I did not understand him. I had never had power over her, and he knew it. How many times had he told me that I belonged to her?

We joined the pack, and I led them to a secluded place near the Paderborn gate where we could remain unseen by guards. The winter sun broke over the top of the palisade, bringing some warmth to our bones. The gate opened, releasing two dozen armored soldiers who spurred their horses down the road toward Lippespringe.

Widukind was smiling under his dirty beard. "And there rides the reinforcements to the garrison, just as you predicted, Gerwulf. How many soldiers do you think remain inside? I see only two guards posted on the gatehouse."

"When the king is in residence, there would be at least a dozen visible on the gatehouse. If it appears so lightly defended, there are likely not many soldiers holding the city, but I cannot be sure."

Widukind was waiting for me to say something else, to provide some secret way into Paderborn, but I knew of no loose timber or weaknesses in its physical defenses. Unlike the hastily erected wooden palisade at Lippespringe, the city wall was reinforced by an earthwork rampart. Trying to breach it with five of us would be futile. There was only one way to get in—right through the front gate—and I was the one who had to do it.

I took off my wolf skin and tossed it to Wichbert. The boy was so surprised, it nearly knocked him over.

"It does not matter how many soldiers there are," I said. "The king has not returned yet, and they may believe I am still the Royal Scout."

We all knew the risk I would need to take, but no one spoke of it. One of the king's messengers might have arrived before us. He likely would have brought news about my attempt to kill the king. If so, the guards would immediately arrest me.

Shivering, I clenched my jaw so tightly that my teeth ground together. I had just evaded certain execution at the king's hands. I must have been as mad as Pyttel to walk right into his city. The shadows of the forest called me to flee and hide in their depths. That would have been the wise thing to do. I would never have taken such a fool's risk for my father and the Wulfhednar, but I had to do it for Vala and our child.

I waited. None of the Wulfhednar tried to talk me out of it, so I left the safety of the forest and strode up to the gate.

"Open up!" I demanded.

"Go away," the guard called from the top of the gatehouse. "We are not admitting vagabonds."

"I am Tracker, the Royal Scout and Huntsman."

He spat. "And I am the queen of Britannia."

"I carry urgent news from King Karl."

He sighed and left, returning shortly with an unarmored man dressed in a linen shirt. His face was bloated and flushed.

"Who is waking me so early?" he blurted.

"Tracker, King Karl's Royal Scout and Huntsman."

"You look like a filthy dog."

I was tempted to hurl a string of insults back at him, but that was not a nobleman's way. I calmed my tongue and spit out the fancy words of a courtier. "I bear great news of the triumphant victory of our most wondrous King Karl, supreme sovereign of the Kingdom of the Franks, God's blessed ruler of Christendom."

When they did not respond, I repeated it in Latin. My Latin was broken, and I had to invent a couple of words, but it was good enough to impress their kind of rabble. If they'd had any real education or standing in court, they would have been with the army at Verden.

"All right, all right." The bloated-faced man waved at the guards. "He is giving me a headache. Let him in so he shuts up."

I was met inside by the guard who had spoken from the top of the gate. He grunted at me with impatience. The second guard joined him. Stinking of stale beer, he almost stumbled over his own feet. They both wore worn leather vests, old discards from real soldiers, and I doubted they had had much training, either. Their bloated captain—or whoever he was—tramped down the stairs, which creaked under his weight. He was unarmed, and his belly was as overstuffed as his face. He scratched his belly and took a closer look at me.

"I do recognize you now." He sneered. "The king's pet. You stink like a brigand. What happened to your horse and clothes?"

"Saxon bandits," I said simply. Providing too much explanation might have aroused his suspicions.

He scanned the bruises and swellings on my arms and face. "They sure beat the piss out of you. So what news is so urgent?" The idiot had not noticed most of my bruises were old and turning green.

"King Karl sends orders to make ready for his triumphant arrival."

He rolled his eyes. "Not another triumphant arrival."

Clearly the king's plans were interrupting his plans to sleep off a hangover.

"I must speak to the commander of the city guard immediately." I glanced around the gatehouse and saw no additional guards.

"The commander is gone. He rode out with most of the city's force to Lippespringe. It was attacked and burned last night by filthy heathens. I would bet they are the same Saxon scum who got the best of you. You are lucky to be alive."

"The Lord God was with me, I am sure." I crossed myself, cringing. God had never been with me. "When I began to pray, they ran, but they managed to steal my purse, horse, and sword—the craven suckers of the Devil's cock!"

My stomach turned at what I had said. I had debased all Saxons, including Vala and our child—and myself—in front of a man I disrespected. My face burned with shame as both the giver and the taker of such hatred. I glanced around, hoping the Raven was not near and had not heard me.

The fat man and the guards were laughing. "Craven suckers of the Devil's cock!" he repeated. "That is good! You are a funny one—for a courtier. Anyway, I am in charge until the city commander and his men return. I suppose you must speak with me."

The ploy to win the trust of the guards and their bulbous headman had worked, but I silently swore never to use those vulgar words again.

"My lord," I said with a bow. "I bring welcome news. The king will be here within a day with his entire army to reinforce your numbers. How many do you command here now?"

"The city commander rode out with our best soldiers and left me with a single rotation of the watch, twelve men. Hardly enough to hold a royal city."

Just as I had suspected. And their temporary leader's best military skill was probably in guarding the beer cellar from everyone but himself.

"Not to worry, my lord," I said. "The king has captured and executed more than four thousand Saxon malcontents and rebel leaders."

"Praise God! It has taken him long enough to quell these suckers of the Devil's cock." He chuckled.

"I carry detailed instructions for you to make the palace ready for his return."

"Not my job. Talk to the steward. Go drag his skinny ass out of bed too."

"I will, commander. And let me assure you the king will return at the head of his army to reinforce defenses here, kill the Saxons who attacked the garrison, and secure the area."

The commander was scratching his belly. "Good. Then we can fuck their women and finally go home for the winter."

The guards laughed until they were interrupted by shouting from outside the wall.

"Open the gate!" a man ordered. "I am King Karl's messenger and bear urgent news from him about his triumph against the Saxon heathens."

The commander tilted his head and rubbed his bloodshot eyes. Even he would quickly realize something was wrong. With a burst of speed, I kicked him in the gut. As he doubled over, I wrenched a spear from one of the two guards and impaled it through his chest. His ribs splintered as I twisted the tip and yanked it out. I lunged toward the other guard, who stood frozen in shock. I rammed my spear through his throat before he could take another breath.

The commander was still gasping from my blow. He stumbled, trying to back away from me, and opened his mouth to shout. The perfect target. I rammed the spear through his mouth, down his gullet, and jammed it through his spine.

Taking the stairs two at a time, I ran to the top of the guard house tower, which had an unobstructed view over the entire city and the wall around it. The city lay quiet. The main street connecting the gatehouse to the church and palace was empty. At the distant end of the city, two guards stood at the palace door, as tiny as insects. Four more were posted on the opposite wall. They were all too far away to have heard anything.

The church bell began to toll, calling the priests and monks to gather for Lauds, the dawn prayer. They were easy targets, and now they would be assembled together in one undefended place. The gods were with us.

I signaled the Wulfhednar and opened the gate. The pack rushed from the trees, hoods drawn. Rotgrim and Abbo jumped the stunned messenger. They cracked open his chest with a flash of their blades, and Widukind tossed my wolf skin and axe to me.

"There are only twelve soldiers in the city," I said, throwing on my fur, feeling its heat flow through my veins. "I killed the commander and two guards. Two are posted at the palace, and four on the far side of the wall—too far to see us. The last four guards are likely off duty, and the priests and monks are assembling now in church to pray. The city is as vulnerable as it is ever going to be."

Widukind grinned. My heart pounded, and blood surged through my veins, firing my whole body. A fury rose within me, a hungering need. The beast was not coming to the others, but anyone who saw the blood-splattered warriors in wolf hoods would be terrified, nonetheless.

I led the pack, weapons at the ready, through the city's back alleys toward the church. A pack of stray dogs crossed our path but caught a whiff of my scent and skulked away, whimpering. Next to the church, a well-muscled man who might have been a soldier vomited in the muddy gutter, his attention on his own retching. Several beggars were huddling in the church doorway, but they scattered as we approached. We heard the monks' holy chanting through the door. I despised the sound of it.

Rotgrim leered. "Ready to kill some Christian sorcerers, Gerwulf?"

I kicked the door open, smashing it against the stone wall. The chanting stopped, and the priests and monks turned toward me. I scanned their faces and did not see Pyttel. Relieved, I strode down the aisle, axe drawn, searching for a holy man to cleave in half, the one most deserving. I was no longer in a war but on the hunt.

The pack was on my heels, spreading out between two rows of monks. They panicked, shouting and tripping on one another to escape us. The sound of steel cutting through flesh soon silenced their screams.

The priest leading the service at the altar grabbed a large silver crucifix and held it aloft like a weapon. "Filthy demons!" he screamed. "God damns you to Hell!"

He had made my choice easy. My eyes locked onto my target, and my muscles surged with a beast's strength. One great swing of my axe planted the blade deeply in his breastbone, cracking it like an eggshell. He fell behind, dropping the crucifix, mouthing his useless curses at me. I jerked the blade free and hacked his throat to shut him up, snarling with each chop until his head rolled free past my feet. Grabbing the head by the hair, I held it high above the altar. My throat roared with a ghastly howl. The sound echoed loudly against the stone walls, and the Wulfhednar paused their attack—their jaws agape at the sight of me.

My rage grew more rabid with every beat of my heart. I could no longer hide the wolf from them, but did not care. Let them see it. Let them share in it and use it against the Christian holy men who had brutalized me. Let them take the wolf in exchange for Vala. Panting and sweating, I howled. The sound echoed up the walls of the church and into the bell tower, summoning the fury to them all.

"Are you not pleased, Father?" I shouted at Widukind and then looked up. "Are you not pleased, Walkyrie?"

Widukind took a torch from the wall sconce and set the hem of the altar cloth on fire. He threw the flame at several monks huddled around a wooden statue of Jesus. They screamed and scattered as the statue caught fire. Then he snatched the silver crucifix and a jeweled chalice from the altar and joined the pack to attack the remaining monks and priests.

My furor had invigorated the rest of the pack, and they cut down the Christian sorcerers as enraged and skilled warriors. They did not cross into the realm of the wolf demon, but the dying monks and priests did not know the difference.

As the altar cloth burned, a flash of steel shot out from underneath and plunged into my calf. I shouted and yanked out a small knife. The blade was hardly large enough to cut an apple, but blood was dripping from the cut. I reached under the cloth and grabbed a young boy hiding underneath. Dressed in the habit of a novice monk, the bony child slid over the blood-soaked floor like a pebble over ice.

"God, deliver me from the Wulfhedinn Devil," he murmured, shivering. "Deliver me. Deliver me."

I held his little knife to his neck. "Your god will not save you, boy."

He trembled so violently that he stopped praying. I loosened my grip on him. The wolf might have killed him, but the man could not.

"Do you know the monk Brother Pyttel?" I asked.

He froze in terror and could not respond.

I took his collar and shook the fear out of him. "Do you know of him? The king's monk?"

"Y...y...yes. He is with the army."

"When he returns, give him a message from me. Tell him Gerwulf was here, and then tell King Karl."

He managed to nod, so I shoved him back under the burning altar cloth. "Stay hidden until we are gone," I said. "And remember it was not your god who saved you."

The pack had been too busy stripping the church of valuables to notice the boy. They continued their pillaging, ripping crosses from the priests' necks and silver sconces off the walls. They set the wooden pews on fire. The smoke and heat of the rising flames obscured the nave. The roof beams caught fire, and one collapsed, crushing a dying monk and barely missing Abbo.

"Gerwulf!" Rotgrim shouted. "We must go!"

They raced from the blazing room, their backs to the boy under the burning altar cloth. He twitched and scooted, trying to keep his habit away from the fire and to stay out of sight. When they had gone, I yanked him through the flames, singeing my arm and part of his habit. Wiping the soot from my nose, I said, "Remember always, a *Wulfhedinn* saved you today."

He had stopped trembling. "Yes, my lord...Wulfhedinn."

I left him to his own devices. The crafty novice, the only one with the courage to fight back at us, would manage to escape the burning building and deliver my message. He would become known as the boy who had survived the attack of the Wulfhednar. They would believe he was blessed by their god, and they would make him an abbot or a saint. I had had no such luck as a novice monk.

I caught up to the pack, and we raced through the streets toward the gate. We howled like madmen, and everyone ran in terror from us as though real wolf demons had invaded their city.

"Awwwhoooo!" Rotgrim shouted. His cry did not have the bite of a wolf howl, but his blood-splattered jaw was open and hungry for more. "We gave them a good fucking!"

"We destroyed the Christian god in his own house," Widukind said.

The Raven hovered outside the gate on a rising current, waiting for us.

Quark! Quark! Quark!

She sang her victory song as she escorted us back into the depths of the Teutoburg Forest. I was sure the Walkyrie and the wolf would return soon to the pack, and Vala would come to me. And I thought of Pyttel's crooked smile when he heard the little novice say my name.

A Good Omen

Wulfhedinn

The raid on the palace church would strike Karl hard, and he would lash back quickly. Without the wolf, the rest of the pack members were still vulnerable, but the elation of victory bolstered them with new energy and power.

We fled through the forest with Wichbert. Widukind had made him wait for us outside the city, but he was already talking as if he had been part of the raid. No one paid him any mind.

We followed the Raven northeast, running as though our legs were linked together. My wolf legs helped carry the others forward, or were they taking me along with their stride? I disliked the feeling, so I decreased my pace to widen the space between us. As soon as I slowed, their chests heaved harder, and they gasped for air. One by one—Wichbert first—they slowed too, but Widukind pushed his exhausted men until we had gone a safe distance from the city.

When we stopped to rest, Rotgrim accosted me, his spittle hitting my face. "You have had the wolf all along!"

"You became Wulfhedinn right in front of my eyes," Abbo said.

"I saw it too," said Erhard.

Rotgrim grabbed my collar. "You have been keeping the wolf to yourself."

I shoved him, knocking him against the tree where the Raven had perched. She squawked and flew off.

Erhard stepped between us, breathless and holding his chest. "I think—Gerwulf was as surprised as we were."

"I do not control the wolf," I said.

"Treulogo! You can summon it any time," Rotgrim said.

"He can!" Wichbert said, unable to stop himself. "I have seen him became Wulfhedinn."

He recoiled quickly, surely afraid I would tell his father what he had done at Lippespringe. I held my tongue, keeping his secret, holding him in my debt.

"The wolf possesses me when it wishes," I said. "If I could command it, I would send it to you and order it to leave me alone."

"Enough," Widukind said. "The wolf has come to one of us. This means the Walkyrie might soon bring it to the rest. Nothing else matters."

"I saw the Walkyrie too. I did!" said Wichbert, panting. "And I felt the wolf."

Rotgrim smirked, and the others ignored him. The boy was not even a good liar.

"This fight has just begun," Widukind said. "We will need to gather many more warriors to join us, whether the wolf comes to the rest of the pack or not."

Widukind kept talking, something about rallying other clans, but as far as I was concerned, my part in his fight was finished. I had proved myself to the Walkyrie, and the wolf had come to me. Vala would come soon too, and then we would flee the butcher king's unending war with the Saxons.

My heart warmed with anticipation, and I lost myself in a vision. Vala was wearing her circlet of white hawthorn flowers. She ran toward me in a field of ripe golden barley. The warm sun shone through her thin linen dress, showing her round hips and ripe breasts. Our son toddled next to her, half hidden by the tall grasses. He called me, his plump, round cheeks rosy with joy. "Father! Father!"

Erhard elbowed me like a child who was not paying attention in church, and I plummeted back to the cold winter air among dirty, blood-soaked warriors.

Widukind was still talking. "We will travel to all the Saxon tribes, Westphalian, Angrian, and Eastphalian. We will spread the news of the butcher king's blood court at Verden and gather as much support as we can for the rebellion," he said. "Then we will head north to the Nordalbian Saxons and into Daneland to seek King Sigfred's aid."

Rotgrim was cleaning his sword with a piece of gold-embroidered cloth torn from a priest's vestments. "King Sigfred does not care about us. He grows fat trading with the Franks. Why would he risk such wealth by helping us?"

"He has sheltered us many times from the king in the past," Erhard said. "When he hears of the massacre at Verden, he will do more."

Widukind nodded. "If Sigfred does not support us, and all of the Saxon tribes fall to Karl, the Christian army will soon be storming his hall."

No one disagreed. Even I understood that the Saxons were all that stood between the King Karl and the Danes.

Widukind sent us out to hunt for dinner. We were tired and hungry and needed to eat and rest. It was midday, not the easiest time to find game, but I bagged a doe while Rotgrim and the others came back empty-handed. I hung the carcass and gutted and skinned it. Our mouths watered, but before we cooked it, Erhard took the heart and made a sacrifice to the Walkyrie.

"We are grateful you have come to one of us," he said. "May the rest of us prove worthy again of you and the wolf. Guide us on our path of vengeance against our Christian enemies to the glory of Wodan and the gods."

The heart was passed around, and we each took a large bite. Its warm, bloody richness tasted better than other organs. So much more than sustenance, the heart of the animal fed us its power. Erhard burned what remained of it, and the smoke rose to the sky. The Raven flew into the smoke and was gone. She had accepted and taken our sacrifice to the Walkyrie.

"A good omen," Erhard said.

We roasted the rest of the meat, licking our chops at the smell of sizzling fat and bone marrow. By sunset, we had filled our stomachs to bursting. Abbo, Erhard, and Widukind lay down to sleep, wrapped in their wolf skins. Wichbert shivered in his nobleman's cloak but eventually dozed off. Rotgrim sat with his back against a tree. His broken nose must have throbbed too much to recline, but he did not degrade himself to complain about it to me.

I was feeling the aftermath of his punch to my gut and wished I had not eaten so much. I tossed and could not rest. When would Vala appear? I wanted to search for her in the woods but was too exhausted to move. I decided to let her come to me. She was close. I felt it with every flap of the Raven's wings as she flew in from the darkness, landed on a branch, and tucked her head under her wing.

The Blood That Binds

Wulfhedinn

Jawoke before dawn. The fire had burned out, and the air was frigid. I pulled my wolf skin closer around me, rolled over, and tried to sleep again. Light emerged in the east, and a soft voice called to me.

Gerwulf.

Rotgrim's snoring nearly overpowered the voice, but I heard it well enough. Vala.

Sweet musk and hawthorn.

Padding quietly around the sleeping Wulfhednar, I set my nose on her sweet, earthy fragrance and tracked it through the woods. This forest was strange to me, and I had no notion of direction, but I did not care. I was headed toward her.

Her scent began to dissipate, so I hurried to catch it before it disappeared. Several times I thought I had glimpsed her silhouette, but it vanished so quickly behind a tree or bush that I could not be sure. I bit my tongue to stop myself from calling out to her. I was still too close to camp and might wake the others.

She was leading me toward the sound of flowing water, a fast-running stream, a river. If she kept going, she would have to cross it, which would slow her pace. The sound grew louder, obscuring the rhythm of her light footsteps. I continued to the river's edge. There, I found her sitting on a fallen tree trunk that bridged the churning water. The trunk was as wide as two men and easy enough to cross. If she had wanted to escape me, she could have done so easily. Instead, she sat there, watching the roaring water cascade over the rocks. She was holding the Walkyrie's mask, her back to me. I moved closer, reaching for her long black hair. Its sleek softness had brushed across my bare thigh when she had tended my wounds in Wodan's Tower. It felt so long ago, or it might have been the day before.

I stopped and pulled away, afraid to startle her, afraid she would leave. I feared she might not be real.

"The Walkyrie understands why you left us," she said. "She knew you were going to run away from the pack." She turned and caught my gaze in her sky-blue eyes, glowing like jewels in the shadows of early dawn. "I knew you were not ready to stay, but my heart broke when she let you go."

I sat next to her on the log, unsure what to say, wondering about the child she carried, our child. She was wearing a loose tunic that hid her swelling belly. Almost six moons had passed since we had laid together at the Raven's Stones on Midsummer Day. Soon she would no longer be able to hide the growing baby.

"I am the woman who carries the union of Walkyrie and Wulfhedinn," she said, as if hearing my thoughts. "I was not supposed to love you. My task was to heal you and lay with you to conceive—nothing more. I should not be here now. I am risking everything."

I reached to stroke her black hair. It felt like silk threads weaving themselves through my fingers. She did not pull away.

"You know what I have done at the garrison and Paderborn?" I asked.

"Yes. A good beginning."

"Beginning? It is done! I burned the king's garrison, and led the Wulfhednar to destroy the king's church and slay their holy men. I risked my life to give the Walkyrie the blood vengeance against Christians she demanded."

"Widukind craves vengeance. The Walkyrie hungers for a different kind of blood."

I dropped the tendril of her hair. "Blood is blood."

"The Walkyrie needs the kind of blood that binds itself together to *stop* the bleeding."

Blood that can stop bleeding? What? The enchantment of the moment shattered. My mind spun like a cyclone of dust. She was making no sense—or maybe she was, and I did not want to hear it.

She took my hand. "Your love must be for the Walkyrie and the pack, not me. It is she who gives the pack its power. You must take your place with them as the son of the leader."

"I did not return to fight for my father or become a leader. I came back for you."

"You do not want me, not the woman I really am. You came back because King Karl and the Franks never accepted you and who you are."

I thrust her hand away. "The Walkyrie is poisoning your mind and holding you and my child hostage from me," I said bitterly. "Or maybe you are trying to poison my mind."

Her jaw quivered. "You do not understand." She swallowed hard and placed my hand on her heart. Her warm breast rose and fell with her breathing. Her flesh was real, but I did not trust the other faces she wore. Yet all three, Raven, Walkyrie, and woman, stoked my need for her—more than a need, a hunger I would not be able to satisfy until I conquered the Walkyrie and her Raven spirit and had the woman to myself.

I pulled her to me greedily and kissed her. Her soft lips parted, eager to join my mine with as much hunger and lust.

Sweet musk and hawthorn.

Her taste enveloped me, and I sunk into it as a rock sinks in the water, drowning, clawing, and gasping for more. Her black hair wound around me with the shimmer of the sleek Raven's wings. The wings interlocked and tightened their grip on me as the Raven's feathers covered Vala's face, leaving only her human eyes. I was helpless under the power of the Walkyrie.

"There is no Vala," she whispered hoarsely in my ear.

The Strength he Needed

Wulfhedinn

Jawoke with a start. The Wulfhednar had already risen and were chewing on cold venison. They snickered at me.

"Dreaming of some Frankish court whore?" Rotgrim asked. "We can see your cock from here."

I scrambled to my feet, covering myself with my wolf skin. "Go fuck yourself," I said and dashed into the woods to clear my head.

But nothing was clear. Nothing was certain, except my longing, the unrelieved aching for her. I hastily satisfied my flesh away from the ears of the pack, but it did little to free my mind. I could not stop thinking of her. I wanted to strip her of the Walkyrie's mask to seize the woman beneath, but there was only one way to do it. I would have to follow the Wulfhednar path until the butcher king was dead and the Franks were beaten and driven back into their own lands.

The thought made me hungry, despite the huge meal the night before and my aching gut, still sore from Rotgrim's punch. I returned to camp and cut cold meat from the deer carcass.

"Have a good shit this morning?" Erhard asked.

"Delightful," I said, stuffing my mouth.

He sighed and shook his head. "Shitting is harder for me than it used to be, especially after feasting on so much meat."

"Eat some grass."

He laughed and his expression darkened. "I will not be put out to pasture to graze on grass like an old goat. I will die in this fight, and so will you."

"We will all die fighting one day," I said.

Leaving the carcass, we moved on, trotting north, deeper into Westphalian Saxon territory. The day was sunny and warm for late autumn, good for traveling. The Raven hovered above us on the warm breeze.

The farther we got from Paderborn and the king, the better I felt. By late morning, we came to the burned-out remains of a village. No one was surprised by the piles of charred timbers rotting in the mud. The place had been destroyed and abandoned long ago. Within a day, we passed several more villages in the same condition.

"Are there no villages left?" I asked.

"In two days' travel, we will be welcomed in the hall of my kin," Erhard said. "They have accepted Christian baptism to protect their families and lands from the king, but in their hearts, they are loyal to the old ways and the old gods. My son is the ealderman there. He and his followers did not surrender at Verden, but when they hear of the butcher king's massacre, they will take up arms and help us muster more men."

The journey to Erhard's village was uneventful, but as we neared it, the Raven shrieked. Her call ran down my spine, chilling me like the sound of metal scraping metal. The stink of freshly burnt wood hung heavily in the air, and I could not shake a feeling of doom. Erhard's face clouded. He set his jaw and ran ahead of us.

The forest opened to reveal the smoldering remains of a village. At the far edge of the forest, several dozen corpses hung from the trees. Men, women, and children had been stripped, beaten, and strung up by their necks. They swayed and turned in the breeze, the twisting of the ropes creaking faintly.

Staring at his family, Erhard's ghost eye twitched once, but the rest of his expression did not change. He went to one of corpses and cut it down, kneeling by its side. It was a young man who resembled Erhard strongly. His son.

"The heads of thousands of our warriors were not enough for that mother-fucking butcher," Rotgrim muttered.

The king will not be satisfied until he destroys us all.
Us.

I pulled my axe to cut the rest of the bodies down, but Erhard stopped me. "I will do it," he said.

"You need help," I said.

I held each of Erhard's family members as he cut their nooses. Together we lowered them gently to the ground. As we worked, the others searched through the rubble. The village and hall had been thoroughly ransacked and destroyed, and there was nothing in which to wrap the bodies. I took off my wolf skin and covered the bareness of one of the women. I did not know if she was a servant or the ealderman's wife, but it did not seem to matter.

Erhard put a hand on my shoulder. "Thank you," he said. "There are others I don't see here. The Franks might have taken them as slaves, but maybe the gods helped some of them escape into the woods."

"We will search for them after we honor your fallen kin," Widukind said.

"You honor them best by finding survivors and tracking down those who have done this. I will attend my family."

"I will stay with him," I said.

Widukind, Abbo, Rotgrim, and Wichbert searched the edges of the forest for survivors. They found a few footprints in the mud, those of two small boys and a women or older girl. They also found a dozen sets of iron shod hoofprints on the road heading north—Scola riders.

"They made no attempt to hide their tracks," Abbo said.

Rotgrim felt one of the charred timbers. "Still warm."

"They will not get far," Widukind said.

The Raven remained with Erhard and me while the others searched the surrounding forest. The Raven was quiet, leaving an ominous silence among us.

No one escaped.

I kept my thoughts to myself as we gathered half-burned logs and cut trees to build a pyre.

The pack returned quickly, carrying three more bloodied bodies, two little girls and a woman.

The pack helped us with the pyre, which had to be large enough to engulf a whole village of people in its flames. Despite the cold, we were quickly drenched with sweat and breathing hard. Erhard refused to stop, although the labor would nearly cripple the old man with aches and pains by morning. Working together with us, he found the strength he needed, and he even appeared to grew stronger as the rest of us tired. The wolf was with him.

He carried his son to the pyre with the care of a mother cradling her baby. Then he took each of the others there. He did not let anyone help him with the task and whispered something to each as he laid them down. Many of them resembled him, but he did not tell us who they were. His mother? Grandchildren? Did he have a wife in this village? Widukind and the other Wulfhednar must have known, but they said nothing, allowing him to mourn in his own manner.

We raised our hoods and lit the fire. Erhard choked back his grief, a hardened man broken into despair. The rest of the pack stared at the growing fire, allowing him to weep without shaming him with pity. When the tears had been shed, his voice rose into the air, deep and lonely. He was Wulfhedinn, and he was singing of his sorrow and calling for his pack.

Only I could answer him. Our howling echoed across the bare treetops as the Raven carried his kin from fire and smoke to the lands of the dead.

Courage and Might

Wulfhedinn

We left Erhard's village behind, following the tracks of the Scola riders, the murderers. We ran silently, with unspoken respect for Erhard's loss. He led the pack with the speed of a man half his age. No one mentioned how the wolf had come upon Erhard. I could feel the beast simmering inside him, ready to burst. Had his grief brought it to him? Or something else? Would he be able to control or even command the wolf?

Fog was settling around us, as thick as the rage we were all feeling. We dreaded what would confront us in the next village. As we feared, ash-filled smoke soon appeared, settling upon the forest, nearly choking us. Every building in the village was burning. Men shouted in a mixed dialect of Saxon and the common tongue. People screamed. Goats and pigs squealed and butted against their pens to escape the flames.

We circled off the road into the brush and crept on our bellies to a good vantage point over the village. Below us, men lay bleeding. Women and children ran in chaos, trying to flee a dozen fully armored Franks trampling through the village on large war horses. Their swords, helmets, and polished mail coats flashed in the light. They were the king's most elite champions—and most vicious cutthroats. They herded the coughing, soot-covered villagers into a group. One of the riders chased down all the livestock, crushing them underfoot or skewing them with his spear. Their dying howls and squeals mixed with human screams of terror and despair.

The rider wearing the best mail shirt and carrying the finest sword charged a youth of about eleven. I recognized Fulco, commander of the elite Scola riders. I'd had little contact with him at court, but everyone knew his reputation, and no one dared cross him. He and his horsemen had been just as ruthless when rounding up the prisoners at Verden.

He rode hard at the boy, separating him from the others, and threw a noose around his neck. A woman screamed, begging for him to stop, but her pleas only provoked Fulco. He pulled the boy to the edge of the forest, threw the rope over a branch, and tied it to his saddle. Then he reined his horse backward, slowly. The rope tightened around the boy's neck. He screamed, still able to breathe, clawing frantically at the tightening noose.

The woman had broken down sobbing. "Please, please, my lord! Mercy! He is too young. My son does not know anything."

"Someone in this village knows," Fulco said. "Who will take us to the rebel Widukind and his pack of wolf warriors?"

When no one answered, he backed his horse farther, raising the boy onto the tips of his toes. "Which one of you will take us through the Teutoburg Forest to the rebel and the lair of the Eater of Souls, the Raven's Stones?"

The woman wailed, and the other villagers clung to their crying children. Several men of the village stepped protectively in front of their families. One of them pulled a small dagger hidden in his breeches and rushed Fulco. Another soldier spurred his horse and swung his blade across the man's wrist, nearly severing it. Dropping his dagger, the villager clutched the slash, trying to stem the spray of blood. Terrified, the others were helpless to do anything.

Rotgrim raised his hood. "Wolf or not, I will make them into maggot pie."

Widukind stayed him with a strong hand. "The time will come—with the wolf."

Fulco backed his horse a step, raising the boy higher. His feet danced frantically in the air. He choked. His mother stood and rushed toward him but was kicked to the ground by another soldier. The boy continued to thrash, his face flushing, his legs dripping with piss and shit.

Rotgrim was ready to jump. "Gerwulf, bring us the wolf!" he whispered harshly.

My fury was boiling as hotly as Rotgrim's. I strained to hear the sound of the wolf beast and feel its power surge through me, but it did not come. It left me an angry, frustrated man.

"I cannot," I said.

Rotgrim glowered at me and turned to Erhard. "Erhard! I know you have felt it. Call the wolf!"

Erhard shook his head. "It escapes me now."

"We must attack as men, as the band of warriors we are," Widukind said.

"We cannot fight them all," Abbo said.

Wichbert paled and scooted away deeper into the forest to hide.

"We will draw them into the woods where we can ambush them," Widukind said.

The boy's lips and face were turning blue. Fulco lowered him onto his toes. He choked, making a stridorous sound as he sucked air into his chest. Some of the color in his lips returned, but the gasping did not stop.

"There is no time!" Rotgrim said.

"We cannot afford to lose the whole pack in a rash attack," Erhard said, drilling through me with his ghost eye.

"Hold my horse," Fulco ordered one of his men and dismounted. "Bring me the pregnant woman."

A young woman heavy with child was dragged to him from the group of villagers. The soldiers tore off her tunic, and she kicked one of them in the cullions, spat at another, and bit a third. Two more rushed her, and she writhed and cried as they pinned her and pulled her trembling legs apart.

Fulco scratched her thigh slowly from knee to groin with his sword. "Witch! I'm going to fuck you with this blade to rid us of the demon growing inside."

Another soldier shoved past him, pulling down his breeches. "Not before I have her."

Fulco turned his blade toward the soldiers. "Your commander is always first."

Some of the village men shouted in protest. They tried to break past the soldiers, but they bashed their heads with their sword hilts and kicked the villagers to the ground.

The girl writhed and spit like a viper. "May the Walkyrie curse your Christian souls and throw you into the draugar's fire!"

The pagan spirits responded to her courage. They rode the wind, blowing through dried leaves and bare branches, unsettling the soldiers. They spun around, twisting their necks to see what was happening, unsure if what they had heard was just the wind or something more. The disturbance grew into a noise as deafening as a hundred thunderclaps.

In a blinding burst of speed, Rotgrim bounded through the brush toward them. His wolf hood obscured his mortal face, and he yowled like a wretched creature suffering eternal torments. Fangs dripping with froth, his eyes flared into flames. All rational thought escaped me as the beast roared inside my own chest, drawing me to follow him. Erhard joined our chorus of bestial fury, and we descended on the riders together.

One of the village men screamed with awe. "Wulfhednar! The Walkyrie has brought them to us!"

The Franks froze like raw recruits in their first battle. In a mad whirlwind, we leaped on the soldiers who were holding the naked woman. Our fangs latched onto their throats and tore them out before they could raise a weapon. Fulco's horse neighed and reared. While he struggled to control his mount, I cut through the rope holding the hanging boy. He fell to his knees, coughing and rubbing his neck. I leaped at Fulco, pulling him off the horse. He fell hard, and before he could catch his breath, I crushed his throat in my jaws. His blood tasted the sweetest of all of them. I hacked through his mail with my axe until it hit the flesh of his gut. Another swipe and his guts spilled.

An unearthly shriek roared from the forest and from under the earth. A deafening sound of pounding hooves echoed across the treetops, louder than a thousand galloping horses. The Walkyrie burst across the sky. Her great black wings flapped, carrying her mount through the clouds. She shrieked with the agonies of a thousand tortured souls, calling for more blood.

The eyes gazing through the feathered mask were Vala's, but the power of the wolf was the Walkyrie's. She brought her fury to Abbo, and he sprang from the forest to my side, the essence of a giant Wulfhedinn, the largest of us all.

Widukind was not far behind, spear in hand. He remained a mortal in a wolf skin, but he threw his spear with a mighty strength and accuracy. It pierced the jaw of another soldier, and he tumbled from his horse onto his head.

The remaining riders spurred and beat their spooked horses to escape us, but three of them were bucked off their mounts and thrown to the ground. Widukind slashed and stab them without mercy. The villagers—men, women, and children—grabbed stones and sticks and swarmed behind Widukind to back him.

Rotgrim, Erhard, Abbo, and I vaulted at the four riders who remained in their saddles. Snarling and snapping, we attacked with a rabid blood lust. We were Wulfhednar, and our lifeblood surged through one another, creating a firestorm of power. We took them all to the ground by the throats.

The riders gasped for their last breaths. Fulco was dying quickly, laying among his scattered entrails. "Keep her away from me...the Eater of Souls..." he pleaded weakly.

Without covering herself, the pregnant woman picked up a sword and ran it through his cullions. "The Raven will feast on your Christian soul, and you will dance in the flames with the draugar," she said.

The fight was won, but the villagers were not satisfied. They pulled off the riders' helmets and crushed their skulls with rocks. They stripped off the mail coats and beat the bodies into pulp, making an easy feast for the ravens. Then they collected the weapons and armor as their trophies.

This was what the king feared most—not wolves, wolf warriors, demons, or the ancient gods. He dreaded the power that could transform a pregnant woman and a handful of peasants into fighters with more courage and might than a highly trained, well-outfitted army. He cringed under the shadow of the Walkyrie, the Eater of Souls, the demon who could embolden an entire people to crush him.

First-Born Son

Wulfhedinn

The villagers crowded around us. The children petted our wolf skins, and the women thanked us and offered a few scraps of food. We did not speak in front of the villagers of how the Walkyrie had appeared and wolf had come to Rotgrim and Abbo, but we looked at each other with glowing recognition of it. She was with us again. Only Widukind now remained outside the wolf, and I was sure it would come to him soon too.

The pregnant woman wrapped herself in the Fulco's bloodied mantle and wore it with more regal bearing than he had ever had. One of the men carried the boy who had been hanged to us. He was still gasping for air, and when he tried to speak, his voice was hoarse. The man set down the boy, and his mother rushed to his side and threw her arms around him, sobbing. Another woman brought a cup of cold water and a wet rag to cool his neck, swollen and raw from the noose. His eyes were bloodshot, and red spots covered his pallid face and neck. He was alert, a good sign, but I had seen people survive a hanging one day and die the next.

"My Lord Widukind," said the man who had helped the boy. "We are honored by you and the Wulfhednar. I am Berard, the ealderman of this village, and this is my only son."

"What happened here?" Widukind asked.

Berard kept his eyes on his son. "The riders rode into the village without warning and burned us out. They were looking for you, Widukind, and the woman who carries the Walkyrie's child in her womb. I am sure they would have killed us all, even if someone had talked."

Widukind told them about the Verden massacre and the killing of Erhard's clan. They listened in numbed silence, too shocked to respond. Then he told them of our successful attack on King Karl's garrison and his church at Paderborn. A dash of hope crossed their faces.

"I will be honored to join your rebellion," Berard said. "When the other clans hear of the king's atrocities, they will rise to the call."

The rest of the villagers stepped forward to offer their service. Many were injured in some way, some bleeding from their heads. They were mostly farmers, skinny boys, women, and bony old men, but they bore their wounds like warriors. They were not fed well enough to labor in the fields *and* train for war, but none wanted to back away from the fight.

"What is your plan, my lord,?" Berard asked Widukind.

"We will spread the word of the butcher king's atrocities against the Saxons and gather those who would join us against him," Widukind said. "We will raid and burn every Christian church and Frankish holding that has been built on our lands.

At the same time, bands of raiders can attack small ports along the Rhine to disrupt the king's trade. After the Yule month, we will hold the assembly of the clans who have joined us. This will give us time to train together through winter. We will be prepared for open battle before Karl rallies his full army for the summer campaign season."

Rotgrim had been shaking his head but could no longer hold his tongue. "Our annual assembly has been outlawed. There will be spies at the settlement at Marklo, where it is always held. The clans will be afraid to attend."

Widukind sheathed his sword. "That is why the assembly will be held in secret, away from Marklo. We will meet at the Grotenburg fortress. There we will elect a war chief."

"You are our war chief," Abbo said. Berard and the villagers murmured in agreement.

"A war chief must be elected by all the tribes and clans. It is our way," Widukind said. "Erhard, Abbo, and I will muster the Eastphalian clans. Gerwulf and Rotgrim will bring you all to the settlement of Lübbecke, where you can rest and recover behind its walls."

For the first time, Rotgrim smiled at me. It was more of a leer, but despite our differences, we were both pleased to be matched with a strong partner.

"At Lübbecke, Gerwulf and Rotgrim will meet with the ealderman, Heinrich," Widukind said. "He is my cousin and has repeatedly rejected Christian baptism and burned churches built on his lands. He has many ties with the chieftains of the Westphalian and Angrian tribes. He will help you to spread word of the assembly and muster warriors for the uprising. Then Gerwulf and Rotgrim will meet with Erhard, Abbo, and I in Treva. From there, we will travel north together through the lands of the Nordalbian Saxons and into Daneland. At Hedeby, I will recruit the support of Sigfred, King of the Danes."

The Wulfhednar were nodding in agreement when Wichbert ran from his hiding place at the edge of the village. He pushed through the villagers. "I will go with you, Father."

Widukind pondered it for a moment, but before he could respond, Erhard said. "Wichbert will go with Gerwulf and Rotgrim."

Rotgrim blustered. Neither one of us wanted to be Wichbert's nursemaid.

"I do not want to go with them," Wichbert said.

Widukind thought about it for a moment and said, "Erhard has made a good choice. I will send you on this mission as a boy. You will present yourself and your brother as my sons to the clans. You will help muster the fighters we need, and return to me as a man."

His sons? What would happen when the elders learned who I was?

"If the warriors of Lübbecke find out who I really am, they will kill me," I said.

"The treulogo will get us both killed!" Wichbert said.

Widukind smacked the boy across the face. "You will no longer use that term when you speak of Gerwulf. No one will."

Wichbert held his burning cheek, fighting tears.

"You are both the sons of Widukind," Erhard said. "You will find a way to do what you must—as brothers."

Berard was squinting at me. He spoke to Widukind. "So this is your first-born, the one who served the butcher king? The bas...?"

He had nearly called me a bastard—and I was sure he would have called me treulogo as well had Widukind not just forbade it. Most of the villagers were gaping at me, likely thinking the same thing.

"Gerwulf is one of the Wulfhednar, and he just saved your ass," Rotgrim said.

I was beginning to like Rotgrim's direct manner of speaking.

"Yes, so he is." Berard bowed his head, and the other villagers followed suit.

Widukind instructed Berard and his clan to gather any provisions they could find for the journey to Lübbecke.

He took the Wulfhednar aside, and Abbo spoke his mind. "Widukind, if we split the pack, the wolf may not come to you. Perhaps we should stay together."

"We do not have to be next to one another," Erhard said, "but we do need to continue to work together as a pack."

"Agreed," Widukind said and instructed us on what to tell the Westphalian and Angrian clans. "This is not the time to drink and sleep the dark months of winter away. Tell them to refortify weaknesses in their halls, dig ditches, and build palisades around settlements and villages. Extra guards and patrols must be posted day and night, and every man, woman, and child who is able must learn to wield a weapon, whether slings, bows, clubs, or blades."

One by one, the villagers gathered around to hear him speak. They clutched a couple silver pieces they had salvaged from buried hordes and a few iron tools that had not burned.

"Our warriors will train daily to keep their skills sharp and their resolve hard," Widukind said. "Through the winter, we will build their strength by felling trees and cutting firewood to stoke the blacksmiths' fires. We will need all the weapons they can produce."

Widukind paused as the pregnant woman moved to the front of the crowd. "Women who are with child must be protected from the butcher king who kills innocent women and children," she said.

"Agreed," Widukind said. "Fortified settlements and fortresses shall offer protection to all pregnant women and those with infants. We will defend our own and grow leaner and stronger, hardened to deal with more, tougher than the Franks. The Walkyrie and the wolf are with us. Our time is now."

The villagers' hollowed eyes brightened, standing out from their sooty faces. Widukind had spoken like a king and given them hope. He was the greatest of us, and I wondered why the wolf had not yet come to him. He should have been the first, but these simple peasants did not realize the wolf escaped him. They revered Widukind like he was a war god. He was everything I was not, but I did not want to be a war god. I wanted to be a man who lived in peace with his woman.

Negotiations

The Monk

After Theoderic's slaughter of the Saxon refugees, I tripled my prayers to God.

Father, Son, and Holy Ghost.
I should have done more.
I should have done something.
I should have done something more.
Unrighteous, by any god.

God was not listening, so I kept my soiled hands tucked away as we rode. My only blessing was knowing Theoderic and his thugs would not cause trouble in the Saxon settlement of Treva. They dared not because it was a wealthy trading town, and the king wanted to keep the peace with traders. The General's riders would also be vastly outnumbered by men capable of defending themselves. Traders knew how to protect their wealth, often keeping personal guards. The settlement would be full of well-trained militia and goons as ruthless as Theoderic's squad.

The journey to Treva seemed endless. Unrelenting icy rain chilled me to the bone, and the General was in agony with every step his horse took. I saw it in his rigid riding posture and drawn face, but his band of cutthroats were not the type to notice or care. The closer we got to the settlement, the more they complained about the rain and the pittance of booty. Captain Lothar grumbled the loudest while he fingered the amber necklace he had stolen from the battered body of the elder's wife. I wanted to rip it from his neck and cram it so far down his throat he would shit it out. I distracted myself from the cold by concocting gruesome deaths for them all until we reached Treva. Then my thoughts turned to visions of beer, clean water for washing, and a dry place to sleep.

Treva lay on the other side of the Elbe River. I was glad the river was too deep and treacherous to cross by horseback. Theoderic was forced to open his purse to pay for a ferry crossing. The Saxon ferryman snatched the heavy Frankish silver coins from his hand before he could change his mind. He eyed us suspiciously as he took us across the river on his tipsy ferryboat. In his business, he knew better than to antagonize customers, especially Frankish soldiers, but his expression did not hide his feelings about us. He and everyone else in Treva relied on keeping trade open with the Franks, but they did not want to become our comrades, either. When Frankish silver was offered, they pretended to embrace the king and the Christian god. When Saxon or Danish silver was offered, they were pagans again.

Theoderic also paid for a room at an inn. I had to share the bed with two of his riders, and none of us liked it, but it was better than the wet, cold ground. Still, I could not sleep. My mind wrestled with images of slaughtered women and children, their murders committed by men snoring next to me. None of them had asked me to hear their confession, and they never would.

I should have done more.

I rose in the middle of the night and walked to the Elbe River to wash. I tripled my sacrifices, but neither the Lord God, the Shepherd, nor Wodan, the Traveler appeared to give me further direction or a reprieve from my guilt. The Raven spirit had told me what the gods all demanded of me. They wanted the butcher king dead and would not appear again until I had completed the deed.

I could delay the dreaded task because I was hundreds of miles away from the king. But my guilt would not be relieved until the deed had been done. I had sacrificed more of my own blood to no avail, and I was hurting and exhausted. Yawning, I returned to the inn before Theoderic and his men woke. After breaking our fast at dawn, we left Treva.

Our Saxon guide navigated us northward through more bogs and swamps. Fortunately, we did not pass any other Saxon villages. I was sure some tiny homesteads were nestled on islands of dry land or were built on posts above the water, but they were well hidden from us.

The drizzling rain was incessant until we reached the drier lands of the Nordalbian Saxons. We rode across their open plains of grassland, an area of good farmland, but our guide did not take us to any farms or settlements.

Captain Lothar and his men were getting impatient. "You Saxon turd! Where are the farms and villages?"

"This is a desolate route, I know," he said, "but it is the most direct path to Hedeby. If you want settlements, we will have to detour far out of the way, and we are almost in Danish lands now."

Lothar spurred his mount next to the guide and stuck his spear tip at his chest. "I do not care. Take us someplace with booty."

"Enough, Lothar," Theoderic said. "These dirt farmers have no valuables for you, and we will learn nothing from them. We have wasted enough time. It is time to get to Hedeby."

Lothar jabbed at the guide's chest before lowering his spear. "We were promised we could plunder on this mission," he grumbled.

"You have had blood booty," Theoderic said, but Lothar and the others did not seem pleased by it.

I was relieved when we crossed into Danish lands. Theoderic would not let his goons disturb the Danes. He could not risk provoking their king on a diplomatic mission. As we neared Hedeby, we passed many intact farmsteads and villages with pens full of livestock and well-stocked hay stores for the winter. The Danish men and women were wearing rings, brooches, bracelets, and necklaces. Many pieces were made of bronze or animal bones, but the wealthiest landowners had silver and amber jewelry and carried coin purses.

Lothar and his men were nearly salivating at the wealth of the Danes. They were a prosperous people who had not been pillaged like the Saxons had. They glared back at us with suspicion and looks of arrogance.

"These Northmen think they are better than us," Lothar grumbled.

"Ignore them," the General said. "We will put these heathens in their place too someday."

He kept the men under a tight rein and did not allow us to stop to talk to anyone. We spent two cold nights camping instead of demanding lodging and the hospitality of the locals.

At Hedeby, we came to an enormous earthwork wall undergoing new construction. Men were digging a series of three ditches at the base of the wall. Women and children carried baskets of dirt to the top of the banks to build them higher.

Theoderic's face darkened. "King Sigfred is preparing to make war."

Our guide shrugged. "Or strengthening defenses against invasion. I heard he plans to extend the wall all the way to the Treene River."

Such a wall would provide complete protection from an incursion from the south. We all knew the Danes would not invest such resources to defend against occasional small-scale raids from their Saxon cousins and neighbors. This was a major rampart built to withstand an assault by King Karl's massive Frankish army.

At the gate, our guide acted as a herald, introducing General Theoderic and requesting a diplomatic audience with King Sigfred. We were acknowledged as high-ranking Franks and were admitted inside the earthworks, but they made us wait outside the city's wooden palisade for King Sigfred's permission to enter the city. The mist turned to rain, then sleet and snow. Sigfred was making us linger long enough in the cold to make it clear we were not his priority. As we waited, we watched the activity on the fringe of the city harbor. The busy port city had been built on an inlet of the Baltic Sea, an ideal locale for trade. I had never seen so many trading ships loaded with freight in one place. There were seafaring ships, coastal trading ships, and many smaller boats. The wealth of Hedeby traders must have dwarfed the coffers of Treva's traders in Saxony and many in the Frankish Kingdom.

Theoderic shifted uncomfortably on his mount. His face was as white as a king's sheets, but his hawk-like gaze remained sharp. Snowflakes melted on his feverish forehead and dripped off his brow, but he did not take his attention off the many ships rushing to the docks. Hedeby's port was a perfect haven from the full fury of a squall blowing in from the sea. I wondered how long we would have to wait outside in the storm.

Something moving at the far end of the sea inlet caught my eye. An unusual ship was cutting through the choppy waves kicked up by the approaching storm. It had a shallower hold than the other ships and was propelled by oars. The hold could not have carried nearly as much cargo as the others, but the ship was fast in heavy waters. Really fast. It had a mast, but the sail was not raised. The men rowing it worked together with the strength and discipline of a well-trained army, and their ship flew by the other vessels as though they were anchored.

The fast ship was astonishing to watch, but the Scola riders were growing bored. They made crude jests about the women working on the rampart until Theoderic turned in his saddle and silenced them with a stony glance.

The wind whipped along the palisade, pelting us with icy snow. Darkness had fallen before we were finally granted an audience with the king. A large guard of three dozen escorted us through the city, and its residents crowded the street to gawk at us. The onlookers pointed to us like amusing curiosities. Lothar and his men bristled, feeling insulted. At Sigfred's hall, Theoderic's injured leg buckled when he dismounted from his horse, and he nearly fell into the mud.

The king's guard demanded we surrender our weapons before we entered the hall. The stiff northerly wind was intensifying, and we were tired of the cold, so Theoderic and his men yielded their weapons. I kept my seax hidden under my mantle, assuming they would not expect a monk to be armed, and I was right. They did not question me, but one of the guards ran his finger around the edge of the bald spot of my tonsured haircut. Puzzled, he and his comrades laughed.

We were taken into the warmth of the massive timber hall, which was larger than many of King Karl's palaces. Inside, three large fires were blazing, lighting up huge oak posts carved with magical pagan symbols and beasts. A hundred or more people crowded the hall, richly dressed and well-armed. They turned to gape at us foreigners.

King Sigfred sat on a brightly painted throne on a raised dais. He waved us forward. I was surprised at his stature—about the size of a boy of thirteen—but he had the lined face and full beard of a man of about thirty. Not all kings were built like King Karl, I thought, but I would not want to raise his temper, nonetheless. Sigfred did not come to rule a kingdom and such a wealthy trading town by being weak and stupid.

"You are welcome in my hall, General Theoderic," he said.

I was not convinced and kept a hand tucked under my mantle on the hilt of my seax.

"Do you bring me news from the south?" Sigfred asked. "I have heard many Saxon nobles and thousands of their followers were surrendering to King Karl. I expected your king to send a royal messenger, not his general, to deliver the official news."

"The Saxon rebels were punished at Verden," Theoderic said.

"Punished? My envoys told me there was to be a truce and a pardon for those who surrendered."

"Your envoys must have heard incorrectly."

"What kind of punishments did your king hand out?"

"Executions."

"Of whom?"

"All of them."

A hush fell over the hall. For a moment, Sigfred was speechless, but his expression remained unchanged. "Sounds like your Christian king took a pagan's vengeance on those who had humiliated him at the battle in the Süntel Hills."

His courtiers chucked, and I covered a smile behind my sleeve. Clearly this king was not the ignorant barbarian the Christians believed him to be.

Sigfred raised a hand to quiet the hall. "Karl's desire to expunge the disgrace of his generals is, after all, understandable. I heard they were drawn right into a Saxon ambush like flies to shit."

Theoderic bristled, shifting his weight off his injured leg. His pale skin grew gray and waxy, and sweat poured from his head. He swayed, gritting his teeth. "We have come for the rebel Widukind."

Sigfred raised an eyebrow, feigning a shocked expression. "Oh, so the Wulfhedinn leader did not surrender with the rest?"

"We captured and executed eight of his wolf warriors."

I held my tongue. In truth, they had captured one Wulfhedinn. The other seven had surrendered.

"Eight. How impressive," Sigfred said. "But not Widukind, the leader."

Despite the tension of the negotiations, my mind drifted to thoughts of Gerwulf. I scanned the hall for signs he and the other Wulfhednar were there. If they were, they would know we were too. They might even be in the hall, behind a curtain or wall, peeking through a tiny hole and listening.

The wind was growing stronger. It howled, shaking the timbers and rattling the shutters. Was it the wind or the wolf?

I hoped for the wolf. The door banged open, and a raven flew in from the storm and perched in the rafters, shaking rain from its feathers.

The sinewy cords in Theoderic's neck tightened, and he swayed again. "I have come to negotiate for the delivery of Widukind and his Wulfhednar."

"Negotiate?" Sigfred asked. "Do you think I have the Walkyrie and her Wulfhednar at my calling to bargain with?"

"You are Widukind's brother-in-law, and it is well-known you have harbored him in the past," Theoderic said. "And you have fostered his son Wichbert in your court."

"I sent my useless nephew away months ago." He waved his hand, dismissing any significance of the boy. Then he locked eyes with Theoderic. "I am a greedy king. Greedy for the benefit of my people. I am not fool enough to bring the wrath of the king of the Franks upon my doorstep. We have been trading together so well, and it has been making us all rich. I sent my ambassador to King Karl's assembly last spring, offering gifts of great value to show my good faith. I was told he accepted them graciously."

"Yes. I witnessed the event myself," the General said.

King Sigfred locked his hands together and leaned forward. He had more golden rings embedded with jewels on his fingers than King Karl had. "I don't give a shit about your god or your war with the Saxons," he said. "But I do want to keep trading."

He pointed toward me, and my heart sank. I had hoped to escape his notice.

"Christian holy man," he said. "If your god is as mighty as you claim, he will use his power to help me bring your pagan rebel to justice. Is this not so?"

I was forced to agree. "Yes, my lord."

"Then Widukind's fate lies in the hands of your god," he said.

Clearly, the little Danish king was well educated about Christianity, and he was clever enough to use it to manipulate his enemies. He had deferred his responsibility of condemning Widukind just as Pilate had washed his hands of the responsibility of condemning Jesus Christ. I liked him, but I did not trust him. I was sure he was lying. Gerwulf and the Wulfhednar were surely in Hedeby.

"You are welcome to stay as guests in my hall for a few nights," Sigfred said. "After you rest, you must return to your king with my greetings, more gifts, and wishes for continued friendship and trading."

I suspected he most wanted to trade for Frankish swords, the best blades made anywhere. He wanted to hoard weapons. Together with his enlarged earthwork wall and the ship that flew across the water like a bird, it added up to preparation for war. I had been a soldier too long not to see it, and so had Theoderic.

I glanced around, hoping to see Widukind's face somewhere among the court. He was not foolish enough to show it while General Theoderic was there, but I looked anyway.

The wind shook the hall. The storm was intensifying, and I was glad to have a warm place to sleep in that night. A shutter blew open, and the raven squawked, mimicking human laughter, as if mocking us. Then Theoderic clutched his leg. The color drained from his lips, and he passed out.

A Chant to the Gods

Wulfhedinn

Darkness had fallen when Rotgrim, Wichbert, and I arrived with Berard and the villagers at Lübbecke. The journey had taken longer than I had hoped. Rotgrim and I could have traveled the distance in less than half a day, but the old men, women, and children had slowed our progress. The Scola riders had burned their carts and killed their oxen, so Rotgrim and I had carried two injured villagers. Berard had carried his son, his head lolling as he passed in and out of consciousness.

Despite the dropping temperature that night, we decided to wait until morning to approach the heavily guarded gate. Lübbecke was no peasant farmstead. The large trading settlement was surrounded by a defensive ditch and wooden palisade. Iron bands reinforced the thick timber gate, and guards stood watch over it. The cold dampness would settle into our bones overnight, but remaining outside was our best choice.

"Why do we have to sleep in the cold?" Wichbert asked.

"Only desperate men approach locked gates at night," I said.

"Gerwulf is right," Berard said. "Ealderman Heinrich and his warriors are fierce fighters and are no fools, especially after dark. His guards may launch arrows first, and ask questions later. I would not approach them until morning."

"You are a peasant," Wichbert said. "I am the son of Widukind, and the ealderman is my kin. He will welcome me."

"The guards cannot see who you are in the dark, you little idiot," Rotgrim said.

"They will know me. I was presented to Ealderman Heinrich and his clan when my father took me on a tour of Westphalia."

"How long ago was that?" I asked.

"I do not know, maybe ten years."

"You were barely weaned from your mother's tit."

"He is barely weaned from it now." Rotgrim wrapped his cloak around himself and lay down. "If the little maggot wants a face full of arrows, I will not stop him."

"Do you think that anyone will recognize you in the dark after so many years?" I asked.

"They...I had not thought..."

"You need to start thinking like a warrior."

"I can think better than you know," he muttered.

He stood and sulked for a long time after the rest us of had settled down to sleep, but I was glad to remain in the forest one more night. Vala might come. I turned fitfully while Rotgrim snored as though he had gulped a whole cask of beer. Berard and the villagers were restless too, but they did not complain about the cold or the pains of their injuries. I knew Berard worried about his son, but his fate lay in the hands of the gods.

By dawn, Vala had not shown herself, which irritated me more than even Wichbert had. I was ready to snap at an easy target. I glared at the boy, hoping he would say or do something to annoy me. He shied away from me and kept quiet while Rotgrim and I discussed how to approach Ealderman Heinrich and his clan.

"When we meet Heinrich, I will speak first," Rotgrim said. "There is much they do not know yet, especially about you, but they trust me."

I agreed. Ealderman Heinrich and his followers had to be handled in a way to encourage their support. Unfortunately, we also needed Wichbert's credibility as Widukind's legitimate son, which annoyed me even more.

We waited until the sun had risen high in the sky. Then Rotgrim and I raised our wolf hoods and led Wichbert, Berard, and the villagers to the gates. A guard instantly recognized us and called out, "Wulfhednar! Wolf warriors approach! They are with Ealderman Berard and his clan."

We were taken inside without question and escorted through the yard toward a timbered hall. It towered above the other buildings in the settlement, its walls three times my height. Next to the hall stood the remains of a burned out wattle-and-daub hut. A charred Christian cross lay on top of the ruins, which were slowly sinking into the mud. Some missionary must have made friends with the ealderman long enough to establish a hovel of a church. Looking at the ruins, I wondered what he had done to anger the ealderman and what the ealderman had done to him.

Two huge wooden pillars stood in front of the hall. Carved out of massive oak trunks, they had been decorated with intricate, swirling designs of trees, leaves, and boars with huge tusks. They were sacred pagan columns that held up their world, a tribute to the gods and the totem boar spirit that gave this clan strength. They had likely burned the little church and killed the priest when he had demanded they destroy their pillars.

I felt the boar spirit's power as we passed between the pillars and under a huge boar's skull posted over the hall threshold. Inside, Ealderman Heinrich was breaking his fast, surrounded by long tables of clan families. Next to him sat a hearty-looking woman who must have been his wife. She was cutting slabs off a deer carcass like a warrior cutting through the neck of an enemy. She and everyone else stopped eating at the sight of us in our wolf skins. We lowered our hoods, and the herald announced us to the ealderman and his wife, Gunda. Heinrich came around the table and embraced Rotgrim with a hearty pat to his back.

"Welcome, welcome, Rotgrim," he said. "It has been too long."

Then the ealderman greeted Berard and the villagers, eying the soot and dried blood on their faces and mantles. "What has happened, Berard?"

"A band of Frankish soldiers. They..."

Heinrich frowned. "Please, you are cold and hungry. Sit and eat, and the women will attend to the injured ones. Then we will hear everything."

Berard and the villagers were given places at the tables.

The Lübbecke elder crossed his arms, considering me. "I do not recognize this Wulfhedinn."

"Ealderman Heinrich, this is Gerwulf," Rotgrim said, gesturing. "He was chosen by the Walkyrie for the pack last Midsummer."

"Gerwulf? I have heard that name."

"He is the eldest son of Widukind."

Heinrich scrutinized me from head to foot. "The half-breed Frank. You served King Karl."

"In the past," Rotgrim said. "He has returned to the pack and proven himself to the Walkyrie—and to me." He put his arm around my shoulder. "He is my wolf brother."

Wolf brother? Stunned, I doubted he was sincere. Then for a moment, I felt he might be.

Heinrich rubbed his chin. "I will accept your word because you are Rotgrim of the Wulfhednar, but there is much I have to ask about this man who now wears the wolf's mantle."

"And I have much to tell."

"I will be glad to hear it." He turned his attention to Wichbert. "I have not seen you since you were a babe." He pinched one of the boy's arms, and he winced. "You are puny. Not much like your father or big brother, are you?" Heinrich laughed. "Well, sit and eat, little Wichbert. Put some meat on those bones so you will grow to fight like a Wulfhedinn."

Wichbert needed more than a few bits of bread and cheese to make him into a fighter. By the way Heinrich had mocked him, it seemed he thought so too. Wichbert pouted but was too cold and hungry to argue or whine. We all were. More benches were brought to make room for the Wulfhednar to sit at the ealderman's table. Then his servants brought us food and beer.

"Why did Widukind and Erhard not come with you?" Heinrich asked, wolfing down slabs of venison his wife had cut.

Rotgrim spoke first. "They are…"

Heinrich interrupted. "Gerwulf will speak, and then you will tell me if he lies."

Rotgrim sat back and gorged himself. "I will."

"So share all the news, Gerwulf, son of Widukind." Heinrich continued to eat but kept a keen eye on me.

"Widukind and Erhard are on their way to the Eastphalian Saxons to muster warriors for a rebellion," I said.

"Now—in winter?" Heinrich asked. "Why?"

"There is a great deal to tell, and not all of it is good," I said.

"I expected as much. What has happened to the craven clans who surrendered at Verden? Did they accept the king's pardon and lick his balls? We feared they would join the Franks to fight against us."

"King Karl betrayed and beheaded them all—more than four thousand."

Gunda rammed her dagger into the table, seething. Her lips curled, and her eyes flashed.

Heinrich furrowed his brow and looked to Rotgrim. He nodded, confirming my story.

"They were promised clemency by King Karl," Heinrich said. "I am ashamed to admit some of those who surrendered were my kin—distant kin—and I warned them not to trust the Christian king, the treulogo butcher king."

Treulogo.

He had said the word with such venom, I understood the full meaning of it for the first time. I would give the Wulfhednar no reason to use it again when speaking of me.

I told Heinrich and his clan all that had happened, the king's blood court at Verden, our attack on the garrison and Paderborn, and the butcher king's new attacks on the Saxon villages. I did not mention how the pack had lost the wolf.

When I finished, the only sound in the hall was the crackling fire. Then I told him of Widukind's plans for the rebellion, and a faint thumping rose over the silence. Some of Heinrich's warriors were hitting the tables with their fists and butts of daggers. Soft and dull at first, the sound grew quickly, and soon everyone had joined in. They pounded the tables harder and harder until the noise exploded like the thunder of Donar. My heart pounded with the beat, united with them in their anger and grief and desire for vengeance. I had become as excited as they were and, for a moment, believed we could not lose our rebellion against the butcher king.

The pounding subsided, and Heinrich spoke. "What about the Danes? They supported us in the past, but will they now?"

"Of course," said Wichbert. "King Sigfred is my uncle, *my* blood. He will stand by us."

Heinrich and his wife looked dubiously at the boy.

"We are on our way to the Danish court to rally his support," I said, stopping short of making promises.

Heinrich grunted. He pulled Gunda's dagger from the table and gave it back to her. He knew there was no guarantee of Sigfred's support or of how much he might give us.

"My wife and my clan warriors have spoken. Our loyalty lies with Widukind. We will back him and the Wulfhednar in his revolt against the butcher king. I will muster the Westphalian clans and join Widukind and the Wulfhednar after Yule at Grotenburg." He raised his drinking horn. "May the gods be with us in our fight, and may we die bravely and with honor in the eyes of the Walkyrie."

Everyone in the hall raised their horns and drank deeply. The warriors pounded the tables again and accompanied the beating rhythm with a mantra to the gods. Rotgrim joined in, and I found myself chanting and pounding the table with my axe handle. Humans and wolves sang together as one. My father and the Wulfhednar might have dragged me into this rebellion, but it had carried me away, and my heart surged. Freeing Vala from the Walkyrie felt closer than ever.

A Friend

Wulfhedinn

Rotgrim and I spent the morning with Ealderman Heinrich, his wife, Gunda, and his senior warriors discussing Widukind's war plan and preparations. Wichbert was allowed to attend the council, but every time he tried to talk, he was silenced by Heinrich. The ealderman only wanted to hear from Rotgrim and me. Wichbert fumed silently, pretending he was bored, rolling his eyes often.

The council agreed that the best plan to quickly cover the most territory was to split into two groups. Heinrich and his men would muster his clan and the Westphalians to the east and the Angrian Saxons to the northeast. His wife was an ealderman's daughter from the Angrian Saxon tribe, and his ties to them through their marriage were strong. Rotgrim and I would rally the

Westphalian clans living to the west in the Hunte River Valley.

"They will respond to the call," Heinrich said with confidence. "The butcher king's deception and murder of Saxons will not go unanswered."

I did not rejoin the enthusiastic table pounding with the others. My mind had wandered, wondering if the other Saxons would accept me, a treulogo, as readily as Heinrich had.

"You are too quiet, Gerwulf," he said keenly. "Do you have something to say? Now is the time."

Before I could answer, Wichbert said, "What if the clans do not trust him? He endangers us all! Rotgrim and I should go without him."

Heinrich kept his focus on me. "A weak boy child with no war experience will not inspire warriors, but the Wulfhedinn son of Widukind will have as much sway over the people as his father."

He waited patiently for my response. I had none.

"You seem unconvinced, Gerwulf, son of Widukind," he said. "Do you not know anything about your father?"

I did not want to repeat what little I knew about Widukind. As a child, I had been told he had raped my Christian mother and cursed her with his demon seed—me. I did not learn the truth about my parents until last summer. Vala had told me that my Frankish mother had been my Wulfhedinn father's lover. I was the product of their forbidden lust, not rape, but a demon bastard in either case.

"My mother never told me who my father was," I said. "I met him for the first time last Midsummer. All I know is he was a rich Saxon noble before King Karl declared him an outlaw rebel."

"He was a rich noble before the king confiscated his estates and lands," Heinrich said. "He *lost* nothing, but he sacrificed everything. Now he fights for the freedom of the Saxons and for the old ways and the old gods. The families of the Hunte River Valley are his clan—your clan. His people are your people, and you carry his Wulfhedinn blood. They will rally around you and your call to arms."

He glanced toward Wichbert, who had left the table and was poking a small puppy with a burning stick from the fire. The whelp was no bigger than a rabbit, but when it snapped and nipped him, Wichbert cried aloud.

"Keep that boy quiet," Heinrich said.

Rotgrim grinned. "I would love to shut him up—my way."

I thought Heinrich might be right. Widukind's clans—my kin—would more likely rally around me than my pathetic weasel of a half-brother. My confidence passed quickly. Widukind was a hero, a legend among his people. I was not—and did not want to be.

By afternoon, Heinrich was giving orders to his men and dispatching messengers to spread the word of the uprising. After a rich and filling dinner, he advised us to rest.

"We all have long journeys ahead of us to cement the alliance against the butcher king," he said and retired with Gunda to his private quarters.

We spent a comfortable night in the warm, dry hall. In the morning, Rotgrim, Wichbert, and I left Lübbecke full of fresh energy. The sky was misty and gray, and Wichbert complained about the dampness as we trotted on the road west to the Hunte River valley.

"Shut up!" I snapped at him. "If you cannot handle the dampness now, you will never survive it as a warrior who has injuries and aching joints. But it does not matter. You will never become a Wulfhedinn anyway."

Rotgrim snickered, and Wichbert's lower lip quivered. He looked truly wounded, but I did not regret what I had said because, for once, he stayed quiet.

The Hunte River Valley ran north through the heart of Westphalia, connecting a string of villages and settlements. As Heinrich had predicted, the elders of Widukind's clan gladly acknowledged me as his Wulfhedinn son. Many embraced me, calling me the lost son returned by the gods.

"The Walkyrie has brought you back to Widukind and the Wulfhednar to free us from the butcher king!" one woman said.

My face flushed, and I could not reply to her. I was embarrassed and wished they did not expect so much of me.

Rotgrim shook his head as we trotted to the next village. "Do not let it go to your head. Your ass still stinks like any other's."

"Have you been sniffing my ass while I sleep, Rotgrim?" I asked, and he laughed.

I quickly tired of repeating the story of the Verden massacre and our attacks on the king's garrison and church. Despite that, every clan ealderman rallied his warrior followers and dispatched riders to local homesteads to recruit more men. Wichbert continued to pout.

After three weeks of following the river north, we were exhausted, despite the generous amounts of beer and food every clan offered us. Then Rotgrim, Wichbert, and I suffered stomach pains and loosening of the bowels for two days. I felt like a dirty dog when we finally arrived at the confluence where the Hunte River flowed into the Weser.

The area was surrounded by vast swaths of swampland and large areas of open water bounded by boggy ground. Much of the area was not solid enough to walk on, but Rotgrim knew his way along its safe paths. Tiny villages dotted the area, built on small islands and bits of higher dry land in the estuary. Although the bogs and swamps had isolated and protected those clans from the Franks, they too were outraged by the king's massacre and jumped to join the rebellion. Nearly everyone had a blood or marriage tie to someone at Verden.

The locals ferried us across the Weser, and we traversed more bogland before coming to open plains and deep forest. After three days, we arrived at Treva on the Elbe River, where we were to meet up with Widukind.

Treva was the biggest Saxon settlement I had ever seen. It was a city with a port and ships and a tangle of streets running through town. Treva's ealderman, Fridenot, welcomed us and gave us comfortable lodging with Widukind, Abbo, and Erhard, who had arrived just before us. We ate at Fridenot's table, sharing news about our efforts to muster backing for the rebellion. Widukind was more talkative than usual, and his face lit up when I spoke of the enthusiasm of the Westphalian tribes.

"You have done well, son," he said. "The Eastphalians are joining us too. In the past, they had bent a knee to Karl in exchange for titles and lands. But they lost many warriors and kin to him at Verden, and they now consider their oaths to him forfeited."

Ealderman Fridenot, a wealthy trader, not a warrior, pledged support in the form of weapons and silver on the condition we kept his involvement secret. Widukind agreed. Fridenot also told us a contingent of Frankish Scola riders had passed through Treva several weeks earlier.

"They were on their way to Hedeby and the court of King Sigfred, but they did not present themselves to me," he said. "My spies tell me they passed through town quietly, staying at an inn. They say their leader was the king's general, Theoderic. A monk accompanied them—a strange monk with a smashed face and a mad look in his eyes."

Widukind and I exchanged glances. "Theoderic is surely going to negotiate with King Sigfred to betray me," he said.

"Fuck the Danes," Rotgrim said. "We have gotten all the support we want from our own clans and tribes. We do not need the Danes."

"We need them more than ever," Widukind said. "We must learn where Sigfred's loyalty lies."

"You cannot risk it," Rotgrim said. "He loves to trade with the Franks for their silver and their swords. We cannot offer him anything to match it, and he may refuse to make another alliance with us. He might even turn us over to Karl."

"I will talk to my uncle," Wichbert said. "He will listen to me."

The wrinkles on the back of Rotgrim's bare scalp deepened. "You are the last one who should speak to him."

"I may be able to discover Sigfred's true intentions," I said, thinking of Pyttel, my greatest ally, who might still be in Hedeby.

The other Wulfhednar stirred, confused expressions on their faces.

Rotgrim curled his fist around his sword hilt and released it several times. "You cannot approach Sigfred if he has already decided to betray us. We cannot lose you."

"I have a friend."

Rotgrim's brows drew together. "You? A friend? What kind of friend?"

"I know this friend," Widukind said.

"I will explain it on the way to Hedeby," I said.

We left Treva with more promises of silver and weapons from Ealderman Fridenot and traveled north through the Nordalbian Saxon lands. The Raven flew with us. Her dark presence helped convince the northern clans to join the uprising. We enlisted every capable fighting man and youth we encountered all the way to the border of the Danes' territory.

The rest of the journey was uneventful. When we arrived within sight of Hedeby's massive earthwork walls, I told the others to stay hidden in the forest while I scouted the gate. I found a good place to observe the comings and goings of the city and waited.

I thought of Pyttel. My friend. I missed him, his ridiculous hair and smashed nose, his babbling to the voices no one else could hear. If he were in the city, he would be itching to escape and find a place to perform his sacrilegious rituals in the forest. I would smell stale beer, sweat, and old animal blood, and he would come before long—if he were still there.

A Spy

The Monk

Father, Son, and Holy Ghost.

Day and night, I clutched my cross, praying for Theoderic's death. His pus-ridden leg wound had to kill him soon. Our stay as guests of King Sigfred had already been extended for weeks as Theoderic lingered in and out of consciousness.

Gerwulf was not in Hedeby. That much had become obvious to me because he would have found a way to contact me if he were. Most likely, he and the Wulfhednar had sought refuge at the Raven's Stones. My heart longed to see him, and I wanted to return to Paderborn as soon as possible. That city lay on the edge of the Teutoburg Forest, less than a day's walk from the standing stones. Gerwulf would surely contact me there.

I pleaded with the old gods for Theoderic's quick demise. He could not possibly survive in the long term, and I saw no harm doing what I could to lessen his time of suffering—and hasten my return to Paderborn.

King Sigfred had never wanted us in his city and had made us feel less than welcome. The weapons of Theoderic's soldiers had not been returned after our initial audience with him. After several nights' lodging in the king's hall, we had been sent to a damp hovel with a leaking roof and given meager food and drink. I thought Sigfred was trying to hasten Theoderic's inevitable passing and get rid of us as quickly as possible. He would have preferred throwing us out into the winter cold, but he could not treat King Karl's general in such a manner and keep in his good graces for trading.

We were not imprisoned in the hovel, but Theoderic's men were escorted everywhere in town. The guards gladly accepted the Scolas' bribes to take them to taverns where the women were blond and young. They did not care what I did and shied away from me, thinking me mad. I was offended, but glad of it at the same time.

Three times a day, I went to one of the city wells to wash in fresh water, but I never felt clean. I needed to go to a spring to sacrifice but was afraid the guards at the gate would demand to know what I was doing or follow me. What if they let me out but did not allow me back into the city? I considered running away from Hedeby and returning to Paderborn on my own, then quickly changed my mind. I would never survive the journey by myself through pagan lands without Theoderic's guard to protect me. I was too much of a coward to try, so I waited.

Theoderic hung onto his miserable life week after week, like a goat clinging to a sheer cliff. He appeared better one moment, worse the next, and better again. Sometimes, he mumbled incoherently in states of fever and confusion. I would have liked to have stuffed a rag in his mouth to kill him myself, but the gods had charged me with assassinating King Karl. My soul could not withstand any more killing—especially a murder in cold blood.

One morning, I could stand it no longer and had to wash, so I left the city, ducking behind a farmer driving a herd of cattle through the gates. If anyone had seen me, that person did not care.

I quickly found a quiet place where a small spring ran into the river. I cut more flesh, this time from both thighs. As my blood stained the water, I implored Wodan the Traveler and the Lord God the Shepherd to relieve me of the task of killing King Karl. They ignored my sacrifice. Neither one of them appeared, but someone else was coming. The footfall of a mortal approached. The steps were irregular, made by someone with a limping gait.

I panicked and ran, trying to throw on my habit without dropping my seax. Blood dripped down my legs onto my feet, and I slipped. Thrown to my hands and knees, I dropped my blade. Before I could recover, the cold steel of a sword pressed against my throat.

Theoderic stood above me, his face a flat-gray color—stony, like a corpse. For a moment I thought he had died and sent his ghost after me, but the blade on my neck felt real enough. How had he mustered the strength to follow me? I should never have assumed he was on his deathbed.

He pressed the blade harder against my neck. "I have long suspected you of sacrilege, and now I have witnessed it myself."

"But my lord, I...I have just been bathing."

"You cut flesh from your own body, like a dirty, heathen animal."

"Yes...yes, but to the Lord God. Did not our Jesus Christ also sacrifice His body?"

My attempt to weave a story in my favor did not work on him as it did on others. He never changed the way he perceived anything.

"I have always suspected you of freeing Gerwulf and helping him escape," he said. "You are in league with him and his demons."

"I...I...am the king's guardian, his confessor. God will suffer no injury to me! I..."

He kicked me in the gut, harder than I thought him capable in his condition. I rolled over, clenching my belly, trying to catch my breath.

"I have been waiting a long time to prove you are a heretic who conspires against King Karl."

My mind whirled. He wanted to cut me open from cullions to throat. I could see it in his eyes, but I knew he would hold his temper like the stone he was. He would take me back to the king for judgment—a far worse fate. I would be chained and beaten like a criminal during the long journey back, to the delight of Theoderic and his riders. The king and his court would convict me of blasphemy and treason, and I would be punished and executed in the most horrible manner. Worst of all, I would die before saving all the souls I needed to save. They would dump my body in unconsecrated ground, damned to become one of the—

The General raised his sword hilt, aiming it at my head. He was going to knock me out. I fumbled, clawing the dirt for my seax, just out of reach. His hand hung in the air, and he managed a half-grin, enjoying my struggles. I hoped his blow would kill me.

A deep guttural sound echoed through the woods. Dark and terrifying, a savage howl rattled the barren trees and chilled my blood. Theoderic startled. He glanced around, raising his blade defensively. The baying grew louder, rabid and hungering for flesh like spirits of the dead—or a wolf demon of the forest.

A dark figure jumped Theoderic and slammed him to the ground. Covered in shaggy black fur, it flashed fangs longer than daggers, glinting with saliva. Its eyes burned with the rage of hell. The seething beast had no human face, but I knew it to be a man—Gerwulf.

He stood on the General's back, pinning him, cracking his brittle spine. The old man struggled feebly. He might have put up a better fight had he not been so ill, but no one was a match for Gerwulf when he was possessed by the wolf.

Theoderic's lips moved. Gerwulf stomped on his head, jamming his face into the dirt, drowning anything he would say. The beast raised his axe, aiming at the back of the General's neck.

"Gerwulf, no!" I shouted. "If you cut him, they will know he was murdered."

The sound of his name broke the spell. The beast faded. Gerwulf lowered his axe and dropped the wolf hood, revealing the man's face.

Without words, we worked together. I scraped together dirt and leaves while Gerwulf held the General still, twisting his head to the side. Bones cracked as I stuffed the debris in his mouth and nose. The old man gagged, but he had little fight left in him. His struggles weakened as his lips turned blue. The blood vessels in his eyes popped, and his face and neck broke out in tiny red spots. His eyes rolled to Heaven—as if he thought he would go there—and he slowly ceased moving.

I jumped into a hearty embrace with my friend, so elated to see him that tears ran down my cheeks. "You are here and well!"

Gerwulf was as glad to see me, patting me several times before letting me go. "We just arrived—the pack and me. We heard you had traveled here with Theoderic, and I knew you would seek out a spring eventually."

I tucked my hands hastily back into my sleeves, a fruitless effort. I could not hide anything from Gerwulf.

He pulled up my blood-soaked habit. "What did he do to you?"

"Nothing yet," I said. "My sacrifice to the gods."

"Peeling off your own flesh for them? Do they really demand such a sacrifice?"

"From me, yes." I lowered my eyes in shame. "But my sacrifice did bring you to me in my time of most need. You have now also repaid me for freeing you at Verden. Be glad of it, and do not try to understand it. You owe me nothing more."

"You will always need me at your back, you lunatic," he said.

He was the only one who called me such names as a token of affection instead of ridicule. We embraced again, holding each other tightly. Then we talked. I shared the events that had transpired since I had freed him, including the price the king had put on his head. I described how Theoderic and his cutthroats had rampaged through Saxony on the road to Hedeby.

"I could not stop him," I said.

"You have stopped him now."

I smiled with gratitude for his words.

"The king is withdrawing most of his conscripted forces from Saxony for the winter," I said. "But he has sent out small contingents of Scola riders to terrorize the Saxons until someone betrays you and your father. They are also searching for your woman."

"We saw the work of Commander Fulco and his henchmen." His gaze was distant, and we shared an unspoken understanding of the horrors we both had witnessed.

"Is Vala safe?" I asked softly, as if afraid of the answer.

"Yes. They cannot get to her as long as she is protected by the Walkyrie."

"Good. I hope the riders you killed are damned to dance with the Devil's draugar and return to haunt King Karl." The words had slid out of my mouth before I could stop myself, but I was not sorry to have said them.

"Draugar? My mother used to tell me tales of such creatures to scare me, so I would become a good Christian."

"She was trying to protect you."

"And I was not there to protect her when the Christian god abandoned her," he said, furrowing his heavy dark brow. I let him brood silently on the memory until he was ready to speak again. "We left Fulco's corpse and the rest of them to rot on pagan soil."

"Their souls are at the mercy of the Raven," I said with satisfaction.

Gerwulf lifted his head as if feeling some sense of justice too. "Will they become draugar?"

"If there is any justice," I said. "So tell me more about your woman."

He squared his shoulders. "The Spirit of Three Faces has shown herself to me, but I fight for the woman and our child—not the Walkyric and the Raven. I must fight with the Wulfhednar to push the Christians out of Saxon lands. Then Vala will be free of the Walkyrie and the Raven, and we will go away together."

Gerwulf was different, and I had to study him for a moment before I saw how. He possessed a spark in his human eyes, which had lightened to deep green color. I had not noticed that when he had fought for King Karl. The wolf skin lay on his shoulders like a mantle of pride instead of a cloak of shame. If I pointed it out to him, he would deny it, but he clearly had found something with the Wulfhednar and his woman that the king or I could not have given him. I was happy for him—and jealous of Vala.

He told me about the uprising he and the Wulfhednar were mustering. While he spoke, he called Widukind his father once, but quickly returned to using his name. Then Gerwulf described his raid on the Lippespringe garrison. To my great shame as a monk, I rejoiced at the news he had led the Wulfhednar to kill priests and monks and destroy the king's church at Paderborn. But I was also afraid for him.

"The king will become more obsessed with capturing you," I said. "The Eater of Souls haunts him and sends her Raven spirit to torment him. He believes he will not have peace until you, Vala, and the unborn babe are destroyed."

"He is right," Gerwulf said. "All of Saxony is answering the call for vengeance for Verden. If King Sigfred and his warriors join us, the butcher king and his god will be destroyed. Have you seen Sigfred?"

"Yes."

"Do you think he will welcome us?"

"He received Theoderic and treated us with marginal political courtesy," I said. "But I know his loyalty lies with the old gods, and he is building strong defenses and the fastest ships I have ever seen. It is obvious his mind is on war with the Christians."

"Good signs." He paused, thinking, then said, "Join us, brother. Renounce Karl and the Christian god and join us. We need men like you with fighting experience."

I laughed. "I am no wolf warrior."

"But you are a soldier. Widukind respects you and will make a place for you."

I ran my fingers through my wet, knotted tonsure. "*Was...* was a soldier. Gerwulf, there is nowhere I would rather be than fighting at your side, truly, but I will be of more help to you and your woman by keeping my position as Karl's trusted adviser."

"Spying is dangerous."

"So is murdering a king," I muttered.

I pretended I had not said it, and Gerwulf pretended he had not heard me.

"I will come to you at Grotenburg when the time is right," I said.

He frowned.

"The gods tell me my path is to stay with the king, for now," I said. "*All* the gods tell me this, even the Christian one."

He belted his axe, unable to deny my usefulness as a spy. "If that is your decision, so be it."

"It is," I said, trying to sound confident of my choice.

Gerwulf kicked over Theoderic's lifeless body. "What should we do with him?"

"I will clean the shit out of his mouth, and we will take him to the road. They will find him quickly there and think he has finally died of his damned pestilent leg. No one will be unhappy about it, and hopefully, no one will care if they notice he's been beat up a bit. Then I will return to Karl's court and be about the business of the gods."

We carried Theoderic to the edge of the road and dropped his body.

"I have to know something," Gerwulf said. "How did you find Widukind when he had evaded Karl's entire army for so long? And why did he not kill you?"

"That is your father's story to tell," I said.

He knotted his thick brow, but the creaking of an approaching oxcart stopped him from pursuing the question. We had to disappear before we were seen. He ducked into the forest, and I ran in the opposite direction toward the spring. I had to try to cleanse myself of my newest sin. Another killing.

I am not a...no...Theoderic is the murderer...soulless killer of pregnant women and children. He attacked me...self-defense and justice...yes. Self-defense and justice.

I convinced myself the pagan gods would see it my way, but the satisfaction of killing him felt good—too wickedly good for the Lord God. I stuffed my filthy hands into my sleeves, but it was too late. God had seen them, and no amount of washing would cleanse them. I would have to save a thousand more souls for this mortal sin, and my time was running short.

Father, Son, and Holy Ghost.
Wolf, Raven, and Walkyrie.

The Sea Warriors

Wulfhedinn

The Wulfhednar and I watched Brother Pyttel and the Scola riders leave Hedeby. Hidden in the woods, we glimpsed Theoderic's shrouded body slung over his horse. I had told Widukind and the wolf pack about the king's plans and how Pyttel had killed the General and become a spy for us. Seeing Theoderic's corpse in a bag cemented the truth of my story.

Staying out of sight, I followed the riders and Pyttel for a couple of miles. The monk's unkempt tonsure flipped as he peered back several times. He sensed I was near. Neither of us knew if we would ever see each other again, but he was right. He could do more for the rebellion by returning to the king than by staying with us.

Later that day, the pack and I presented ourselves to King Sigfred. He embraced Widukind as honored family. Danish nobles, guards, warriors, and townspeople crowded into the hall to see the Saxon Wulfhednar. They gaped at us with a mixture of awe and curiosity.

"What are they staring at?" I whispered to Erhard.

"They have no Wulfhednar. The Walkyrie has not brought the wolf spirit to their warriors for many years, and we are a wonder to them."

King Sigfred released his embrace with Widukind with an ominous expression. "Brother. King Karl's general and an entourage of Scola riders have been here. They told us about the executions at Verden. King Karl wants your hide and demands I deliver you to him. That Christian bastard has become a boil on my ass." Sigfred's eyes settled on me. "Who is this Wulfhedinn? I do not know him."

"My oldest son, Gerwulf."

"Your son the Christian woman whelped? Hmm…Gerwulf, of whom I have heard so much, the Wulfhedinn in the service of King Karl."

Widukind put his hand on my shoulder. "Gerwulf has forsaken the butcher king and his Christian god and returned to the Wulfhedinn pack. The wolf is strong in him, and he has strengthened the pack's bonds with the Walkyrie. He killed five guards at Karl's garrison, drove the rest to abandon their posts, and set the palisade on fire. He did this by himself."

Widukind's words glowed with pride as he spoke of me, and I felt stronger, as though I could defeat any enemy.

He continued, "Then my Wulfhedinn son led us in a successful raid on Paderborn. We destroyed the king's palace church and killed all his monks and priests there. Gerwulf has earned his place as one of the wolf warriors."

King Sigfred sat on his throne. He scratched his beard and

tapped a ringed finger on the throne's carved arm. "Impressive," he said. "The gods and the Walkyrie favor you, Gerwulf, son of Widukind. You are welcome in my hall." He glanced toward Wichbert. "I see you brought him too."

Wichbert's face beamed, but his uncle did not even meet his gaze.

"This is not a family visit," Widukind said. "You know why I have come. It will take more than small-scale ambushes to avenge those killed at Verden and drive the Franks from our lands. I need more warriors, weapons, and silver to build and supply a strong army. I need your support."

Sigfred's ring continued to tap softly. "Karl's numbers are too great, his horsemen too powerful, and his iron workers make the finest swords. He has conquered most of the Christian lands and subjugated many peoples. You cannot beat him with a few Wulfhednar and a mob of peasants, even with my warriors. No one can beat him in open battle on land."

"Honor and vengeance must be satisfied!" Widukind said. "I will not let the murder of thousands go unanswered, and neither will the rest of the Saxon tribes."

Sigfred shook his head. "It is winter, too late in the season to fight, but I will offer you and the Wulfhednar refuge here through the winter."

"We cannot sit around all winter. Karl has sent his cutthroat Scola riders throughout Saxony. They are destroying villages and farmsteads, killing everyone who refuses to betray us."

"You must concede your loss. Saxony has been defeated. Let the Franks have it. A rash rebellion will not help your people."

Widukind's gaze went cold. "I do not strike rashly."

"You know you cannot defeat King Karl's entire army."

"And you cannot let him trample us into the ground. The

Saxon tribes are the only barrier between him and your lands. If Saxony falls, the butcher king will be on your doorstep with his god and his army. He will not spare you because you have traded with him. His army will trample Daneland, storm Hedeby, and take over your trading port."

Sigfred sighed. "I am aware of his ambitions, but neither you nor I can defeat him in open battle. We must fight him in a different way."

Widukind narrowed his eyes. He was angry, but he was no fool. I knew he would consider any tactic that might prove useful despite being insulted by the bearer of it. "Tell me what you speak of," he said.

"Ships."

"Saxon ships are not war ships, and the merchants who man them are not warriors," Widukind said.

Sigfred rose from his throne with a smug smile. "I will show you."

He took us from his hall through the streets of Hedeby toward the sea. A deafening noise grew louder as we neared. Merchant ships, boats, people, and piles of trade goods jammed the city docks.

To the north lay a large shipyard where dozens of men were chopping, sawing, and hammering. The smell of wood shavings and hot pitch overpowered the scent of the sea. Workers used long tools with flat, sharpened ends to peel the bark from massive trunks of oak. Others split bare trunks into planks. In another area, men riveted overlapping planks of wood together to build a hull. In total, there were eight ships in various stages of construction.

"These are my longships," Sigfred said with pride. "We use the best oak, green wood, rather than seasoned wood, because it is easier to shape without splitting or cracking. These ships have shallow drafts and are lighter and faster and more maneuverable than any merchant vessel or other war ship. With oars and sail, a band of warriors can take them across the sea and penetrate deeply into Christian lands by river. They are so light that they do not need a port and can be beached and rapidly put back out to sail."

"They are beautiful," I said.

"Their beauty is in their speed and versatility," Sigfred said. "With my longships, we can strike without warning from rivers and escape to sea before the butcher king and his commanders even know we are there." He pointed to a ship in the inlet, flying across the water. "And I am building dozens more."

The ship sped past all the others like it was gliding across ice. The rowers worked together as a team, propelling it forward. They were a band of sea warriors, bonded together, like my pack of wolf warriors.

"A team of warriors who train and row together like this might fight together better too," I said.

"Exactly!" Sigfred said. "You understand quickly, Gerwulf."

"When will you be ready to launch these fast war ships?" Widukind asked.

"We will begin late next summer with a few raids on small, unprotected villages."

"Karl will have ravaged all of Saxony by then. We need your support now."

"Saxony is lost!" Sigfred said. "But there is a chance you can still defeat him with my help—if you bring the power of the Walkyrie and the wolf to me."

"No one, man or Wulfhedinn, controls the Walkyrie," Widukind said. "She will grace the Danes as she has in the past, when you have earned her blessing."

Sigfred crossed his arms. "You are my brother by marriage. I respect your cunning and courage as a war chieftain, and I like you. I know you are not blind to the overwhelming odds against you. Have patience and join my sea warriors next summer. Together we will become the wolves of the sea and bring the Christians and their god to their knees."

"I need to act now. I cannot wait."

Sigfred's face clouded, and he dismissed Widukind with a wave. "We have discussed this long enough. You know my offer. You are tired and need to rest to think clearly. There is mead and food and a warm place at my hearth for you and the Wulfhednar."

Widukind pulled his wolf skin about his shoulders and stormed back toward Sigfred's hall. The rest of the pack followed. I knew he wanted to storm out of Hedeby, but he had a cool head that tempered his hot blood. He would take advantage of Sigfred's hospitality for a few nights, allowing us to eat and rest, while he tried to convince the Danish king to change his mind.

I lingered next to Sigfred, admiring the beauty of the longship in the inlet. Unlike the other vessels, it thrived on the choppy current, cutting through it instead of battling against it. It moved as gracefully through the water as the wolf ran through the forest.

The rowers took their ship out of the bay, turned it, and raised the sail. The wind caught the huge square canvas, and they rowed as well. The combination of man and wind power returned the ship to port with many times the speed. I imaged the places such a ship could take me, Vala, and our child—far from the reach of King Karl.

"You like my longship?" Sigfred asked.

I nodded.

"You are a natural born sea wolf. I can see it in you. You would make a good ship steersman, even a sea king," he said.

"I do not know anything about ships or the sea."

"I would have my best sailing master teach you. You would learn quickly. And I would give you your own ship and crew of my best warriors—if you joined us."

"Widukind will not join you now."

"I am not asking Widukind or his pack. I am asking *you*," he said. "I can see the wolf is stronger in you than in the others of your pack. I am descended from a line of ancient wolf warriors, just like you, and you have the power to bring the wolf spirit back to me and my warriors."

I was so struck with awe of the longship that I could not respond.

"Widukind is the hero of a lost cause. He is a pauper, and I can offer you so much more than he can," he said. "What is he to you? You do not even refer to him as your father—and he never acted as a father to you."

I turned and glared at him for reminding me of a past I was trying to forget.

"Oh yes, I know your story," he said. "You do not owe Widukind anything. Bring the wolf to me, and you will command the best of my warriors, your sea wolves, and sail under your own banner. I will have my woodcarvers create a Wulfhedinn figurehead to mount onto the sternposts of your ship to terrorize the Christians. You can keep most of the booty you claim."

For a moment, I imagined combining my wolf powers with Sigfred's skilled Danish warriors and his wonderful longships—with the Raven and the Walkyrie flying above us. We *would* make a frightful army, but Hedeby was a long way from Karl's garrisons. Sigfred could protect himself behind his massive earthwork while he prepared for his war from the sea. The Saxons had no such wall—only a few hill forts. Sigfred had plenty of time before the

Frankish horsemen would threaten his city and his trade, and he was using Saxony as a sacrificial buffer between him and King Karl.

For the first time, I felt a kind of loyalty to the pack and my father, such as he was. I did not like how Sigfred was trying to manipulate me away from them and into yet another war. He clearly knew of my disloyalties of the past and thought I would be an easy mark to bend to his will. Joining him would make me a treulogo again. Worst of all, I would lose Vala and our child forever.

Perhaps someday I would sail away from them all with Vala and our baby on a beautiful longship. Someday when the wars were over.

"I will not leave my father and my pack," I said, walking away.

He called after me. "Go. Carry out your doomed rebellion. I will welcome you as part of my sea army once you come to your senses…if you survive that long."

Coward

The Monk

Jdreaded returning to Saxony from the land of the Danes.
Captain Lothar was in command of our party now and had
hired a new guide. The greasy Danish trader promised to take us
through many Saxon villages and settlements on the way back.
He was a man of middle years with several black teeth. He told a
long story about how his betrothed, a girl of twelve, had run off
with a Saxon boy. He told it so often, Lothar smacked him across
the head to shut him up. We were all glad for it.

Lothar believed the trader would be anxious to avenge his
dishonor—and he was. He and the Scola riders terrorized two
farmsteads, slaughtering everyone. They found little booty, and
no one was willing to betray Widukind. The trader eventually
located his betrothed and her lover in a northern Saxon village,

and after settling his vendetta with them, he left us on our own.

Soon after, the weather changed, and the temperature plummeted, and we rode hard back to the Lippespringe garrison. The garrison overflowed with the tents of King Karl's army. God's bones! He had not yet released the men for the winter. He was keeping them busy—and warm—by rebuilding sections of the wall Gerwulf had burned.

As we rode through the gate, a crowd gathered, curious about the body draped over Theoderic's horse. We were told the king was in Paderborn, so we rode on as speculation about the General's death spread.

It was a short ride to the city, but my fingers were so numb with cold I could hardly feel the horse's reins. I longed for a warm fire. At the same time, I dreaded the king's reaction to Theoderic's death and wished the trip had been longer. The stink of Theoderic's corpse after it thawed would not help matters.

The king's chamberlain, Engel, hurried across the courtyard to greet us. "By the grace of God! We thought you were lost or killed by Saxons on the road." He scowled at the shrouded body. "Oh, dear. Is it…?"

"General Theoderic's leg festered again during the journey north," Lothar said. "It killed him this time."

"The king isn't going to like this."

"It was his time," I said, blowing on my frozen fingers. "He is out of his pain and with God now."

Engel directed Lothar and the riders to take the body into the palace. He sent me to the church to find the king.

"He is laying plans to rebuild it, sparing no expense," he said, rolling his eyes. "He has been waiting impatiently for you. Perhaps you can advise restraint on his spending."

So there is more silver for you to pilfer, I thought.

The church's roof was gone, and what was left of the nave was a burned-out shell. Large sections of the stone walls had collapsed in the heat of the fire, and the remains were likely too unstable to salvage. The king must have ruptured a blood vessel in his head when he saw it.

Outside the ruined walls, stone masons were cutting and shaping new slabs of rock into building stones. Despite the cold, the king was clearly determined to rebuild his church as quickly as possible.

I found Karl poring over a parchment on the stone altar, surrounded by builders and a few nobles. He wore a heavy cloak of fox fur, but his nobles where shivering in their woolen mantles. They looked at me, and the king grinned under his drooping moustache. "Brother Pyttel! Blessed be to God! I had begun to think you would not return until spring—or worse. Did you..."

I lowered my head. My guilt-laden hands were safely tucked away from his sight. His face darkened.

"My king, I must speak with you urgently." My unusual brevity had made it clear to him something was wrong.

His face clouded. "We will go to the palace."

He was nearly running, and I had to lift my hem to keep up with his long stride. The chamberlain took us to the room where they had laid the General and left us alone.

Karl rushed to the General's side. "What has happened?"

"His old leg injury became inflamed and festered badly again," I said. "By the time we arrived at King Sigfred's court, he was feverish. He took to his bed for several weeks. He fought hard, and we thought he might recover several times, but the fever finally took him."

Karl stared at the General's face, distorted, bloated, and blue. His grotesque eyes, partially preserved by the cold, stared at me, accusing me. I was sure the king would see my guilt and know. My heart thumped as I waited for him to say something, but he ignored me and tore open the leg of Theoderic's breeches. The poisoned leg was thawing, and a rotting stink rose and assaulted us. I could hardly stand it and had to breathe through my mouth, but the king did not react. He was in shock, and I dreaded what he might do when the numbness lifted and his grief and fury set in.

He drew his sword. My hand fell to the pommel of my seax, ready to fight back, but he turned from me and laid his blade on the General's chest. Then we stood together in vigil. As time passed, I stole glances at the king. His expression was flat, unchanging, and I was unable to determine if he suspected me of anything or if—or when—he would burst into a violent rage. I needed to soothe him and allay any suspicions he might harbor, so I started lying.

"I gave the General Last Rites before he died."

He put his hand on Theoderic's shoulder. "I am glad you were there so he would not die without God's grace in a pagan land. You have done a great service for him and me."

"Thank you, my king. I was honored to be of assistance to your greatest commander."

I did not sound convincing, but the king was distracted and did not seem to notice. I had wanted to leave Theoderic's putrid body in the forest. Then the Raven could have feasted on his putrid soul and taken him to Hell to dance with the draugar. If the rumors of the roving soulless ones were true, no one deserved such a fate more than he did.

I tried to comfort the king to further dispel any possible suspicion of me. "In his last words, the General told me about his great pride in you and how he had always been honored to serve the mighty King Karl of the Franks, God's chosen king. He regretted not seeing you again and sent you his love and most noble praise before he passed."

A thin smile passed Karl's lips. "He was already an old man when I was a youth, but he was tougher, more cunning in war, and more loyal than any of my other generals. He taught me more than my father ever did."

"Let us pray, my king, for the deliverance of his soul," I said.

Karl knelt, folded his hands, and bowed his head. His long blond hair fell forward, and the back of his neck was laid bare. He closed his eyes. The gods had presented my fate right in front of me.

The mark of the beast. Kill him. Justice demands it.

My hand was still resting on the pommel of my blade.

Do it for Gerwulf and all the innocents, or the butcher king will slaughter them all.

The room was empty. No one would see the act, but the guards were right outside the door, and they would hear it. The king was too strong a warrior to kill quietly, and his royal guard would burst in and kill me on the spot. I was not ready to face death; I had not saved enough souls to fulfill my penance. My knees weakened, and my fingers dropped from my blade. I folded my hands and mumbled a long prayer in Latin. I spoke the words of prayer passively, like the coward I was. When it was over, I silently beseeched the gods to give me the courage to do what needed to be done and face damnation for it.

Father, Son, and Holy Ghost.
Wolf, Raven, and Walkyrie.

My courage never came.

Karl crossed himself and stood. "General Theoderic's time has passed, and I will miss him at my side."

He was calmly accepting the General's death, which meant no one else would question it or suspect me. I should have felt relieved, but my soul burned with shame. I had missed my chance to rid the world of the tyrant, the beast. Worst of all, I had condemned Gerwulf and the Saxons to face the king's onslaught in order to save myself.

I needed to wash. Sweat poured from my forehead. The king would never let me leave his side in his grief. I feared I could not bear the distress of it until the smell of roasting barley permeated the air, partially covering the fetid smell of Theoderic's corpse. God's bones, I thirsted desperately for a beer. Then, to my surprise, the king released me.

"I will call for you in the morning," he said. "Bishop Erembert left last week for Worms, and I want you to give the General's funeral Mass tomorrow."

"The General did not favor me. Perhaps his own confessor would be a better choice."

"I favor you. You will do it."

"Yes, my king. It will be an honor, and I would like to pay my respects to your mother and Prince Pepin as well."

He straightened his broad spine and shoulders. "I sent them away from the rebels to the Thionville palace for their safety and to keep the company of Queen Hildegard. Now, I must attend to other matters."

I knew he had sent them away for other reasons. I was not surprised. He was likely weary of dealing with his overbearing mother and his clever and cheeky hunchback son. He had greater matters demanding his attention.

"The heathen swine are taking their vengeance for Verden," he said. "And my church and garrison must be rebuilt. Commander Fulco and his Scola riders were expected to report back weeks ago and have not yet returned. I fear they have been taken by the Wulfhednar. I need to make more plans to hunt those bastard Wulfhednar and the Eater of Souls. I will destroy them if I have to behead every last pagan in Saxony."

Killing him would have been righteous, no matter the god.

I had failed in that task, but I could do right in other ways. Yes, other ways, better ways. I would weave the story to temper his raging heart.

"Verden was your final victory against the Saxons," I said gently. "There are not enough of them left to be a serious threat to you. I have seen much of their lands on the way to Daneland. There are few of them left but old men and hungry women and children. The men of fighting age who remain are witless, frightened peasants—not trained warriors."

"As long as Widukind and his wolf warriors live, no one is safe," he said. "They are devils who destroy churches and murder priests and monks. They threaten every innocent, God-fearing soul in my kingdom. As God's chosen king, it is my sacred duty to protect them."

The Saxons threaten your trading wealth and your pride.

"Be assured, my king," I said. "The Scola horsemen will bring the Wulfhednar to heel and find the woman who carries the Walkyrie's child. The Saxons will give him and the woman up. I am sure of it. They are helpless and defeated and too terrified to resist any longer. And I bring good news from King Sigfred, as well. He remains our ally and has vowed not to harbor or support Widukind and the Wulfhednar. There is no need to spend money and resources on this war."

"Are you convinced of Sigfred's sincerity?"

"Absolutely. The man is obsessed with trade and silver. He knows keeping your friendship and your trade is the best way to make himself rich."

"You have done well," he said. "But I have more concerns. My nobles are restless and need a firm hand to keep them in line. It will be more difficult without the General at my side."

"Then you must exercise reason and restraint so as to not incite them," I advised cautiously. "Release them and their men from service for the winter. By spring, I am sure you will see the Saxon threat has vanished."

He scratched his beard. "What does God say?"

"God speaks in His own way, but He..."

Someone pounded on the door, demanding entry, shouting about the queen. The king opened it, and a royal messenger almost fell into the chamber. His teeth chattered, and his brow and moustache were crusted with ice. He must have ridden all night.

"My king! Forgive the interruption, but I have urgent news from the Thionville palace...about the Queen Hildegard."

"What is it?" the king demanded.

"She is having trouble. She may lose the child."

The king's jaw fell, and his face paled. He began to pace, his hands gripped tightly together behind his back. "The Raven demon now haunts my wife! I must destroy these pagans or..."

"No, my king. God is telling me something else..." I fell to my knees and raised my cross, shouting. "The Lord is telling me now...He says..." I choked and clutched my throat, throwing myself to the ground. I flung my limbs in jolting spasms.

The king shook me. "What does He say? Tell me!"

I gasped for breath and coughed a few times. "He...the Lord...He says you must withdraw your forces from Saxony. Go to your queen. She and the unborn child need you the most. God says all will be right once you are at your wife's side."

The king paced, scratching his beard. "Have you seen the queen?" he asked the messenger.

"Yes. She cannot leave her bed. The physicians are most concerned."

The king sighed and spoke to me. "Tell God I will release the army, as He wishes, but I must leave a small occupying force in Paderborn and the other strongholds we hold in Saxony."

"That is understandable, my king," I said.

"I will leave for my palace at Thionville tomorrow after Theoderic's funeral Mass. I order all clergy to say prayers for the queen's health as well as the General's soul."

"Yes, my king," I said, rising slowly. "A most wise choice, and I will pray for her and the child, night and day."

He ran his fingers through his hair. "Brother Pyttel, I want you to stay by my side, but I need you more here in Paderborn. You will stay here to supervise the rebuilding of my church and the missionary work with the heathens. These tasks are more important than ever, and I trust no one else with them. And pray daily, intercede with God for the life of the queen and my unborn son."

"Of course." I bowed.

Karl and a large entourage of courtiers, servants, and Scola soldiers left the city the next morning. He took Theoderic's body and would deliver it personally to the General's widow on the way to his palace in Thionville.

Throughout the next days, the army filed out of the Lippespringe garrison and the city. They took the Hellweg west, back to their lands in Francia. I viewed the endless procession from atop the gatehouse. Scanning the edges of the forest, I knew Widukind's spies were nearby, watching.

Unity

―――――∞∞――――

Wulfhedinn

The Wulfhednar and I began our journey to the Grotenburg hillfort after several nights in King Sigfred's hall. We were disheartened by our failure to secure King Sigfred's support for the uprising. I said nothing to the others about Sigfred's offer to me, tucking it away in my mind. I had greater concerns. I knew Widukind was troubled the wolf had not come to him yet. I feared he would ask me about it, but he occupied himself with more practical matters as we trotted back to Saxony.

"We should have the beginnings of an army mustering at the assembly when we arrive at Grotenburg," he said several times, as if to convince himself of it.

Since Sigfred's refusal to support us, he seemed less sure of himself. The others were unusually quiet, even Wichbert. I daydreamed about the Danish longship as we trotted through the bogs and forests.

We took a route passing through several dozen villages, settlements, and farmsteads to recruit more men. Word of the uprising had already spread, and most of the ealdermen were preparing to join us. We saw blacksmiths working the forges, making new weapons, and farmers loading grain into carts to sustain their families and our army at Grotenburg. Almost everyone had a relative who had been killed at Verden, and they all hated the butcher king, his church taxes, and the Christian god behind it all. The ones who had been baptized renounced the faith, and every village mission church and chapel we passed had been burned recently.

Farther south, we met up with more clans on their way to the Grotenburg assembly. As we continued, more joined us until we had grown into an army. It was a mixed force of mounted warriors carrying spears, swords, and shields, and experienced infantrymen armed with spears and axes. The clan ealdermen rode with their personal guard. The wealthiest wore mail armor and owned the best swords. We also gathered many free and half-free farmers. They carried daggers, small seaxes, and farm tools as weapons.

Many of their families had come along, herding livestock and driving the carts of grain and other necessities needed to sustain an army. The peasant men, women, and children far outnumbered the seasoned warriors, but I had seen what the fierce grit of unleashed peasant fury could do. With training and cunning strategy, it could be wielded effectively against Karl's disciplined Frankish army.

As we marched, I thought about the longship and about how much farther and faster it could take me on a journey than my wolf legs. I tried to forget about it, but the ship kept gliding through my mind like it had done on the sea.

At a crossroads, a band of three dozen mounted warriors greeted us. They carried high-quality swords, spears, and shields. The leader, a man with a round, open face, dismounted and approached us.

"Widukind! Cousin!"

Widukind's eyes lit up, and they embraced.

"You are most welcome to join us, Sidag."

I recognized him instantly. He was yet another of Widukind's cousins, an ealderman of a large, prosperous clan whose lands lay half a day's ride south of Paderborn. King Karl had made him a count. Count Sidag. He had accepted the title in exchange for fealty to Karl.

Sidag turned to me. "Gerwulf! So the stories are true! Tales of your return to the Wulfhednar are on the lips of every man, woman, and child. You have finally heeded the call of the Raven spirit."

"You are a hard man to track, Sidag," I said.

He chuckled. "You are a hard man—or wolf—to evade. Fortunately, the Raven spirit was with me and not you. Ah…a different time for us both. Someday, we will have to have a beer and reminisce about it."

"It was not so long ago," I said, "I would have killed you if I had found you. Why would you trust me now?"

"We are two of a kind, are we not?" He winked at my puzzled expression. "We are both treulogos, becoming Christians and swearing fealty to King Karl."

Treulogo. I despised the name, and I could not seem to get rid of it. I snapped back at him. "You *willingly* accepted baptism. I had been forced into Christianity as a child. I was raised to believe Karl was my true king. You *chose* him. I am less a treulogo than you."

"Maybe you are right, but we both were misled. Our hearts have always been with our people and the old gods."

"You traded honor for land and title from King Karl, like Hessi and the other greedy Saxon nobles."

Widukind stepped between us. "Sidag cooperated with Karl to try to negotiate peace and save our clans from more ravaging by Karl's army—and he spied for us. You know this, Gerwulf. The General sent you to track Sidag down after he discovered his true allegiance."

I resisted thinking rationally about the matter but had to admit he was right. The General had sent me, the Royal Scout and Huntsman, to track Sidag—and I had failed to catch him.

Sidag grinned. "You are more hot-headed and stubborn than your father and had to find the calling of your heart the hard way. Now your single-handed destruction of the king's garrison is already legendary. I wish I could have seen Karl's face when he saw his church in ruins!"

Sidag seemed the kind of man who only jested with those he respected, and Widukind appeared to trust him, but I was not convinced of him yet.

He gestured to a youth of about fifteen years. "Son, come here!"

Alric had a wide face like his father's, and he slid off his horse in the same manner. Sidag had given the boy as a court hostage to ensure his loyalty to the king. I had watched the formal event at Karl's assembly in Lippespringe last spring and wondered how and why the boy had escaped to join his father.

Sidag put an arm around Alric's shoulders as though he would never let him go. "You remember my son. The king treated him more like an honored guest than a hostage. He treated him so well that I feared he would prefer to stay at court than join us. He had it all, good wine, feasts, silk tunics, and women…"

Alric flushed. "Father!"

"But his heart is faithful to the old ways and the old gods.

He risked his life to slip out from under the king's watch after the news of my betrayal reached Paderborn." His voice rang with pride. "Since then, we have been in hiding in the north boglands with my wife's family. Once we heard word of the massacre and Widukind's uprising, I knew it was time to return to our lands in Westphalia and muster our clan for rebellion."

"It is too dangerous for you," Widukind said. "You are an outlaw now, and your estates lie right next to Paderborn. Karl's spies are thick there. They are just waiting for you to show your face again."

"I do not fear the king," Sidag said. "My people are loyal to me and the old gods. They would not betray me." He had a fierce bearing of resolve about him, which I understood. I was even beginning to trust him. Like his cousin Widukind, he was not going to back down. He was my cousin too, and he needed all the hope we could give him.

"We also have a spy," I said. "Pyttel, a monk, court scribe, and close adviser to the king."

"I remember the monk," he said. "The one with the crushed face, a lunatic, they say. You trust this Christian holy man?"

"He spoke out against the king's actions at Verden, and he helped me escape execution. He is loyal to us, and I trust him like no other. He has reported Karl is withdrawing most of his army from Saxony for the winter. The small occupying force will likely spend the winter behind the walls of the city, drinking and whoring."

Sidag thought for a moment. "Widukind, do you trust this monk's word?"

"He has proven himself to me," he said.

Sidag mounted his horse. "Then I trust him too. Someday I want to hear more about this strange monk over a few horns of beer, but now it seems my timing is as good as it will get. I will meet you in Grotenburg as soon as possible with as many as I can rally."

Sidag, Alric, and their band of warriors spurred their horses hard into a gallop and disappeared down the road.

I wondered if Widukind would ever tell me how Pyttel had found him and what he had done to gain his trust. Someday I would ask him.

We continued our slow progress with our rag-tag group of rebels. As we neared Grotenburg, we met with more Saxons joining the rebellion, peasants mostly. When we stopped to make camp for the night, they went into the forest with their bows and slings and brought back fresh game for dinner. Their skill was helping keep bellies full, and an army needed to be well fed.

One day, a rabbit bounded across the road in front of us. A girl of about eleven stepped forward with her sling and killed it with a single shot to the head. It had dropped in a blink.

"For the Wulfhednar," she said, presenting it to Widukind.

He accepted her offering. "You have the fire of the Walkyrie in your blood," he said, and she beamed.

"A precisely aimed shot at a tiny skull on a moving target," I said.

"Impressive," Rotgrim said.

"Hunger can make warriors of us all," Widukind said.

"A skilled child with a sling can also stand up to a giant," Erhard said. "Karl's missionaries tell the story of how a boy killed a giant with a sling—the only good Christian story I have ever heard."

Rotgrim aimed his spear at a tree and launched it at a knot resembling a face. It hit squarely. "If children can kill running rabbits from fifty paces, they can crack the bulbous heads of the Franks."

We laughed and rode on, discussing strategies using peasant slingers and bowmen in the uprising. More Saxons joined us, and by the time we arrived at Grotenburg, we were a force of more than a thousand. Several hundred more were waiting for us inside the hillfort gate, including Ealderman Heinrich and his wife, Gunda. They greeted us with two dozen fully armed warriors. Berard had also arrived with his clan.

"How is your son?" I asked Berard.

Berard's expression hardened. "Dead. His throat swelled from the hanging, and he lost consciousness and never woke."

"I am sorry," I said.

Rotgrim cussed. "I will wrench retribution from Karl's bony, Christian neck."

I silently made the same vow. Karl was the real demon, the slayer of many innocents in his war on the pagan Saxons. No one would be satisfied until he lay dead.

Widukind, Erhard, and I spent the rest of the day taking inventory of weapons and supplies and a census of everyone who had gathered for the assembly. In addition to the Wulfhednar, we had five dozen experienced warriors and as many sons of nobility. The youths all had had a horse and some level of training and were a fearless bunch, eager to prove their manhood in battle.

The peasant recruits had brought an assortment of hunting bows, slings, wood axes, small seaxes, and farm implements. Grotenburg's smiths fired the forges night and day to make enough iron spear and bow tips to arm everyone able to fight. They also modified the farmer's scythes into spears and their sheep shears into seaxes and daggers. Iron weapons arrived from smiths laboring in settlements throughout the area. As promised, Fridenot, ealderman of Treva, sent two carts of spears and seaxes, half a dozen swords, and a small chest of silver.

"Every Saxon tribe has sent some form of support, including more fighting men than I could have hoped for," said Erhard, who seemed to know everyone.

A feeling of unity filled the crowded hillfort. Nearly all of Saxony had come together to drive the Franks and their despised god from their lands. Yule had passed, and we trained daily during the month of the Cake Moon, the coldest of the year. The fire in the hall was stoked day and night as the weather turned frigid. Two large storms buried the training grounds with snow and ice. When the storms passed, we broke the ice and shoveled the snow aside. Training continued, and I did not hear many complaints about the cold. Our enthusiasm for the uprising heated our blood, and we worked all the harder to keep warm.

On the full moon of the Cake Moon, we sacrificed a goat and left its organs for the gods. The women baked honeyed breads and brewed special winter beer, and we feasted to honor the gods, the Walkyrie, and our ancestors who had been slain by our enemies.

As the weeks of winter passed, I spent less and less time thinking about the longship and sailing away with Vala. My mind and days were filled with responsibilities. There was much to be done to prepare for the uprising, and one of my tasks was to train women and girls in the use of slings and bows. They worked hard, eager to match skills with their husbands, sons, and brothers.

I also instructed and drilled the noble youths. They were more difficult to teach, despite the fact they had had some weapons training. They were unaware of how little they knew about battle but were convinced they were masters of everything. Wichbert was the worst of the lot. Training them required many hours of besting them in sparring with wooden weapons. I sent them back to their mothers banged and bruised until they understood their place. Most learned quickly, but Wichbert and a couple others never got any wiser.

The days warmed and were growing longer as we approached the month of Hreda's Moon. The snow and ice were melting, and we drilled in the mud and damp mists. I spent most evenings with the Wulfhednar and elder warriors by the fire in the hall, discussing training progress and debating tactics.

Night after night, I waited for Vala. The Raven was always near, flying overhead or perched on the Grotenburg palisade, as if supervising our preparations, but Vala never appeared. I longed to see her and wandered the forest after the others had gone to sleep. Searching for her, I visited the Raven's Stones many times, but she was never there. The Raven tagged along each time, squawking for me to return to my obligations at Grotenburg.

I was getting bored of my duties. The tactical discussions and debates in the great hall droned on endlessly. I grumbled that we were talking in circles and there was no need of more discussion. One evening, Widukind finally agreed.

"We have talked long enough," he said. "We must agree on a final plan and act now to attack Paderborn and our strongholds stolen by the Franks. If we wait any longer, the butcher king will have his entire army assembled for the summer fighting months."

Everyone concurred, and we spent the rest of the night finalizing plans, but my mind was drifting. I heard bits and pieces about how to best distribute weapons and the responsibilities of the ealdermen officers, but nothing mattered to me but Vala.

I knew she would be heavy with child and ready to deliver soon. I needed to ensure she was safe and healthy. I wanted to put my hand on her belly and feel the baby kicking inside her. It had been so long since I had seen her; I had to know she and the baby were real, that all my efforts would not be in vain. A vague reassurance came from the Raven's continuous presence, complete with her guttural croaking and mocking cackling. It was not enough.

An Urgent Message

The Monk

The weeks of deep winter were crawling by at Paderborn. I was overseeing the work on King Karl's new stone church, but unrelenting freezing temperatures had stopped the mixing of mortar, and all work ceased when two huge storms covered the city with snow and ice.

I said daily Mass and heard countless confessions, forgiving most of the sinners with light penance or none at all. Slowly, my tally of saved souls was rising. Otherwise, there was much time for drinking. I often helped the soldiers and stonecutters and masons empty a flagon or three, feigning some sort of spiritual discussion with them, but Gerwulf and the rebellion were always on my mind. I wondered how the Wulfhednar's preparation for the uprising was progressing and when they would attack.

Despite the cold, I made several trips to the spring near the Lippespringe garrison to sacrifice and pray for Gerwulf and the rebellion, but the Shepherd and the Traveler remained obscure. The water was so icy that it was painful to bathe in. Everything else had frozen over, but God surely kept the spring flowing to punish me.

The lean weeks of Lent were observed—marginally by the soldiers. I looked the other way when they hunted for fresh meat and could not pass on their offer to share it with me. They appreciated my light penances.

I fantasized about meeting Gerwulf at the spring when the weather warmed. The scene repeated endlessly in my mind. I missed him so much, it hurt more than the icy water. I was tempted to go to Grotenburg to see him, but it was a day's journey away, and my absence in Paderborn would be noticed and questioned—or I might be followed. The danger was too great to risk the trip until I had useful information for the rebellion. So I waited.

The weather finally broke at Easter. Work on the church continued, and I celebrated Mass in the half-built nave, but I had no heart for it. The resurrection of God's only son no longer offered hope for my soul. Jesus Christ might have died for the sins of man, but not for mine.

I took to pacing on the palisade walkway every day, watching for the Raven and other signs of Gerwulf. The sun was shining and warm on the afternoon when a royal messenger galloped to the gate. I called for the commander, and we ran down the steps together to meet him.

"Queen Hildegard is dead," the messenger said. "She gave birth to a girl, but she and the baby have both died."

The commander's mouth gaped, and he shook his head. Then he ordered the captain of the guards to assemble the city's officers and nobles.

"What happened?" I asked.

"She has had trouble carrying the child the since the Verden executions," the messenger said. "Her condition worsened during Lent, and she gave birth to a stillborn, a girl. The queen died soon after from childbed fever. The king is mad with grief and rage. He believes the Eater of Souls has cursed him."

My legs felt weak. The king would blame me. He would remember I had told him God would save his wife and babe if he withdrew his troops from Saxony. I had practically promised it. Karl would see me for the traitor I was. I leaned on the gatehouse wall to keep from collapsing in panic.

The messenger continued. "The king has sent envoys to every duchy in the kingdom to summon his nobles. They are to gather at Paderborn with as many fighting men as they can muster for a full invasion of Saxony within three weeks."

The city commander groaned. "Does he think we can walk right into the Teutoburg Forest and capture a demon? Has he forgotten what has happened every time he tries to invade that cursed woodland? He *is* mad."

"He will have to march the army around the forest," I said, knowing the king might, in his arrogance and anger, try to breech the forest. Then he would quickly discover it and the Raven's Stones were no longer protected by the Walkyrie's powers.

The time had come to go to Gerwulf and warn the Wulfhednar. I had to leave immediately.

"Let it be known, commander," the messenger added, "any noble who holds a stronghold in Saxony who fails to present with his soldiers for duty will be guilty of treason and executed."

"Tell the king that Paderborn's soldiers will be ready," the commander said, looking at me. "Brother Pyttel, you look ill."

"Yes…yes. I do feel a bit faint. The news of the queen and the baby is a great shock. I need to rest and pray. I will retire to my chamber and offer a Mass for the souls of the queen and the child later today."

He waved me off. "Go."

With unsteady steps, I sought the refuge of my cell. It would not be a safe place much longer. The king was sure to take his anger out on me, but he was likely too distressed to have thought to send an order for my arrest with this messenger. It would come soon.

I donned a heavy mantle for the journey and strapped my collecting basket on my back. I would have to go on foot because the stable grooms would question me if I took a horse. The guards at the gate were accustomed to my comings and goings and did not stop me. I had always forgiven their multitude of sins, and they never harassed me or inspected my basket. It usually contained a goat's heart or other offerings to the gods, but that day, it was light on my back. In my haste, I had packed only a slice of bread and a flask of beer. I should have brought more food, but it did not matter. My hunger would be satiated soon enough.

War Chieftain

Wulfhedinn

Widukind and I were sparring in the Grotenburg yard, demonstrating spear fighting techniques to Wichbert and a group of boys. I thrust at Widukind from the hips to show the boys how to maximize the power of their skinny upper bodies, but they were not interested in my hips. Their attention had drifted to a group of girls across the training yard. Their curvy hips swayed and their new breasts jiggled as they trained with their slings. I swatted Wichbert with my spear shaft, who had his eye on a particular girl with long blond hair.

I pointed at the girl. "If you let tits distract you during battle, someone is going to take off your head. Then you will have no chance of bedding the woman with said tits."

The other boys jeered Wichbert, and before we could continue the lesson, a commotion rose at the gate. One of our patrols entered, leading a bound prisoner. A Christian monk.

"A spy!" The patrol captain yanked the rope, throwing him to the ground. "We caught him near the wall. He claims he knows Widukind and Gerwulf."

Pyttel looked up at me and grinned through a mass of matted hair. "I bring urgent news of the king, my lords."

"Let him go," I ordered.

The captain hesitated. "But he is a *Christian* holy man, and we can have some fun with him! Let's string him up by his balls!"

"Does he even have balls?" one of the boys asked. "Don't they sacrifice them to their God?"

"I most assuredly have them," Pyttel said, "and they are far bigger than yours."

The other boys laughed.

"Free him," said Widukind.

The captain shrugged and cut Pyttel's bounds. He stood, brushing the hair away from his eyes and smashed nose. Glancing at his hands, he tucked them into his sleeves. "Queen Hildegard has died giving birth, and her baby died too."

The training yard fell into silence.

"The king is convinced they were cursed by the Walkyrie," Pyttel said. "I am told he is mad with grief and will take his vengeance on the Saxons. He is returning to Paderborn as we speak and making plans for an invasion within three weeks."

Wichbert aimed his blunted practice spear at Pyttel's throat. "Liar! The monk is a Christian spy, trying to save his neck."

"Shut your mouth, boy," Widukind said.

Wichbert's chin trembled. His humiliation was all the worse because it had happened in front of many warriors and other boys his age. He slammed down his spear and pushed his way through the gathering crowd.

Widukind did not order anyone to chase after him. He had no time to coddle boys who were not ready to be men. Instead, he called an immediate council of the Wulfhednar and the clan elders.

The hall filled quickly for the meeting. Everyone's attention was on Pyttel. With his bloodied monk's clothing and his battle-scarred face, he was a strange curiosity to them.

"Who is this?" asked Ealderman Heinrich.

Another ealderman narrowed his eyes at Pyttel. "Why is a Christian monk sitting here at Widukind's council table like an honored guest?"

"Because he killed King Karl's best commander, General Theoderic," Widukind said.

The assembly sat in stunned silence until Widukind spoke again. "Pyttel has proven himself invaluable to me and the rebellion. He also saved Gerwulf from execution by the king."

"What do you have to say to us, monk?" Heinrich said.

Pyttel tucked his hands into his sleeves, cleared his throat, and repeated the news of the king's wife and child and his plan for invasion. "I wish I knew more details of the butcher king's plans but..."

"You have helped more than you know, Pyttel," Widukind said.

Pyttel's words had rung true to the ealdermen. Their expressions had softened when Pyttel had called Karl the butcher king. Already Pyttel was gaining their trust. He was a clever one.

The conversation broke into several small discussions about the numbers of weapons and fighters we had. Widukind listened without speaking. The Westphalian clan ealdermen, including

Heinrich, disagreed with the Eastphalians about the best use of the most experienced warriors. Soon, the discussions splintered into heated arguing.

Widukind stood, halting the ruckus. "Ealdermen of the clans! First, as is our custom, we must elect a war chieftain. Then he will consider the council of every man here before making final decisions about strategy and tactics."

"My Lord Widukind, you are our war chieftain," Heinrich said.

Widukind shook his head. "The council must vote on the matter."

"You are right," said Ricmod, one of the Eastphalian ealdermen. "It must be done in the old way, the right way, so there can be no further arguments."

"I propose Widukind as our war chieftain," Heinrich said.

No one offered another candidate, and Widukind was elected unanimously.

"Good," Erhard said. "Now we can move forward as one people, one fighting force, as is the will of the Walkyrie."

The ealdermen and Wulfhednar slapped the table with their palms, indicating their agreement. Without a thought, I joined in.

Darkness was falling before we had heard everyone's ideas and opinions about tactics and strategy. Widukind considered all the arguments and came to a decision.

"We will keep a tight watch on the Lippespringe garrison," he said. "When Karl launches his invasion, we will draw the army toward Grotenburg. We will bait them along until they are pinched between the bog and the slope of the hillfort. His ranks will be forced to march single- or double-file on the narrow road. This will render his army nearly helpless against an ambush. His horsemen will have nowhere to ride, and his foot soldiers will have nowhere to retreat."

The Wulfhednar and clan elders pounded the table in agreement.

"We will have plenty of time," Ricmod said. "The king will have to march his troops far to the west or east to circumvent the Teutoburg Forest before he can penetrate deeper into Saxony."

The Wulfhednar exchanged brief glances. We had kept our secret well. No one else had discovered the Teutoburg Forest was no longer protected by the Walkyrie's magic.

Talk continued about the best ways to enhance the effectiveness of our force, which was mainly comprised of archers and slingers. It was agreed they should attack in ambush from cover of the forest or from behind the palisade walls.

"Once we have weakened the king's army and taken as many as possible with arrows and stones, our warriors can attack," Widukind said.

I was beginning to see how an ambush could succeed against a force so much larger than ours. We were planning as a single fighting force with a single objective. Our enemy was a king who was ruled by his pride and emotions and who might become reckless. Still, we needed more warriors. I wondered if Sidag had had any success mustering more men and if they would arrive in time.

Berard interrupted my thoughts. "And who will draw them to the fortress?" he asked.

Every eye in the room turned toward me, the obvious choice for such a mission. We all knew the task was best done by someone who knew and understood both armies. I was also the perfect bait for King Karl.

I pulled my wolf skin around my shoulders and stood. "I will do it."

Pyttel looked at me with his usual jittery expression. He wanted to argue with me, to stop me, but he had been a soldier in the past, long enough to understand the task had to be mine.

"So it is agreed," Widukind said.

During the next couple of weeks, we doubled our training and held drills and practice ambushes on the road that ran between the bottom of the fortress hill and the bog. Pyttel participated in the training to prove himself to the Saxons. Wichbert did not appear. No one had seen him since the day Pyttel had come.

"Good riddance," Rotgrim said. "The pus-headed worm ran back to the Danish court with his tail up his asshole."

"He will not find his life easy there either," Widukind said.

"He is nursing his pride," Erhard said. "But the fragile pride of a boy can be a dangerous thing."

I gave little thought to Erhard's words and agreed with Rotgrim. Good riddance. My mind was occupied with thoughts and images of Vala. She was still avoiding me. Some days, I was impatient and frustrated. At other times, I fretted and worried something had happened to her. One night, I decided I had to find her, and instead of scolding me, the Raven guided me through the darkness toward the Raven's Stones.

Strength

Wulfhedinn

I ran to the Raven's Stones, hoping Vala would meet me along the way. She had to know what was happening. The Raven spirit saw everything and must have told her about the death of Karl's wife and baby and his plans for vengeance on the Saxons. She had to know I was worried. Every step without seeing her heightened my disappointment, frustration, and fear. She would not do this to me. The Walkyrie must have been keeping her from me. The Raven cackled and mocked me, whispering in my ear.

Vala has always been free, you fool.

I stopped and stared into the sky, but the dirty scavenger blended into the darkness. I pretended she was not there and refused to believe what she had said. The spirit was a master of bewilderment. I must not have heard her right.

She has always been free.

Her meaning came louder and clearer to me, but she had to be lying. The Raven and the Walkyrie had always been the deceivers and had held Vala and me in their enchantments. I ran faster toward the stones, trying to escape the sound of her flapping black wings.

She has always been free.

I called for Vala, and when she did not answer, I screamed until hoarse. I kicked the dirt and cursed all the gods until breathless. Falling to my knees, I fought the sting of tears, unable to mask the truth and my pain any longer. Perhaps Vala was the deceiver. The thought brought agony beyond enduring.

No…she loved me. She must—

Sweet musk and hawthorn.

It was too early in the spring, and Vala's hawthorn blossoms had yet to bud, but her fragrance filled me with longing and joy. With soft steps, she emerged from behind the trees, cradling her belly. It had grown so large that I thought it might burst. I marveled at her beauty and wondered how the growing child had not torn her apart. Such things were a mystery to me and frightened me more than any battle. I wanted to run and embrace her, but I was afraid and did not move.

"Why have you not come to me?" I asked.

"I have."

"The Raven came. Not you."

"But I am her."

"The Raven told me you are free, and always have been." I wanted her to deny it and feared she would not. "Is it true?"

"No—and yes," she said.

"What does that mean?"

"I…I love you."

She was confusing and maddening me again. I wanted to drill her for more answers, but she was shivering in the damp air, so I wrapped my wolf skin around her and set about building a fire. Then I sat next to her, and she leaned into my arms. We did not speak until the fire had warmed us.

"If you are free, why did you not leave the Walkyrie long ago?" I asked.

"I could not."

I leaned away from her. "Would not! You wanted to trick me into fighting your battle. That is what you wanted of me all along!"

"This *is* your battle. You must face King Karl, or you will never be free—we will never be free."

"I left King Karl for you and was beaten and almost killed for it. Why is that not enough for you, for her?"

She took my face in her hands. "I wish it could be, but even now, you do not understand."

I pulled away. "No! It is finally clear to me. You have played me for a fool, again."

"You are wrong. I have risked everything for you! I want you, more than you can understand, but love is forbidden to the woman who wears the mask of the Walkyrie. Forbidden! I am defying her every time I think about you and dream of running

run away together. I long to be together in a place where we are
not haunted by her and the Raven spirit."

I took her hands in mine and stared into her eyes. "Then go
now with me. Escape her cursed forest and her standing stones.
The next war—the uprising—is coming. We can be gone before
it begins. We could go to the Danes. Their king has offered me
one of his ships. I will learn to sail it, and we can go away together,
far away from this land, over the sea."

"Then you would be beholden to Sigfred." She pulled away
from me. "You, Gerwulf, are the deceiver—fooling yourself. You
still refuse to see that you and I will never be alone in this world. If
you want me, you must accept all of me, the Raven, the Walkyrie,
and my Wulfhednar. We are all in your blood. We are your pack."

"I do not want a pack!"

"The pack has given you something you would never have
had by yourself or with the Franks. You have become one of us."

I stomped to the edge of the firelight and turned back. "I
only want you."

Her face twisted for a moment. The wolf skin fell open, and
she clutched her belly. Standing carefully, she began to pace.

"Come with me now," I said. "If you love me, destroy the
Walkyrie's mask and come with me now. I cannot destroy it, but
surely you can."

"I cannot. It would ruin everything."

"You can, but you *will* not."

"You are right." She pulled something from under my wolf
skin, her mask of Raven feathers, and began to lift it to her face.

Without hesitation, I snatched it from her and threw it into
the fire. The steel edge of my axe had not destroyed it, but perhaps
the power of flames would. The feathers quickly lit up, curling as
they burned into ash and vanished into the cinders.

Vala pushed me away. "Get away from me! You will never understand. You will never be anything to anyone." She grimaced, puffing and clutching her belly. Then she screamed, falling to her knees, writhing in pain.

I went to her side and reached for her but she leaned away from me, gasping. "Leave me!" she croaked.

After several moments, the worst of her pain passed, and her breathing softened. I feared I had hurt her by burning the mask. The pain struck her hard again. She moaned and panted until it passed and took another deep breath.

The baby was coming.

Ignoring me, she gathered leaves and moss and piled them close to the fire. She stopped to grit her teeth and panted. I could see the strain in her face as she labored to release the contraction of her womb and exhaled once it had passed.

"You cannot have the baby now, not here," I said. "You must go back to the Raven's Stones."

"I cannot return there without the mask," she said.

There was nothing left of it, and I was the one who had destroyed it. How could I have been so senseless? I had just obliterated the Walkyrie's protection and doomed her to give birth as a mortal in the cold forest. What had I done?

Her breathing and grunting grew louder until she shrieked with a sound of agony unlike anything I had heard before. I was terrified to step inside the realm of birth. I wanted to run from it, leave it to a midwife and other women, but there were none in the Teutoburg Forest, except Odilia.

"I will get Odilia from the farm for you," I said. "She must know what to do."

"Only you can do this. You must live the fate you have created for us."

"But I..." The truth of it hit me hard. I could not abandon her now.

I went to her side and helped her settle down on the bed of leaves and moss. She rested and gathered her strength. Then she stood, dropping the wolf skin and stripping off her tunic.

"I must walk," she said.

The flickering firelight lit her naked, pale body. The air was cold and damp outside the ring of fire, but the glow from the flames bathed her swollen belly in warmth. She paced back and forth several times and cried out, leaning heavily against a tree. I froze, unsure what to do. Was she dying? So many women died in childbirth. I thought of Queen Hildegard. She and her baby girl had died. I shivered with terror. What had I done?

Sweat poured down her furrowed brow, and her face twisted in agony. I took her hand, and she clung to it as if it were a life-line keeping her from falling off a cliff. She focused on the sky, searching perhaps for the Raven. The power of the Raven spirit and the Walkyrie would not come now, and it was my fault.

Vala worked through countless rounds of pacing, pain, and relief through the night. Each round came faster and harder. Sometimes she sat or lay down between rounds. She was exhausted, and I worried it was taking too long. What if the baby would not come out? I should have fetched Odilia.

After another round of pain that seemed to last forever, Vala squatted over the bed of moss, pushing and grunting. She sat and leaned back on her elbows and a wet, squirming infant fell into my hands and screamed.

"It is a girl." I said, trying not to drop her. I felt her body heat escaping rapidly from her fragile body through my fingers.

"Dry and wrap her—quickly now," Vala said. "Then you must tie the cord in two places and cut it in the middle."

I took off my tunic and tore it in half, drying the baby and then swathing her. Then I cut a piece of my wolf skin to bundle over the linen. Pulling the leather thong from my hair, I tied the cord and cut it with my axe. I picked up the baby, and she stopped crying, becoming calm and content in my arms. She gazed at me with bright, blue eyes as though she already knew I was her father.

Vala rose to her feet like a warrior who had survived a battle greater than any war a man could fight. In her mortal vulnerability, she had become her most powerful and delivered the daughter of the Wulfhedinn and the Walkyrie into the world. She was a warrior like no other, and I understood why she had been chosen as the woman for the Spirit of Three Faces.

She dressed herself, keeping her back to me and the baby. I wanted to hold the tiny, beautiful creature forever, but she needed her mother.

"Will you feed her now?" I asked.

Vala did not turn around. "You must take her to the Walkyrie, to the chamber at the top of the Raven's Stones."

The baby's tiny fingers slipped out from the wolf skin and clutched my thumb. Her grip was stronger than I would have expected. In cradling the delicate creature, I felt both weaker and stronger than I had ever been.

"I will take you both back to the Raven's Stones, as soon as you are able," I said.

"You must take her, without me," she said. "I have fulfilled my purpose. The child is the Walkyrie's now. Only she can keep and protect her."

"I will not leave you here and abandon our child at the stones!"

"If you ever want to see either of us again, you must surrender her freely."

"Never! We must go together now."

"You burned the Walkyrie's mask. None of us will be safe until you give the baby to her."

"But she needs to eat."

"The Walkyrie will provide." She choked suddenly, unable to hold back tears. "Go! Quickly now. Take her away from me. If I hold her, I will be unable to let her go."

Her tears were tearing my heart apart as much as the thought of leaving my baby girl in the cold stone tower.

"What if there is no bridge into the chamber?" I asked.

"If you go willingly with your sacrifice in your arms, the bridge will be there for you."

I wanted to fight, to argue, to find another excuse to avoid the horrible task.

"She needs a name," I said.

"She is not ours to name. Now go! Before it is too late. You must do this, for me and the baby, for the pack, and for the future of the Saxons. Most of all, you have to give her up for yourself."

I held the baby protectively against my chest, daring the Walkyrie to tear her out of my arms. Her tiny pink fingers clasped my dirty, calloused thumb with a strength beyond her size, but she was not clinging to me. Her grip was reassuring, comforting. If our newborn girl possessed such might, and Vala had the grit to birth and relinquish her, I had to find the courage to do what needed to be done.

The Naming

~~~

Wulfhedinn

My baby girl squirmed in my arms as I climbed the stairs up the stone pillar. I moved slowly, trying to delay what I had promised to do. I searched the sky for black wings or any sign that the Walkyrie would come immediately and accept her. With every step up the steps, I fought the impulse to turn back. Bundled in my wolf skin, she was mine. I could steal her and take her far away, but if I failed to offer her to the Walkyrie, I would lose Vala. And her Raven spirit would haunt me to the end of my days for my betrayal.

I could not leave our infant alone on the cold stone altar of Wodan's Tower, so I vowed to stand guard over her until the Walkyrie came. If she did not come by dawn, I would take her back to Vala.

I was halfway to the chamber when I heard something. Men's voices, jangling mail armor, and trotting iron-shod hooves. Scola riders were coming from the south from the direction of Lippespringe garrison. They were heading straight through the Teutoburg Forest, directly to the place where I had left Vala, alone and defenseless. How had they discovered the Walkyrie no longer protected the forest?

A scream rang through the woods. Vala.

I froze, clutching the baby. She cried, sensing my panic and distressed by her mother's screaming. Vala's voice echoed around the giant stones, shaking me with more fear than I had ever felt. They had found her—and I had burned the Walkyrie's mask, her protection.

I had to go to her, and taking the baby to the top of the stones would delay me. Running back with an infant in my arms would slow me and endanger the baby. Yet I could not bear to leave her alone at the Raven's Stones. I remembered giving my cloak to Vala. I had left behind my axe too. Without them, without the wolf, I was as helpless as the kicking, screaming infant in my arms. I had no choice but to leave her in Wodan's Tower. I had to have faith the Walkyrie would come, accept the child, and protect us all. Until then, I would do what I could to protect Vala, without weapons or the wolf skin.

I ran the rest of the way up the stairs and found the plank bridge in place, as Vala had said. The crossing into Wodan's Tower was easy—a good omen. The chamber was bare except for the altar under the little round window. I expected the Raven to be perched there, but it was empty. I hesitated. What if I *had* destroyed the Walkyrie by burning her mask?

Vala's shrill mortal cry rang across the treetops, more desperate than the scream before.

You cannot destroy the Walkyrie so easily.

Vala's words. She had said them when I had chopped the Walkyrie's mask with my axe. I had to believe it was still true, despite having burned the mask. I laid my baby girl on the flat stone, kissed her wrinkled forehead, and tucked the wolf skin tightly around her kicking arms and legs, hoping it had some power to protect her.

I turned to go and stopped, unable to leave her without a name.

"I will call you Frida," I said. "It means peace. And fuck the Walkyrie if she does not like it."

Frida continued to cry, but I had to tear myself away from her. I crossed the bridge and ran down the stairs. At the bottom, I searched the sky, listening for the thundering of the Walkyrie's great black horse, but the woods were silent. Changing my mind, I turned to take Frida back when Vala screamed again.

Taken

Wulfhedinn

Running as fast as my mortal legs could carry me, I feared the worst. Frida's cries and Vala's screams engulfed me like a nightmare that would not let me wake. I had never needed the wolf so desperately, but I knew it would not come. I had destroyed the Walkyrie's mask and, with it, the power of the pack of wolf warriors I had helped to rebuild.

My heart pounded as the smell of war horses and soldiers grew stronger. The perfumed stink of one of them was as pungent as the nobles of King Karl's court. It was a familiar scent—too familiar. I knew who it was before I saw the bright blue mantle through the tangle of branches. Dressed like a prince, Wichbert flourished his sapphire cloak and a new sword. The hilt sparked with gold and a ruby jewel. The price of his betrayal.

The little brat had run to the king and had told him the pack was broken and the Teutoburg Forest was no longer protected by the Walkyrie. He had revealed our darkest secret to our greatest enemy and had led a patrol of riders there, brandishing his new mantle and sword like trophies.

Treulogo.

The boy in royal blue was the image of a truth liar in every way. He sat tall on a fine warhorse—a part of his reward no doubt—among the dozen mounted Frankish riders he had guided into the forest. He wore a smug expression, pleased with himself. He had sold himself to become a king's boy—a noble slave, as I had done. And neither of us had understood what we had done to ourselves.

The Scola riders were heavily armed with swords, shields, and spears. Through the brush, I saw they had surrounded Vala. Two of them had grabbed her and held her roughly. She had stopped screaming and did not struggle. Defeated, she stared vacantly into the fire where the Walkyrie's mask had burned. I swallowed hard, sickened.

I wanted to tear Wichbert and his blue mantle to shreds, but my wolf cloak and axe—all the power I possessed—were in the hands of the Scola captain. Unarmed, I had no chance against a dozen Scola riders. They would kill Vala if I attempted to jump one of them and kill him with my bare hands.

One of the soldiers shook Vala, his tight grasp digging into her arm. "She is bloodied like a woman who has recently given birth," he said. "She must be the one the king is looking for."

The captain fingered an amber necklace around his neck. "Is this woman the Eater of Souls?" he asked Wichbert.

"Yes, Captain Lothar. I am sure of it," he said. "No other woman would give birth so near the Raven's Stones."

"Have you ever seen her?"

"No...yes...I mean..."

A mounted soldier reined his horse near Vala and kicked her belly. She doubled over, held upright by the soldiers.

"She does not look like a demon to me, captain," he said. "She has no fight in her at all."

Lothar chuckled. "If this is the Eater of Souls, we have nothing to fear in Saxony."

Several others laughed.

"I told you the Walkyrie has no power anymore," Wichbert said.

Captain Lothar examined my blood-soaked wolf skin and sniffed it. "This *could* be the cloak of a Wulfhedinn."

Wichbert nodded vigorously. "It is. It is Gerwulf's!"

"Woman, have you lain with a wolf demon and borne its child here?" Lothar asked.

Vala raised her head and stared at the fire. "Yes."

"Where is it?"

She did not take her eyes off the flames. "Dead."

The soldier holding her shook her. "What did you do with your demon child?"

"Sacrificed to the Walkyrie."

The fire sparked and popped, and the Raven shrieked with the agony of countless damned souls. She hovered above us, and my heart soared in her dark presence, feeling the hope of the spirit. She shrieked again, spooking the Scola's horses. They threw their heads, fighting the reins, side-stepping nervously. Two of them reared, nearly throwing their riders.

"That fire stinks like burning flesh," said one of the riders, struggling to control his mount.

The Raven dove through the flames and past the faces of the soldiers holding Vala. She grazed their cheeks with her claws, screeched, and vanished into the sky.

They released Vala and grabbed their scratched faces. "There are wicked spirits and demons in this forest!" one of them said.

Lothar rolled up my wolf skin and tucked it behind him on his saddle. "We will return to Paderborn now and take this woman to the king."

"But the little weasel says we are within a short walk of the Raven's Stones," another of the riders said. "We have come this far. We should be the ones to find it."

Lothar's eyes darted around the area lit by the fire. "We have gotten close enough for now. We must get this woman to the king first."

They bound Vala's wrists and hobbled her ankles so that she would not run. Staring blankly at the fire, she did not resist. Her blue eyes reflected the sparks snapping from the flames. Lothar held her tether and yanked her hard as he spurred his horse. He led his riders back on the path that had not existed before that night. Wichbert's dishonor had opened an easy route for them through the Walkyrie's forest. *Treulogo.*

Waves of self-hatred and guilt gripped me. My destruction of the Walkyrie's mask had been as selfish an act as Wichbert's treachery.

Defenseless but unable to leave her to her fate, I followed them. Naked without my fur, the wolf would not come to me. I was afraid to attack Lothar and his riders but even more terrified of letting them take her to the king. My heart was breaking with every step I took farther from the Raven's Stones, where Frida lay on the stone altar. My little girl would not survive long in the cold there.

I stopped. I had to go back for her but could not abandon Vala either. I had to act quickly or risk losing both of them, and I needed help, *anything*, just a small bit of faith to latch onto. I tried to reason with myself. The Raven had appeared, so the Walkyrie must have come for Frida. She was an innocent babe. The Walkyrie would accept her, despite my failings, but Vala, the woman, was helpless and unprotected without the mask. I continued after the riders, unsure what I could do to help her.

The forest opened for the riders like a gate, allowing them to race forward while it closed around me. It squeezed me, ripping my flesh with thorns. I soon lost sight of them, and the sound of the heavy clopping of their horses' iron shoes faded. A deeper pain hit me harder than any wound I had suffered before. I could not move forward, so I changed direction, climbing straight up a hill. As dawn was breaking, I reached a place high enough to see over the treetops. From there, I had a view for miles to the south. In the distance lay the Lippespringe garrison.

The wall I had burned had been rebuilt, taller and thicker than before. The garrison was packed with tents, both inside and outside the palisade, and more soldiers were camped there than I had ever seen there. The Scola riders and Vala were approaching the gates. They would soon deliver her to the king with the news of the safe route through the Teutoburg Forest. Then Wichbert would guide the whole army straight to the Raven's Stones. All hope would be destroyed for Vala, our child, the Wulfhedinn pack, and the Saxons—for all of us.

Us.

My mind spun with images of what they would do to Vala. The king would take his vendetta against me out on her. I wanted to storm the gate and free her, but I was a mortal man, a treu-logo—not the kind of man my father was. I could not fight them myself. I needed an army to fight an army. I needed an army led by a hero—Widukind, my father.

I had to warn them that the Teutoburg Forest had been breached, and the king's invasion would come quickly. Karl would march straight through the forest to destroy the Raven's Stones, the haunt of the Walkyrie, and now my daughter, Frida.

Captain Lothar led Vala through the gate. As it closed behind the riders, I turned back toward Grotenburg, hoping she knew I had not deserted her.

Protectors of the Raven's Stones

Wulfhedinn

J ran to Grotenburg, pushing myself faster and harder than the wolf could have taken me. Ealderman Berard and his archers were practicing outside the walls. I dashed past their targets, glad to see most of their arrows had struck with precision, and sprinted through the open gates. In the yard, Widukind and the other Wulfhednar were training a group of new arrivals with quarterstaffs.

When they saw me, the Wulfhednar lowered their staffs. Pyttel came running across the yard, followed by a group of boys with their slings. Heinrich and Sidag and their men gathered around. Rotgrim strode toward to me, the folds on the back of his neck furrowed with anger.

"Where have you been?" he demanded. "You were supposed to lead quarterstaff training today."

I panted and caught my breath. "I need to speak with the Wulfhednar—in private. Pyttel as well."

"In my chamber," Widukind said.

I looked twice to ensure no one had followed us, barred the door, and spoke in a low voice. "A Scola patrol has breached the Teutoburg Forest and rode nearly to the Raven's Stones. They have reported back to Lippespringe where Karl has assembled the largest force I have ever seen. The entire army will be marching through the forest soon."

"How did they know they could breech the Walkyrie's forest?" Abbo asked.

Erhard leaned on his staff and spoke the obvious. "Someone told them it was unprotected. There were only a handful of us who were aware of that."

Widukind gave me a hard stare. He knew who it was. They all knew.

"Wichbert was with the patrol," I said.

Widukind did not appear surprised. He listened quietly without questioning my story or accusing me of lying.

"You let a Frankish patrol go?" Rotgrim asked, shaking his staff at me. "You should have ripped them to pieces."

I shook my head. "The wolf did not come to me. I could not hear its howl or feel its fury, and they were fully armed Scola riders—twelve of them. They would have overpowered and killed me. Then I could not have warned you."

It was not a lie, exactly. But I did not have the balls to reveal the whole truth. I could not bear to tell them about Vala, the baby, and what I had done with the Walkyrie's mask.

"The Raven would have warned us," Rotgrim said.

"Maybe. And what if she did not?"

"You should have…" Rotgrim said.

"They would have killed him," Erhard said, examining me with his dead eye.

"It is better you stayed alive," Widukind said. "The priority now is to strike fast and follow the plan we have laid out. We will lure Karl's army away from the Raven's Stones to the Grotenburg, where we can set the ambush."

Rotgrim shook his head, deepening the muscular rolls on the back of his neck. "King Karl will never forget the mistake his commanders made at Süntel. He will not let his army be drawn into another ambush."

Pyttel stepped forward. "If I may speak?"

"Let the monk speak," Widukind said.

"The king will forget," Pyttel said. "The loss of his wife and baby has devastated him, and his fear of the Eater of Souls and thirst for vengeance controls him beyond any reason or logic. It is his greatest weakness."

Rotgrim snorted at Pyttel. "His commanders may not be so willing to lead their followers into the Walkyrie's forest."

"I think they will," Pyttel said. "Karl has lost his greatest general, Theoderic, and his remaining commanders are young and inexperienced, the sons of his commanders slain at Süntel. They are brash and reckless and will do anything to prove themselves to the king."

"And who will draw them here?" Abbo asked.

"I promised to do it, and I will," I said. "I will lure them away from the Raven's Stones to the base of the Grotenburg hillfort."

My father laid a hand on my shoulder. "Then Rotgrim can enjoy ripping out the throats of the Scolas," he said.

Rotgrim pulled his sword, checked his blade with his finger, and licked his lips. "I always hated horsemen. Real men do not sit on horses to fight."

"We will post the most seasoned warriors along the route to support the pack," Widukind said. "And archers will be staged with them where they have clear shots of the army line."

"And what do we tell our warriors?" Abbo asked. "When they hear Karl breached the forest, they will know the Walkyrie has left and taken the wolf spirit with her. They might lose faith in the rebellion and flee."

"We must show them we are still the protectors of our clans and the Raven's Stones," Widukind said. "The Walkyrie has brought the wolf to everyone in the pack but me, and if we falter now, it may never return to me. We must rally our courage as men, as the mortals we are. Only then will the Walkyrie return the wolf to me and restore her full powers to us and the Teutoburg Forest. If we fail, we will fail every warrior, peasant, woman, and child who is risking everything to fight this war."

Rotgrim shook his sword it in the air. "Man or wolf, I will cut down the Franks and their butcher king and trample them into steaming piles of shit!"

Erhard and Abbo pulled their weapons, crossing the blades with Rotgrim, shouting, "To the Walkyrie! To the wolf! To the glory of Wodan!"

Widukind joined them, and I was suddenly aware of the loss of my axe. I raised my fist and howled like a man, and for a moment I thought perhaps the wolf answered.

Pyttel fell to his knees in front of Widukind. "I swear by all the gods to keep faith with you, Widukind, my war chieftain. I vow to always protect you and your Wulfhednar and every Saxon to the greatest extent of my ability."

"Get up, monk," he said. "My warriors do not kneel. They

prove themselves by their actions, not their words."

Pyttel stood. "Good. I am better at saving people with a seax than saving souls with prayers."

"But what do we tell our warriors?" Abbo asked again.

Widukind's expression hardened. "We tell them Wichbert's dishonor broke the pack. With his betrayal to the butcher king, the Walkyrie vanished."

"You are branding your son as a traitor."

"He has done it to himself," Widukind said.

He called an assembly of the clan ealdermen while I prepared for my mission. Brother Pyttel tagged along with me to the armory like a fretting mother hen.

"Where is your wolf skin and axe?" he asked, thrusting his hands on his hips.

"It does not matter now."

"You cannot approach the Frankish army without your wolf skin. You will have no defense. What will you do if they capture you?"

"My best defense is the pack, the rest of the rebel fighters, and you."

He and his crooked grin shadowed me inside the armory. He stood by quietly as I handled several spears and axes and chose the best of each.

"I will go with you," he said.

"No, you crazy monk. Our warriors need you here with them." I slid the axe into my belt. "I must do this myself. You must stay to sacrifice and pray to the Walkyrie for her favor. Then you will fight. Now, give me your cloak. I need the hood to hide my face, and it is so filthy, no one would mistake it for a monk's cloak."

He frowned briefly at the offense, rolled his eyes, and laid it over my shoulders. "Find your wolf skin soon. I want this back."

"No one steals what is mine and keeps it for long."

He raised a brow. He knew me well enough to understand I was referring to something more than a wolf skin—and that I did not want to talk about it.

I sniffed his cloak and grimaced at the stink. "I will return it as soon as I possibly can."

He laughed and saw me to the gate.

The Trap

Wulfhedinn

The ground quaked. Hundreds of Frankish war horses and thousands of infantry were on the march. Karl's army had advanced on the Hellweg, the king's road from the Lippespringe garrison, and were funneling into the Teutoburg Forest. A road through the tangled trees and brush was opening for them, as if the Walkyrie was welcoming them. The road was wide enough to allow four horsemen to ride abreast, and they advanced steadily toward the Raven's Stones and the farm. I had to divert them quickly away from there to the narrow path between the Grotenburg hill and the bog. There the riders would be pinched into riding only one or two abreast and make easy targets.

Wichbert rode with the foreguard, leading the way. The king travelled beside him, holding the Holy Spear like a scepter of God's power. He was accompanied by several priests and surrounded by his personal guard, bearing the royal banner. Vala walked behind the king's horse, her hands and ankles bound in chains, held by the butcher king himself.

She was alive! But her face was pallid, almost ashen, and she was struggling to keep up with the horse. Fresh blood smeared her tunic and dripped from between her legs.

I longed to call out to her, to tell her the whole Saxon army were preparing to attack Karl. If only I could give her that hope! Maybe the Raven had brought her the news. Maybe she had faith in me. Maybe.

Behind the king's entourage, a long line of elite Scola horse-men rode, led by Captain Lothar. Considering his position at the head of the Scolas, he must have been promoted to commander—his reward for bringing in Vala, no doubt. I wanted to leap at him and crack open his chest, but I steadied myself. Such a rash move would doom Vala and our entire ambush.

I studied the approaching army and did not recognize the other young Frankish commanders. One of them led horsemen, and the others lead units of men-at-arms. Their chins were smooth, and their faces were eager, too eager. Pyttel was right about them. Although they were at the helm of well-trained units, these untested young generals were a weakness in the king's offense.

The vast infantry marched behind the professional soldiers. Conscripted peasants trudged along like they were going to a day's labors in the fields. They carried a variety of weapons. Some had wooden spears and fair-sized seaxes, but many had little more than a dagger or farm tools. Their eyes darted nervously, and many were mumbling prayers, as were some of the Scola riders and soldiers. Some were wearing necklaces of black feathers—raven's feathers. A strange token for Christian men. Were they protective charms? Clearly, they were not all convinced that the Teutoburg Forest was free of the Eater of Souls and the Wulfhednar.

I hooded my face, scuttled through the brush, and stopped to wait behind a huge oak tree. When the advancing foreguard came within earshot, I stepped purposely on several dry branches. They cracked and snapped sharply.

"What was that?" one of the foreguard asked, squinting through the trees.

The lieutenant halted his men, and they drew their weapons, jittery as cats.

"A fox in the underbrush," Wichbert said.

"Be silent," the lieutenant ordered, listening.

I stepped on more branches, making a loud cracking sound no fox could make and no fighting man could ignore.

"Grifo, take two men to investigate," the lieutenant said.

Grifo clutched the feather charm on his chest. "Only two?"

The king reined his horse to the foreguard, tugging Vala's chain. "The Eater of Souls is my prisoner, and I have sent her demons back to Hell. Go now! There is nothing to fear. I possess the Holy Spear, and God is with us."

Grifo rubbed the back of his neck and hesitated before choosing two men. They spurred their horses toward my hiding place. Another path opened for them through the tangled thickets, and they grinned with new confidence, urging their mounts faster. When they got within ten paces, I darted across their path, brandishing my axe and spear.

"There!" one of them shouted. "An armed scout!"

"Take him," Grifo ordered.

A well-aimed spear grazed my shoulder. It had left barely a scratch, but I clutched my shoulder as though I was more seriously injured.

"Ride him down," Grifo said.

They spurred their horses, and I trotted just ahead of them, leading them farther from the Raven's Stones and closer to Grotenburg. Changing direction frequently, I made it more difficult to target me through the thick forest. Every time I turned, they were forced to slow their horses to turn and wait for a new path to open for them. When I had led them far enough, I crawled into a crevice beneath a fallen log and waited for them to get frustrated with the search. I wanted them to quit the chase, return to the king, and bring the whole army back in my direction, away from the stones and the farm.

The clopping of their horses' hooves slowed and stopped within a few paces of my hiding place.

"We lost him," one of them said.

"He was injured. He could not be far," another said.

"He is taking us away from the army," Grifo said. "I do not like it. We should report back."

They rode away, and I shadowed them back to the army.

"He kept drawing us farther away," Grifo told the foreguard lieutenant and the king. "Then he was gone."

"He might be luring us…" the lieutenant said.

"Cowards! The Eater of Souls is my prisoner," the king said with a hard yank of Vala's chain. "*We* are the ones baiting the trap."

Without consulting Wichbert, the king ordered the army to advance on the new path, diverting them away from the stones and the farm. Wichbert opened his mouth to protest, and changed his mind.

I moved ahead of the advancing army and continued to pull them closer to Grotenburg. I knew that when they were in position, one of our own archers or slingers might inadvertently hit Vala. Or once under attack, the king might use her as a shield or kill her. I had to do more than get him and his army to Grotenburg. I had to rescue Vala before they got there.

A Single Power

Wulfhedinn

Karl and his army progressed through the Teutoburg Forest, heading away from the Raven's Stones and the farm, as I had hoped. After about a mile, I darted in front of them, keeping my face hidden under the hood of Pyttel's cloak. I scampered away like a terrified rabbit flushed out from hiding. One of the foreguard spotted me immediately, and Karl gave the order to follow.

I played cat-and-mouse with them for several miles, pulling them closer and closer to Grotenburg. At the same time, I pondered different plans to free Vala. Every idea was as unlikely to succeed as the next—except one. I tried to push it from my mind, but there was no other way.

Surrender to King Karl.

I must have been as mad as Pyttel. The king had proven what he would do to enemies who submitted to him, and he would ensure my fate was far more brutal than a quick beheading.

It must be done, for Vala, for the pack, and all the clans and tribes.

I realized I had been deceiving myself. I was not alone in the world. The Wulfhednar pack had given me more than the king ever could have, and Frida, my baby girl, was a sacred gift from all the faces of the Walkyrie. For the first time, I wanted Vala—every bit of her—woman, Raven spirit, and Walkyrie. She, Frida, and her Wulfhednar were in my blood. I was one of them.

This *was* my war, and if I did not face the king, none of them would ever be free.

In dying for them, I would never be more alive.

I dropped my spear and axe and walked into the path of King Karl's advancing army. Throwing back my hood, I raised my hands aloft in compete surrender.

The foreguard stopped, jaws dropping.

"The Royal Scout!" the lieutenant said.

I stepped closer. "I am Wulfhedinn, son of Widukind, and I yield myself to you in exchange for the life of the Saxon woman you hold."

The king's guard reined their horses around Karl, creating a tight wall of protection.

I walked within range of the foreguard's spear tips. "That woman is a poor peasant's wife. Release her, and I will take you to the Raven's Stones."

Karl cocked his head and smirked. "Take him," he ordered.

The guards hesitated. Vala stared at me with a blank expression, as though she did not know me.

Karl thrust my wolf skin over his head. "Do not fear him! I hold all his power in my hands, and I have the Eater of Souls in chains. He and the Wulfhednar are helpless."

The foreguard pressed close to me, leveling their spears at my throat and chest. With perfect aim, the foreguard lieutenant threw a noose around my neck and pulled it tight. He yanked me to my knees, collapsing my throat. I grasped the rope, instinctively thinking to pull the lieutenant off his horse. Choking, I stopped myself and submitted to him as he secured the rope around his saddle pommel.

Karl pointed the Holy Spear toward me. "You are a damned bastard and a traitor who will burn in the flames of Hell," he hissed. "And you will beg for that before I am done with you."

Wichbert had reined his horse back several steps, but I was choking and coughing too much to pay him any more notice.

The king glanced from me to Wichbert and back to me. "Your brother?" he asked.

Wichbert swallowed hard and nodded. "Half-brother."

"A family of traitors. This is why I must rid my kingdom of heathens. They are Devil-worshippers, with no conscience and no soul! This land must be cleared of them and their demons so that God-fearing Christians can live in peace and prosperity."

Grifo and several soldiers got off their horses. Grifo kicked me in the face, knocking me to the ground. The others followed, their blows coming from all directions. They were not going to kill me quickly, and the Walkyrie or Pyttel would not rescue me again. I was helpless to stop them.

"Let the woman go!" I shouted hoarsely, trying to protect my face and head from their blows.

The faces of my Wulfhedinn pack flashed in front of me—
Erhard, Rotgrim, Abbo, and Widukind. My father and my wolf
brothers. For their sake, and the sake of Vala and all the Saxons,
I had to convince the king to release her.

"Let her go! Let her go!" I pleaded between kicks, but the
beating continued. I despaired, knowing what a fool I had been
to believe they would free her in exchange for me.

Darkness fell, and an image of Wodan's Tower floated in front
of me. The Raven floated above it on warm sunny currents rising
between the standing stones. My body lay in the chamber. Little
Frida was on the cold stone altar. Bundled in the scrap of my wolf
skin, she was lifeless, and no breath passed through her blue lips.

The Raven flew through the little window and perched on
the altar. She spread her feathers, wrapping them around Frida.
My baby girl whimpered. Sickly sounding at first, her cry quickly
grew into a lusty scream. A feisty little fist of five perfect fingers
punched through the wolf skin, and the Raven took her, carrying
her through the window to the Walkyrie.

I fell back into a void, tumbling toward the flames of the
Christian Hell to which I had damned myself. The fires were
swelling, their heat like a red-hot forge, blistering and charring
my flesh. I had but a moment to offer one last hope to Vala.

"The Raven took Frida!" I shouted, but my words were lost
and unheard in the crackling fires and sparks of Hell. "She is safe
with the Walkyrie."

Damnation engulfed me, the fate I had feared and fought
my whole life. I deserved it and would let it take me—but not
while Vala was still in chains. From the shadows inside my soul, I
summoned a rumbling, booming howl. It wailed with a force that
could be heard from the top of heaven to the fires of the Devil. It
rang through the forest and carried me from oblivion back to Vala.

The rope was crushing my windpipe, but it no longer mattered. This howl did not pass through my throat or from a distant wolf demon to me. It came from deep within, from the spirit of my father and my wolf brothers, and their fathers and brothers before them.

I am Wulfhedinn.

The wolf had not come to me. It *was* me. Karl possessed my wolf skin, but he could not control its spirit. Strength surged through my limbs and the beast echoed in my cry with more power than it ever had when I wore its fur on my back.

My pack, my brothers, answered my call. One by one, Wulfhednar voices rose through the trees, deafening the soldiers. I recognized the cries of Erhard, Rotgrim, and Abbo. Then came another, a howl not unlike my own.

Widukind.

The soldiers stopped beating me. They spun around, trying to see the demons they knew were there. The horses whinnied and bucked. Their riders struggled to control them and draw their weapons. They glanced from one direction to the next, struggling to determine what was coming at them and from where.

Excitement surged through me. I jumped up with renewed strength and snapped the rope around my neck like a thread. Three Wulfhednar bounded from the forest. Erhard, Rotgrim, and Abbo attacked like a pack of rabid wolves—huge creatures, with fangs like razors and snarling muzzles capable of shattering a man's arm in their jaws. I saw Erhard's ghost eye ignite with fire, Rotgrim's fervent hunger, and Abbo's tremendous size. And another joined us, one who embodied all of their best qualities, the greatest Wulfhedinn of all.

My father.

The Raven screamed for blood, and the Walkyrie answered. Her giant black wings spread wide as she charged across the sky on her black mount, spear in hand. She shrieked with the wrath of hellfire, and her mount's hooves thundered, kicking up black clouds, shaking the ground. No one but the pack could see her, but every pagan warrior could feel her presence, and every Frankish soldier was struck with terror by her squall. Huge branches snapped, and trees toppled, crushing at least ten of Karl's men.

I looked to where Vala had stood in chains. She was gone, her bonds shattered into iron shards on the ground. Joy and understanding overtook me with such intensity that tears rolled down my cheeks. I should have seen it months ago. Vala had never needed the Walkyrie's mask, and I had never needed the wolf skin. We needed each other and the pack. To love Vala was to love the Walkyrie and the pack as one.

Until that day, I had given them nothing of myself, but the pack would never be broken again as long as I embraced them. My heart surged, and the spirit of wolf, Raven, and Walkyrie joined the pack, heating our temper, fueling our strength. We growled and howled as one force, a single power that would knock King Karl to his knees.

A cloudburst released a tempest of sleet. Shards of ice bit into the flesh of the Franks. Empowered by the wolf, we were numb to its sting, but Karl's men trembled with cold and fear. Ice sheeted over them. Their frigid fingers clutched their weapons so rigidly that they would be unable to wield them with skill.

The Walkyrie galloped back and forth over the battleground. With a swoosh of her horse's tail, vines and thickets began to creep across the road from the forest. They blocked the army's path with impenetrable brush and thorns, and a rapid retreat became impossible. They were trapped in their fate and at the mercy of the Walkyrie and her pagan army.

My father tossed me an axe, and we set upon the stunned foreguard. I tore apart Grifo, and my brothers took down several of his stunned men. They had no time to wield weapons, and the Wulfhednar's howling overpowered their screams as our blades and fury ripped them apart.

The rest of the army broke down into chaos, and I lost sight of the king. I bounded toward the place where I had last seen him, felling Scola riders with my axe like wispy saplings. The rest of the pack continued their assault behind me. Choked by the encroaching forest, the horsemen could not wield their spears and swords effectively. Steel rang on steel, but their stunted thrusts and slashes often missed their targets. When they did hit us, the wolf fury made us impervious to their blades. We grew fiercer with every blow we shouldered. We were fearless and would triumph over the butcher king and end his war. We were immortal.

Then I glimpsed the king. He had turned away and was attempting to retreat. His personal guards shouted, shoved, and jabbed at their own soldiers to make way for him. His withdrawal spread disorder down the advancing line, from the Scola riders, to the men-at-arms, to the peasant infantry. His young commanders panicked and abandoned their units. They tried to escape with the king but were caught in the mass of confused and frightened soldiers. The commotion was breaking down discipline, making them more vulnerable, but it had also created an impenetrable barrier between me and the fleeing king.

I bared my fangs, howling with a savage drive to kill him. I needed to feel my jaws tear his flesh, and my claws ached to crush his bones. I craved vengeance for what he had done to Vala and me and all the Saxons, and I had to destroy his precious Holy

Spear. But he was out of reach. My moment to strike had passed. I had to let him go and finish the battle in front of me.

A flash of sapphire blue caught my eye on the edge of the forest. Wichbert's cloak, the price of his loyalty, was hanging in the thorns of a hawthorn thicket. The craven boy had run, shimmying through the brush and mud to escape us all. Karl would blame him for leading them into an ambush, and he could never return to us. *Treulogo*. He belonged nowhere and to no one. I doubted he would survive the night in the forest.

The foreguard was decimated, and we had taken down at least a dozen Scola riders. Widukind gave the signal to pull back. We scattered into the forest where our best warriors were waiting behind every tree, rock, and bush, poised for their attack. Several dozen well-armed warriors I did not recognize appeared, snaking down through the woods from the top of the ridge. They were led by a small, stout man wearing the finest mail shirt I had ever seen. King Sigfred of the Danes. He darted to my side.

"Fighting without your ships?" I asked.

"Fuck King Karl," he said. "And this forest is hardly the place for ships, but they are still waiting for you in Hedeby. My offer stands."

"Perhaps, someday."

He fell back to his men. Brother Pyttel, seax in hand, peeked out from behind a tree. He winked, twisting his crooked forehead and smashed nose. Around his neck hung a new amulet—a glossy black feather. He and King Sigfred had made their choice, as had I.

The Walkyrie flapped her great wings, opening a path ahead of Karl's army. They had no choice but to move forward, closer to Grotenburg. In their panic, many dropped their shields. Some hacked at the dense vegetation, hoping to escape the rampage through the forest, to no avail. Others beat their horses to drive them past other riders, causing their mounts to rear and kick one another. Men were thrown and trampled, and the air was soon filled with the stink of blood mixed with shit from the loosened bowels of terrified men.

The Frankish soldiers pushed forward, soon reaching the clearing below the Grotenburg's rampart. There they found themselves wedged between the hillfort and the bog. The chaos intensified when the Franks saw the hillfort looming over them on the cliff. Above the gate, a banner waved, bearing the emblem of a black stallion—the great black steed of the Walkyrie.

"A fortress! Shields!" officers cried to their units, but it was too late. Our first volley of arrows had been loosed. A hailstorm of iron arrows plummeted down on them from the fortress ramparts and from hidden places in the forest. Men and horses fell, creating more obstacles for those pushing from behind and others who were trying to turn and flee.

Some soldiers ran or drove their horses into the bog to escape the arrows. They quickly sank into the soggy ground. Trapped in mud, their screams rose as they descended into the bottomless muck. They thrashed and clawed futilely to grasp something solid until the mire rose over their heads and silenced them.

More volleys of arrows rained down in an inescapable deluge of deadly steel points. Widukind signaled the slingers with a howl. They threw a torrent of rocks from their positions, aiming with lethal accuracy at the bare heads of soldiers without helmets. Other archers positioned in the forest loosed several rounds of arrows.

When most of the riders had been thrown or knocked off their mounts, Widukind signaled to begin the next wave of the attack. The Wulfhednar, the Saxon warriors, and the Danes sprung from the woods and fell upon what was left of the forward line. Sidag stormed from the forest with his warriors, followed by Heinrich and Gunda and their men, Sigfred and the Danes, and the rest of the clan fighters. They descended on the riders who had been unhorsed, the men-at-arms, and the peasant infantry.

My father, brothers, and I attacked the Scola riders who remained mounted. Lothar was spurring his horse, shouting orders, unheard above the din. I leaped at him, knocking him from his horse. My axe cleaved his chest, and I shredded his throat. All around me, the pack was slaying the last of the riders. In the middle of it all, Brother Pyttel swung and stabbed his seax into flesh and bone with the ferocity of a warrior of Wodan. Seeing him fight with such vigor, shoulder-to-shoulder with pagans, I doubted he would ever want his monk's cloak back.

Blades flashed, and steel rang on steel until we waded in the blood of our enemies. It flowed into the bog, flooding the sodden ground. Sacrificial blood. Pyttel gripped the Raven's feather on his chest, resting his hand on his heart. He looked to the sky, and I thought he might have caught a glimpse of the Walkyrie.

Farther down the path, the remaining men-at-arms and infantry were fleeing on the heels of the king. They raced against the closing of the thorny forest around them, trampling each other to squeeze through. Rotgrim led a charge against the remaining infantry. They offered little resistance and were taken down quickly. If the king survived the forest and the assault of our warriors, slingers, and archers, he would be left with few real soldiers.

The pack gathered to howl, voicing our unity, joyous in the satisfaction of vengeance fulfilled. The sleet continued, turning to rain and washing the blood off our wolf faces.

It was time to collect our injured and the handful of slain warriors. Hordes of ravens swarmed and blackened the sky, attracted to the scent of battle. We quickly stripped the Frankish corpses of their weapons, armor, and coins and left them to the ravens' feast. Climbing the hill to the Grotenburg fortress, we anticipated our own feast to celebrate victory and honor our brave dead.

Wulfhedinn Son

Wulfhedinn

The Grotenburg hall was alive with firelight, dancing, and music. We toasted the honorable ones we lost in the battle and relished the evening, drunk on beer and victory. The Walkyrie was vivid to us all, and there was no sadness. We knew the Raven had feasted on our fallen comrades' blood and would carry them on her black wings to the great hall of Wodan.

The festivity was a far humbler affair than King Karl's banquets were, but the laughter was pure, the elation contagious, and the food and beer tasted all the more satisfying.

Musicians played flutes and beat on drums. The beat was uneven and the flute notes sour at times, but no one cared. We danced and drank and drank and danced. Rotgrim, Abbo, and Brother Pyttel frolicked like drunken fools and kissed every girl, woman, and man who was willing, which was most of them. Even the men posted on watch did not mind their duties. They would be relieved soon enough, and everyone would have time to join in a feast that would last until the beer was gone, several days at least.

Erhard sat next to the open fire, content to rub his aching joints in its warm glow. My father and I joined him. Pyttel twirled several times and fell away from the dancing. Catching his breath, he plopped down with us, brushing sweaty hair out of his eyes. His tonsure had grown out in a ragged manner, and no one would guess he had ever been a monk. Refilling his cup, he belched loud enough to wake the gods.

"So the Holy Spear has been proven powerless—again," he said.

"Perhaps," Erhard said.

No one voiced the obvious. We knew the war was not over, and our victory would be short-lived. Scouts had reported they had seen Karl alive and riding hard to Paderborn. He would quickly muster more troops from other areas of his massive kingdom and retaliate. The thought encouraged us to drink and feast all the heartier so that we could forget it for a short, blissful time.

King Sigfred joined us at the fire. Widukind raised his drinking horn and toasted him. "Brother."

"I was angry with you when you left Hedeby," Sigfred said. "I even tempted Gerwulf with a lavish offer to leave you and the pack, but he refused. His honor and loyalty gave me much to think about. He is why I support your rebellion, but I still have hope the pack and the Walkyrie will join us as wolves of the sea."

"We will stay here and protect our lands," Widukind said. "The Wulfhedinn pack is whole, and the Saxons have been united against a common enemy under the banner of the Walkyrie."

Sigfred sighed. "I see your power is here with the Walkyrie in the Teutoburg Forest—for now."

"Righteous by any god!" Pyttel raised another toast, but before he could drink, three young, giggling women pulled him back to the dancing.

Widukind stared into the fire. "Tomorrow we will throw Karl's fallen soldiers into the bog as sacrifices to the Walkyrie and Wodan."

"Out of the reach of the Christian priests," Erhard said, taking a drink.

No one had spoken of Wichbert. My father drank several more horns of beers in silence, staring into the flames. He seemed unaware of the festivity around him.

"Fate has determined all our paths," he said.

I knew he was thinking of Wichbert, so I remained by his side, giving him time to say more if he chose. Erhard rose slowly, rubbing a stiff hip and a huge bruise the size of a soup bowl on his forearm. Sigfred returned to his men, leaving my father and me alone.

He turned to me and said, "I have lost one son, but the Walkyrie has brought me the other, my first-born, my Wulfhedinn son. Soon we will talk about your mother and why I did not kill your monk when I first saw him. But not tonight."

His face darkened, and his chin dropped. His slumping shoulders aged him, and I realized how old he really was. My father looked tired and worn, as though he were hiding something in the shadows of his soul. Something he could not tell me about yet.

"We all have secrets," he said. "Someday you will tell me how the king got ahold of your wolf skin and captured the woman who bore the Walkyrie's child."

"The child is alive and well, in the Walkyrie's care," I said. "Your granddaughter, Frida."

He gave me a big warm smile, and we toasted and drank without words, sharing the fire's warmth. I wished Vala and Frida were there, to feast and celebrate with my father and me. I missed them. I reminded myself they were safe, but doubted they would ever come back to me as woman and child. They belonged to the Walkyrie, the Raven spirit, and the Wulfhednar, not me. Through them, Vala and little Frida would always be with me, in my thoughts. I tried to feel satisfied, but I wanted more than a memory.

Restless, I left the hall. The noise of the feast faded behind me. The full moon lit my way as I crossed the training yard. The air was still, and the Walkyrie's banner lay limp on its pole above the gate. In the silence outside the walls, I looked down at the battle site. The path between the hillside and bog was empty. The bodies of Karl's slain had disappeared.

I thought the moonlight was playing tricks on me, so I walked down the hill and found the moon shadows empty. The ravens had eaten their fill, leaving nothing for the Christian priests to bless and bury.

The satisfaction of victory waned quickly on that empty battle site. I wondered if the Saxon warriors were any different from the Frankish soldiers they had just sent to Hell. I was a half-blood and had fought on both sides of this war. I had resisted it, but I could not escape it. Fate had brought me to my pack, and I would continue to fight for those who needed me and those I loved.

In the emptiness of the battlefield, I pictured Vala waiting for me, hiding in the shadows as she always did. I knew she would not be there. Swallowing hard, I struggled to accept my fate and content myself with the brotherhood of the pack. Perhaps on a warm spring day, I might catch the occasional whiff of sweet musk and hawthorn. I did not want to wait, so I set out for the Raven's Stones. Her memory would be strong there and might fulfill me for a short time.

The stones towered above, the mighty pillars, giant shadows

of the gods. They were almost alive in the moonlight, but the place was empty. I was afraid the memories of her and Frida would fade over time. I did not try to stop my tears as the Raven screeched above, carrying the souls of a thousand Christian corpses left without consecrated burial. An army of roving soulless ones to haunt the King Karl.

Righteous by any god, Pyttel would say, but I had had enough of memories and ghosts. I needed to go somewhere alive, somewhere where Vala's image was vibrant, where I could imagine peering into her sky-blue eyes and feeling her soft flesh and tender kisses. It would be a place where she could rock and nurse little Frida bundled in my wolf skin—a place like the heaven Christianity promised but would deny me. I had seen such a paradise existing in this lifetime, and it was nearby.

The farm.

I left the Raven and her stones behind and ran there. Nestled in its cozy glen, it slept peacefully. The hall was dark, the windows shuttered for the night. Across the farmyard, firelight flickered through an open window of the little cottage.

Sweet musk and hawthorn.

I closed my eyes and inhaled her scent's earthy, sweet essence. It drew me down the glen toward the cottage. The door swung open as I approached, and Vala appeared in the threshold. She beamed like a farmer's wife greeting her husband after a day in the fields. She wore a simple woolen tunic and cradled Frida, bundled in the scrap of my wolf skin. I wrapped my arms around them, savoring their warm mortal flesh. I clutched them tightly, clinging to our moment of peace and heaven. For the first time, I felt at home in my own skin.

"It is good to see your dark eyes turn green again," Vala said.

Moonbeams fell through the open window, bathing us in silver radiance. A soft call drifted from the forest through the glen. Frida cooed and thrust her little fist in the air as the Walkyrie, the Raven, and the wolf soared across the moon and vanished.

Afterword

Travel into the History and Lore of a Dark Age with the Author

I am a time traveler.

My passion as a writer is to journey with readers into the wonder of long ago. I love being your tour guide to my vision of a mist-shrouded primeval era. My greatest hope is that while you are there, you will be entertained and perhaps discover your own visions and revelations.

I have been obsessed with learning about the Middle Ages since childhood. It probably began with a love of fairy tales and fables. At age eleven, I saw the skull reliquary of King Karl, better known as Charlemagne, in the Aachen Cathedral, in Germany. On that first trip to Germany, I learned that the bones, skeletons, and fleshy bits of saints and other objects were showcased in cathedrals all over Europe. As an American Catholic kid, I was fascinated. Why did my forebears preserve bones and artifacts in holy places? Why didn't I have cool skeletons and a Holy Spear in my church?

I also learned relics were revered and worshipped by Catholics for their supernatural powers to protect, heal, and bestow blessing—or luck. Seemed rather pagan to me. When I questioned the practice, the nuns who taught my catechism insisted relics wrought miracles, not heathen magic. To this day, I don't understand the difference.

I sensed there were many more such mystifying stories buried in our forgotten past. Stories that reveal strange and engrossing secrets about our forebears and ourselves. Stories that have not been told, but are alive in ancient memories and in our imaginations.

Since then, I have traveled to countless medieval and ancient sites, including many places in The Wulfhedinn Series. A favorite destination is the Teutoburg Forest and the Raven's Stones, better known as the Externsteine. This natural formation of giant standing stones inspired my series. The Externsteine is located near Horn-Bad Meinberg in North Rhine-Westphalia, Germany. This area is the homeland of the historical Widukind and the Westphalian Saxons. It's also the land of my ancestors, whose line goes back centuries there. Still surrounded by primeval forest, the Externsteine is as shrouded in enchantment today as it was in Charlemagne's time. My fictional characters, Gerwulf the Wulfhedinn and Vala the Walkyrie, came alive to me while visiting this amazing place.

In researching The Wulfhedinn Series, I spent many hours discussing Charlemagne, Saxons, Franks, and Danes with medieval historians, museum curators, military experts, and other authorities on Germany's Early Middle Ages, also called the Dark Ages. This kind of debating is a rabbit hole I love to fall down. However, I realized was more interested in the unknown than the known, and how it might have *felt* to live long ago. The resulting series is a fantasy tale, a creative mix of history, mythology, lore, and legend—with lots of speculation and pure fiction. I hope it brings the past alive in your mind's eye.

The Wulfhedinn Series is set against the backdrop of Charlemagne's campaigns against the Saxons in eighth-century northern Germany. The major events of the campaigns are based on actual events, but are highly fictionalized. These include the disastrous ambush of the Frankish troops by the rebel Saxons, Charlemagne's bloody revenge at Verden, and the battle of Grotenburg, which is located about five miles northwest of the Externsteine.

Many of the secondary characters are drawn from real people. They include King Karl, General Theoderic, Brother Pyttel, Horse Master Gallo, Chamberlain Adalgis, Count Worad, Count Sidag, King Sigfred, Abbo, Queen Mother Bertrada, Carloman, Queen Hildegard, and Prince Pepin. Except for Charlemagne, very little is documented about these figures, so their character traits and actions are make-believe or speculation. I did, however, infuse selected bits of Charlemagne's documented personality into his character.

Most of the fantasy elements in the series are inspired by the Christian and Germanic pagan traditions and beliefs of the time. The Saxons and their neighbors and relatives, the Danes, shared a similar culture, language, and religion. The common foundations of these elements go back centuries before the tribal divisions of Saxon and Dane, whom we now commonly call the Vikings.

The Wulfhednar or "wolf warriors" are rooted in the Úlfhéðnar, a type of berserker warrior who wore wolf pelts into battle. Also known as warriors of Wodan, they invoked the wolf spirit and fought with its ferocious frenzy. The Wulfhednar were believed to be nearly immortal when in their trance-like battle fury, which made them immune from the effects of fire and iron. Some folklorists believe the tales of these raging wolf warriors evolved over time into the werewolf legend we know today.

The Walkyrie/Eater of Souls/Spirit of Three Faces is inspired by the Norse Valkyries and the Saxon wælcyrge and wælcyrie. These female spirits are associated with ravens, and possess related and overlapping qualities. The most well-known view of them is as shield maidens who chose the bravest slain warriors for afterlife in Wodan's Hall (Odin's Hall, Valhalla). Through the ages, they have played various roles and been viewed in many ways, such as war-goddesses, witches, death angels, corpse eaters, and choosers of the slain.

Other elements loosely grounded in Germanic tradition include the Raven, the draugar (roving soulless ones), the Traveler, forest spirits, and treulogo (truth liar, oath breaker).

In addition to the Externsteine and Grotenburg, many of the locations in the novels are based on real places. Some still exist today as modern cities and locations in Germany. They include Paderborn, Bad Lippespringe, Lübbecke, Treva (modern Hamburg), Eresburg, Verden, and the Hohenstein Plateau in the Süntel.

The site of the medieval Danish city of Hedeby and the earth-work wall of King Sigfred (the Danevirke) now lie within the northern German state of Schleswig-Holstein. This is because the border between Denmark and Germany has changed throughout the centuries, which highlights the close relationship and some-what hazy distinction between Danes and northern Germans.

The same could be said of the Saxons and the Franks, who were also a Germanic tribe. In the era of the Wulfhedinn Series, the Franks were Christianized. However, in the past, they had had a culture and polytheistic religion related to that of the Saxons. Unfortunately, the differences between Frank and Saxon won out over their similarities at the massacre at Verden.

I have always been a traveler, a searcher, and a collector of stories. I grew up in the middle-class Chicago suburbs in the '60s and '70s, an outcast book nerd who struggled to fit in. My rebellious nature and thirst to find my tribe and experience a bigger world took me from high-school dropout to teenage runaway to Grateful Deadhead. Then I embraced marriage and motherhood and eventually earned my degree as an RN. The ER trauma center called to me, and I spent 20 years there, healing wounds and sharing the worst days of people's lives with them. I moved into journalism and became an editor and eventually a fiction author. Over the years I have explored many passions, from reading to hiking and camping in mountain wildernesses to exploring remote castle ruins. Other hobbies include mountain biking, motorcycling, and running, and I am obsessed with playing ice hockey.

Throughout all these realms of time and place, I have gathered the stories of others and my own experiences. Both creep into my novels, consciously and unconsciously. I learned much about survival as a runaway teen, and the meaning of unconditional love as a wife and mother. Playing ice hockey, largely with men, has tested me beyond all physical and mental limits and shown me how tough I can be. It has taught me how to take a devastating hit and get up and keep going, even when injured and hurting. My ER experience has also taught me much about injury and pain—physical, emotional, and psychological.

I have discovered that the farther I travel from my comfort zone and the present time, the more similarities in the human spirit I find in our collective story. Even a man possessed by a wolf demon—or an author—hungers to connect with humanity, belong, and give and receive love.

I welcome you to join me on the journey.

Catherine Spader

Get updates on future releases in The Wulfhedinn Series and learn more about the historical and mythological elements of the stories at https://catherinespader.com/.

CPSIA information can be obtained
at www.ICGtesting.com
Printed in the USA
LVHW030028010322
712228LV00004B/51